TURKISH
RONDO

ALSO BY ANNE STEVENSON

A RELATIVE STRANGER

A GAME OF STATUES

THE FRENCH INHERITANCE

COIL OF SERPENTS

MASK OF TREASON

TURKISH RONDO

by

ANNE STEVENSON

WILLIAM MORROW AND COMPANY, INC.
New York   *1981*

Library of Congress Cataloging in Publication Data

Stevenson, Anne.
    Turkish rondo.
    I. Title.
PR6069.T449T8   1981   823'.914   81-3967
ISBN 0-688-00638-8   AACR2

Printed in the United States of America

First Edition

1 2 3 4 5 6 7 8 9 10

CHAPTER 1

The shot echoed round the myrtle-scented hillside, the sound ricocheting from ancient stones, sending birds wheeling into flight.

I called out to Bernice: "What was that?"

She shrugged. "Someone killing a snake?"

"You mean the man from the taxi. There's no one else here."

"There are two horses tethered up there."

"Soldiers?"

"I don't know," she said. "I didn't see the riders."

Silence was settling down once more upon the site, broken, neglected, half-hidden in a tangle of trees and bushes, the stone-carved doors and windows of the tombs we had found almost buried in a sea of yellow sage.

"Very important," the taxi driver had said, pulling up to a sudden halt at a bend in the road. "Temple, tombs . . ." He had waved his hands expressively.

The other passenger had immediately got out and set off up the track, slippery with sheep dung. The driver, tipping his cap forward over his eyes, folded his arms and composed himself for sleep.

"Not long," Bernice said in her careful Turkish. "Twenty minutes, then we go on."

The driver did not bother to reply. He knew all about us. We wanted ruins. He had provided ruins. What more could we ask?

It took us twenty minutes to climb up the slope. There had been nothing to see from the road and little to see when we got there. Some marble columns sprawled among the myrtle thickets, all that remained but for a broken arch of a small temple that once stood here; two or three rock tombs hacked out of the hillside, their façades where one could discern them through the encroaching maquis split open, the stone cracked. Higher up, Bernice told me, returning from an exploration, there were the traces of walls, perhaps the remnants of a fort, one of the many that line the route from Xanthus to Myra, its stones now crumbled or taken by the peasants for their houses centuries ago.

There was a poignancy about the small abandoned settlement, more evocative and touching in its own way than the great show-places of Ephesus or Aspendus. A peaceful place to rest, to gaze on the distant glimpses of the Mediterranean, to contemplate who had once been buried here, who had fought here, who had worshiped in that graceful little temple in the bright days of Alexander.

Bernice wandered away, sketchbook in hand. I sat down beside the path, leaned my back against the trunk of a young tree and closed my eyes. A light breeze lifted the heat and carried to me the soft breath of the sea, mingling with the scent of honeysuckle. Drugged by warmth, contentment and the murmuring of insects, I had been half-asleep when the shot was fired. Now I looked at my watch. We had been here nearly an hour.

There was a noise from above, and the stranger who was sharing the taxi with us came down the path, moving quickly and lightly for a man of such heavy build. He stopped below us to get his breath, wiping his florid face with a handkerchief. Bernice called to him: "Tell the driver we're coming." He turned and plunged on down the hillside, making no reply.

We were no more than a few minutes behind him. When we reached the road, he was getting into the taxi. The engine was running. As he slammed the door shut, the taxi drove off, accelerating rapidly, vanishing in a spume of dust and exhaust smoke round the corner, out of sight.

We stood in the middle of the road, staring after them, not quite believing it had happened.

"We haven't paid the driver yet," I said at last. "He'll be back."

"If he does come back, it'll be when it suits him," Bernice remarked. "We might be stuck here for hours."

Then we remembered the gunshot, and the tethered horses, and the way the stranger had leaped from the taxi the moment we stopped, heading up the hill intent and purposeful.

"The driver knew those ruins were of no real interest," Bernice said. "This was all arranged. That man paid him to stop here, paid him to get him away fast. The fact we'd also booked seats in the taxi was just our bad luck."

The more we thought about it, the more certain it seemed that we had strayed into someone else's personal drama. The man had been meeting someone or, when we remembered the two horses, intruding on a meeting.

"A blood feud?" I suggested. "An unfaithful wife?"

We climbed back up to the temple, half expecting to find corpses strewn among its fallen columns. But we found nothing. The two horses with their unseen riders had gone as secretly as they had arrived. There were no bloodstains, no bodies, not even a slaughtered snake. The hillside dreamed on in the gathering heat of the day, as quiet and deserted as its graves. We set off back down to the road.

"We might as well start walking as wait here," Bernice said, and we began to walk towards the west.

That summer was not perhaps the best time to visit Turkey. The political situation, the revolutions on its borders, the terrorist attacks, the imposition of martial law had created a tension even foreigners could not wholly escape. We got used to the convoys of army trucks streaming past our buses on the dusty roads. Rumors and counterrumors made even the stolidest a little edgy. And more than rumors. In Antalya, two weeks before we arrived, another American had been shot. But apart from this, or perhaps despite it, the tourists were unaffected. Very few could speak or read Turkish. The talk in the cafés, the headlines in the papers meant nothing to them. Isolated in their tourist hotels, guided and guarded round the tourist sights, they could still enjoy a very pleasant holiday on that magnificent, uncrowded coast. Bernice had had to drag me from the beaches of Antalya.

Bernice and I were cousins. She was a tall, stately brunette inclined to plumpness and rather disconcertingly dedicated to archaeology. With her looks, her kindness and her intelligence, she must have been a totally unexpected delight to any professor whose dig she graced. She was three years older than I. When we were young children, this had been an almost insuperable gap, but the older we grew, the less important it became. After my mother remarried and went to live in Canada, it was Bernice and her family who offered to take me in while I finished my schooling, and while I was at the university, it was their home I returned to most often in vacations. In fact, when I went to London in October for a further course, it would be the first time I had been completely on my own. Her parents had retired to France, and Bernice was on her way to Greece for a year's stay.

As a Hellenist she wanted to take in the Turkish sites before she went on to Athens. I was there to keep her company. Even Bernice hesitated at going round Turkey on her own.

We traveled the cheapest way to make the money last longer. If the village people we encountered, the bus drivers, café owners and hotelkeepers we dealt with were puzzled or shocked by two young women traveling alone in that Muslim, male-dominated country unescorted by any husband or father, it was an attitude rarely shown openly to us. We stayed where we could afford to. As the days went by and the money grew less, our stopping places became more primitive and the food we bought simpler. We lived on yogurt and fruit, and as a result, I was struck down by diarrhea. Stumbling along unlit cement-floored corridors in the middle of the night in search of a foul-smelling box with a hole in the floor is not the most comfortable of operations in that state of health, and in the end I rebelled. That is how we came to be staying in a clean modern hotel in Antalya, where rest in a room containing only two beds instead of three or four, and a few days of lying on a beach instead of bumping along in a bus, cured my illness and bleached my fair hair a shade lighter.

I didn't realize then how important that decision had been. But for that illness and those days of relative comfort which ate into our funds and shortened our trip by a vital margin, I might never have become involved in all that followed. My life might have continued along its quiet, predictable path, untouched by fear and loss and tragedy or by the pain of a love distorted by doubt. But when we gathered up our possessions, counted our money and set off again on a limpid morning, it was not to go east again, past Side to Silifke, as we originally planned, but on a route taking us back towards the Aegean coast.

The night before the episode at the ruins we had reached Finike. In the morning we discovered that the bus which daily made the eight-hour journey to Fethiye lay stranded with a broken axle two miles from town, and we were forced into the extravagance of a taxi. For the first part of the journey we had the company of a dentist and his wife on their way to a family occasion. Though we had initiated the hiring of the taxi, he took as if by right the front passenger seat, his plump wife, crushed in the back with us, edging her silk-clad thighs away from our crumpled jeans, her profile mute with disapproval. Her husband, on the contrary, was delighted to have the opportunity of conversing with foreigners and, swinging bodily round in his seat, fired eager questions at us in a mixture of Americanese and German. When I replied in German, he reached over to seize my hands, congratulating me on my race.

"Good soldiers, good workers. Germans very good!"

He told the taxi driver in Turkish that we were Germans.

"They are English," the driver replied gloomily. "They are going to Xanthus to look at ruins." He shook his head at our folly.

The dentist was disappointed that we had been spending our time visiting Greek and Roman monuments.

"They are not Turkish," he said. "They are not the real Turkey."

Why are foreigners always looking for forgotten things? Why do they not come to see the new things we have done, the modern things, business, industry, roads?" He began to ask me about English sports cars.

They left us at Demre, and the driver went off to look for more custom. We followed him to a teahouse and took seats out of the sun, sipping glasses of tea and listening to the gossip of the old men over the backgammon board while we waited for him to find his passengers and strike his bargains. We were inured by now, if not resigned, to the unimportance of time in country districts. And we were glad to be still and relatively cool. Even Bernice was feeling the effects of the rough ride from Finike.

As it happened, though he had spent several minutes in deep conversation with a man in a corner of the teahouse, when the driver summoned us, it was to continue in an empty cab.

"I hope he's not going to charge us for all the seats," Bernice murmured.

About a mile out of town the same man was waiting by the roadside. He was square in shape, arms and shoulders bulging through the worn jacket of the ubiquitous baggy suit. The taxi stopped beside him, and he got in without a word, bringing with him the smell of tobacco and sweat. His face beneath his cloth cap was like a piece of rock, seamed with cracks and fissures. His hands, as he sat with them planted on his knees, looked hard enough to fell a sheep.

"Is he going all the way?" Bernice asked the driver.

He nodded. "Yes, all the way."

"In that case, he can have this seat." Bernice had taken the front seat for comfort. Now doors were opened and places changed. The driver ground the gears and drove off. Bernice winked at me and opened the window we had closed against the dust. The man gave no thanks and made no acknowledgment of our presence. He settled himself into the seat and said something to the driver in a low, harsh voice.

"They are foreigners, but they understand Turkish," the driver replied.

The man grunted and thereafter kept silent.

And now two hours later we had little doubt that he was responsible for our abandonment on this lonely mountainous road.

"Frances, he was the man the driver talked to at the teahouse," Bernice suddenly remarked. "Why should he arrange to be picked up out of town?"

"Because he didn't want anyone to know where he was going?"

"We know where he was going."

In view of the shot we had heard, the mystery of the whole affair, that was a slightly disturbing thought.

After a while I said: "That must be why they left us. He will be miles away before we can tell anyone what we have seen."

"Why should we tell? There is nothing to tell."

"There probably is," I said, "but we shall never know what it is."

The taxi came back for us about five o'clock. During those hours we had been passed by only two vehicles, a minibus and a jeep, both going in the wrong direction. Apart from a few grazing goats, they were the only signs of life we had seen.

The driver was clearly stricken by guilt at his behavior to his country's guests. He gathered us into his car as if we were forsaken lambs. He explained his actions by saying that the passenger had been an important government official who would have made trouble for him if he had not done as he was asked. However, he didn't tell us where he had taken him.

On our expressions of indignation, our fares were immediately reduced to half price. He had found us a reasonable hotel in Kaş, and tomorrow he would personally drive us to Xanthus, wait for us and drive us back, all at a reduced cost and at great personal inconvenience to himself. With stony faces we accepted all his offers. At Kaş we relented and asked him to eat with us and learned his name, which was Mahmud, and heard about his sons and his wife, and his views of the state of the country, which was that the Russians were arming the Kurds and inciting them to rebellion and that his eldest son, who was doing his national service, had been sent to the frontier and had reported much activity there on his last visit home.

When he left us the following day to drive back to Finike, it was as old friends. Before he went, he found us a lift on a truck to Muğla, and from there we made our way to Marmaris and a steamer back to Istanbul.

The steamer was old and slow, calling at every minor port along the coast. There was a constant movement of people on and off at these stopping places, peasants, laborers, families carrying what seemed their whole households with them, officials aloofly superior, keeping their distance from the crowd, crop-haired soldiers, foreign students, even a group of Kurds, the women dressed like gypsies with strong, unveiled faces and shrill voices, the children shy and silent. At the times of prayer the deck was aripple with bowing heads; between ports it looked like the aftermath of a battle, men stretched out in careless sleep tumbled against each other, the women like mourning figures hiding their faces behind their dark headcloths.

The first night we slept on deck, while the dark water slid by and some insomniac idled away the hours with the playing of a flute; but our quiet corner proved to be near the outlet of an unseen ventilator, and a mingling of smells filtered through to us: fuel oil, burned mutton fat, a fishy stench of unmistakable decay. In the morning Bernice was ill, shivering with what might have been heatstroke or might have been something worse. I moved her to a more open but shaded part of the deck, staking our small piece of territory out with our baggage, and went to find the purser.

He was a tall, thin man with a long, grave face and the weary expression of one who has long ceased to be surprised at the vagaries of fate. When he heard my story, he took me into his cramped office, waved me to a seat and handed me a tiny cup of dense black coffee. He sat opposite me, sipping his own coffee and smoking a cigarette. His middle finger was stained yellow with nicotine.

"We do not have many cabins, and they are all taken," he said. "It is not a boat for tourists, you understand. Most visitors book passages on the larger, faster boats. More comfortable. First class. They arrange for their cabins before they embark." There was the slightest hint of reproach in his mild manner.

"I understand that," I said. "But we weren't sure when we would be traveling."

"As for doctors—" He sifted through the papers on the table in front of him and let them fall negligently. "We have no doctors on board."

"One of the officers," I suggested, "might have some medical knowledge, or there might be medicines on board—"

He shook his head slowly from side to side. "Do you want to get off," he said, "at the next port?"

I didn't intend to be shifted quite so easily. If I had had spare money to offer, it might have been simpler. I could see that he was puzzled that I was a foreigner and apparently not rich.

"Are you sure there are no cabins free?" I persisted. "Might not some of the passengers have left at the last port?"

He considered the end of his cigarette. He looked up at me with sad spaniel eyes. He sighed.

"Come with me," he said.

There were eight doors in the passageway along which he led me. He paused before the eighth and knocked. A woman's voice invited us to enter.

The cabin was large. It gleamed with brass and mahogany and reeked with a heavy, musk perfume. It had two berths. Seated on one of them, reading a magazine, was a woman in her early forties. She seemed to be constructed entirely of circles, from the round face with the sloe black eyes and dimpled chin to the swelling bosom and curved stomach straining against the tight dress to the small fat feet shod in expensive French shoes. Her black hair was waved and curled and shining with health, and the total effect, in spite of the clothes, the scent and the diamonds encrusting her fingers, was of the comfortable, welcoming dumpiness of a favorite nanny.

The purser introduced her. "This lady," he explained to me, "is the wife of a director of the shipping company."

He proceeded to speak to her in Turkish too rapid for me to follow, but from his gestures towards me and towards the vacant berth he was putting forward eloquently the story of our plight. The lady looked at first bewildered, then solemn, then sympathetic. She waved the purser to silence and, grasping my hands, spoke to me in excellent French. Of course, my friend must come and share the cabin. No one needed the other bunk. And she had medicines in her luggage she was sure would help. She would give me the address of a doctor in Istanbul in case my friend had not recovered by the time we arrived there. And tomorrow I could have her berth. She was leaving at the next port to join her husband.

I was as effusive as I could be with my thanks. She laughed, and patted my shoulder, and said since she usually spent the day in the saloon playing bridge, it would be no trouble to her at all.

"Fetch her at once," she cried, shooing us out of the door. "Don't leave her with that mob up there another moment."

Outside I thanked the purser and asked the price of the berth.

"There is no charge, Miss Howard," he said. "It is a cabin reserved for directors of the company and their families. I told Madame your father was also the director of a shipping company."

Without comment I handed him the money I had estimated to be the cost of a cabin. Without comment he slipped it into his pocket.

I spent most of that day in the cabin nursing Bernice. She had a high fever and was racked with fits of shivering. Our benefactress Madame Ağaoğlu produced tablets she was sure would defeat any fever.

"Could it be malaria?" she wondered.

"Surely not," I said. "Not in these days."

"The region you have been traveling in was once infested by malaria. My grandparents would never go there for fear of it. It is supposed to be clear of it now, but when you see symptoms like your friend's, you wonder. And traveling as you tell me you have been doing, in crowded buses, mixing with peasants—I admire young people of today, especially young women, for their independence, but I think perhaps your father might have overdone the freedom he has allowed you. A little more money, a little more comfort in your journey might have avoided this trouble. Of course, it could be an infection from the food. Heaven knows what you have been eating. I will send you something I have supervised myself. No, not a word! And make sure you eat it. You will need to keep up your strength to look after your friend."

A little later a steward arrived with a tray loaded with food: grilled cutlets, salad, a pilav with chicken, a dish of eggplant, a bottle of red Turkish wine. I ate about half of it, and Bernice took some plain rice. By nightfall the shivering had stopped and she had fallen into a quiet sleep. Madame Ağaoğlu was still in the saloon, engaged in another battle at the bridge table. I decided to go find a place for myself for the night on deck. I gathered up my things and opened the cabin door. As I did so, the door of the cabin opposite was opened and a man came out. The passageway was dimly lit by one small electric bulb, but there was enough light for me to recognize him: the man from the taxi. It was a totally unexpected shock. I slipped back into the cabin and closed the door, wondering, even as I did so, why I was avoiding him, why I should feel guilty at seeing him. He should be the one avoiding me after his cavalier treatment of us, stranding us on a deserted road in the afternoon heat. But some instinct warned me not to confront him, not to challenge that powerful, stony presence.

He had gone when after a few minutes I set out again and began to make my way back to the deck.

It was late. The deck passengers had already settled down to sleep. Apart from the muffled throb of the engines, the ship was quiet. But not restful. My acquaintance from the taxi had left behind him a trail of menace, concocted entirely out of my imagination but none the less real for that. I found it eerie to walk along the shadowy corridors and empty companionways, and when I turned a corner and came across a tableau of violence, it seemed almost inevitable. One man stood facing two others. They seemed to have trapped him against the ship's rail, leaving him no escape but the sea. It was too dark to distinguish his face beneath the peasant's cap he wore, but in that first instance I had the impression of height, of concentration and a nervous catlike tension. The next moment one of his attackers sprang at him, knife in hand, ripping it upwards in a savage movement that could have killed if it had made contact. The tall man sidestepped, missing the blow, and caught the other's wrist, bending it back to force away the knife. The second attacker moved close in, waiting his chance.

It was then I came to life. I was carrying a haversack, stuffed full of clothes and books, and I swung it hard into the back of the second man, knocking him off-balance with the surprise of my attack. I began to shout, too, saying anything to make a noise, to bring other people to the scene. The intended victim seized his chance and almost flung the first man directly at the second. Already thrown by my assault, he went down, smashing his head against the metal rail. His partner leaped over him and vanished into the darkness. He struggled to his feet and scrambled after him, hands clutched to his head. I stopped shouting. No one had come.

The tall man brushed himself down. He seemed quite unmoved by the incident.

"Thank you," he said in Turkish. "That was a brave thing to do." Then he paused and laughed, staring at me in the dim light. "I'm sorry. I thought at first you were a boy. I only saw your outline, with the trousers." He added in English: "I'm very grateful to you."

There is no mistaking your own tongue spoken by a native, as opposed to a good linguist with another mother tongue.

"You're English," I said.

"Yes."

"Are you all right?"

"I could do with a drink. Couldn't you do with a drink?"

"I wouldn't know how to get one. There's no bar on board." I had forgotten the half-finished bottle of wine in the cabin.

"I've got some raki. Follow me."

I paused. His calmness was more disturbing than a more normal reaction would have been, of anger, excitement or relief. The episode had terrified me. There had been such an intensity, such a grim purpose in that attack.

He came closer to me. "What is it?"

"Shouldn't you tell the captain what's happened? Get a search started? They might catch those men if you acted fast."

"I doubt it. They'll have melted back into the crowd. Would you recognize them again? I wouldn't."

"You don't know them?"

"That's an odd question. Why should you think that?"

"I got the impression, I don't know why"—I spoke hesitantly —"that you all knew each other, that they'd been hunting you—" I broke off.

There was a short silence. Then he said: "They followed me when I left the main deck. Most Turks still have the fond belief that all foreigners are wealthy, so no doubt they seized the opportunity for a little armed robbery."

"But you don't look like a foreigner. The way you're dressed . . . No one would guess at first glance that you were a foreigner."

He took my arm in a gentle but insistent grasp. "Come on. I

don't think we should hang about here, do you? And I really could do with that drink."

He guided me to a secluded part of the boat deck. "Wait here. I'll be back in a moment."

When he returned, he was carrying an old-fashioned cardboard suitcase tied shut with a leather strap. He put it down with a triumphant gesture in front of me. "Everything the traveler could require." He squatted down beside me and opened it, producing from the melee of shirts, socks, sweater and books two plastic glasses, a plastic bottle of mineral water and a half-full bottle of raki. He poured two generous measures of the spirit, added water and handed me a glass. He raised his own glass to me in the gesture of a toast.

"What shall it be?" he said. "To travel? To adventure? Or perhaps just 'Thank you.' For saving my—" He paused, then completed it. "For saving my few remaining liras."

I sipped the cloudy liquid. It warmed and soothed me. Perhaps it was that that made me careless, speaking my thoughts in a way I would never normally have done.

"You were going to say 'for saving my life,' " I said. "Those men meant to kill you."

"You have an overactive imagination," he said. "Forget what you think you saw. It was an everyday scuffle. Soon over, soon forgotten. It happens all the time."

I raised my head and met his gaze. There was a lamp fixed to the bulwark beside me, and its light fell on us. We were isolated in that pool of light. It created a sense of intimacy. Beyond the light, people moved, murmured, turned in their sleep; within it, we were enclosed in a cell of silence.

When he sat down, he had pulled off his cap. Strands of thick brown hair had fallen forward across his forehead. In repose his face had a grave, sculptural quality, all planes and angles. When he smiled, it was with an enormous charm. I thought him well aware of that charm, but that didn't stop it from having its effect.

He poured more raki into his glass. "And what exactly are you doing here," he asked, "wandering about on this boat alone?"

I told him briefly what I was doing there, what had happened to Bernice.

"So you're not alone," he said. "That's a pity. But you're quite right to take such care of your friend. Western systems can get knocked out by bugs the natives take in their stride. I seem to have become immune to most of them, thank God. And of course, this helps." He took another drink. "Excellent antiseptic. Have some more."

I shook my head. "Are you working in Turkey?"

"I have in the past. I've done some teaching. But I'm really a glorified tourist, like you. I wander round, looking at things." He paused. "You were wondering about my clothes, I think, and this perhaps." He touched the battered suitcase. "I haven't much money, and they're cheap and convenient." He was wearing a shabby jacket and trousers with a collarless shirt. His shoes were worn and cracked. His clothes made no difference to his attraction.

"It's easier to see the country if you're anonymous," I said.

He smiled gently. "Not only beautiful but intelligent. What a pity that you're not alone."

"You said that before. Why is it such a pity?"

"Because now I can't ask you to come with me when I leave the boat tomorrow."

I looked up into his face. He looked back at me with a steadfast, serious expression I was to remember later, when I had to make judgments on tenuous evidence.

I said: "Would you have asked me?"

"Yes. Would you have come?"

"Yes," I said.

He sighed and reached across me for my glass. "Let us have one more drink together before we part. I must go in a moment. There is someone on this boat I have to see."

"About what happened?"

"You really must," he said, "forget what happened."

We finished that last drink together in silence. Then he put the glasses and the bottles back into the suitcase and refastened the strap. He stood up and offered me his hand to help pull myself up. The clasp of our hands was like an electric shock. As we stood together, hands locked, he closed his mouth on mine. His breath tasted sweetly of the raki.

"I don't think we shall meet again," he said, "but you never know." He stepped out of the circle of light and was gone, lost in the darkness.

I spent that night on the floor of Madame Ağaoğlu's cabin. She had insisted on it when I went back to check on Bernice. Bernice was still sleeping, her forehead was cool and there was normal color in her cheeks.

"You see, I told you those tablets would work." Madame Ağaoğlu had been watching me from her bunk, exotic in a silk nightdress, smoking a Turkish cigarette. "Now where are you going?"

"Back on deck," I said. "I just wanted to see she was all right."

"What nonsense! You cannot possibly go back up there alone, to sleep amongst those peasants. It was bad enough when there were the two of you. You can sleep on the floor here. Put this blanket down. It will be quite clean. And take a pillow. You will be more comfortable here than on the open deck, and if your friend needs you, you will be here."

She was quite right. I hadn't liked leaving Bernice but had thought I had no choice. Now I chose to stay.

I didn't sleep until it was almost morning. For the first time in my life I had learned that someone could cause you pain merely by existing. I didn't know his name; he didn't know mine. Tomorrow he would be gone. Even if I got up now and searched the ship for him, it would make no difference. It would be better to forget the whole incident. As I listened to Madame Ağaoğlu snoring gently like a purring kitten, it was already developing a dreamlike quality in my mind. By tomorrow I could convince myself it had never happened. I had imagined it all, the meeting, my own emotions, my own certainty. As last I slept.

The boat docked at six. I went up with Madame Ağaoğlu to see her safely off and thank her once more for her kindness. Before she left, she gave me a card with her Istanbul address. "I shall be back there at the end of the month, but that is no use for you. Never mind, when you come to Turkey again, look me up. Take care."

She was one of the last off the boat. I had waited to carry some of her belongings for her, and so I was too late. He must have gone as soon as the gangway was put down. But if I could not see his tall figure among the departing passengers, there was one I did recognize: impassive of face as ever, the man from the taxi was also leaving the ship.

The rest of the voyage was uneventful. Bernice slept much of the time. I read or wandered over the ship, watching the other passengers, watching the coast, gazing with blank mind at the changing colors of the sea. She was the one who had been ill, but we were both behaving like convalescents. Our journey had possibly been too long. Now that there was no effort to be made, the strains of travel, like a long-hidden weariness, began to tell. That, at least, was how I explained my state of mind to myself.

There were, as far as I heard, no other attacks made on passengers. Bernice was so horrified when I told her of the incident that she overcame my first decision to do as the Englishman had asked and forget what I had seen. My conviction that it was an attempt not at robbery but deliberate murder I had witnessed began to seem melodramatic in the light of day.

"If those two men are still on board, other people could be in danger," Bernice urged me. "You must tell someone."

So I went back to the purser.

He listened gravely, hands clasped before him in an attitude of prayer.

"Why does not the man attacked himself make the charge?" he asked me.

"He has left the ship."

He shook his head. "So no doubt have the thieves. You should have reported this at once, Miss Howard, not waited until morning. There is little we can do now. You can give no clear descriptions, the man concerned has gone and you cannot give me his name. However"—he shrugged—"I will inform the captain." He added politely that he was thankful I had not been injured in the attack.

"You will be safer at night in the cabin. It is quite satisfactory?"

"It is very comfortable, thank you. By the way, who had the cabin opposite, number seven?"

"Number seven?" He seemed puzzled by my query but took a list from a drawer and ran a finger down it. "A Mr. N. Okyer. Why? Is he troubling you?"

"No, no. In any case, he is no longer on board. He went ashore this morning."

"I do not think so. He is booked through to Istanbul." A sudden understanding lit his face. "Ah, you wanted his cabin, too?"

I laughed and left him.

A little later in the morning the purser came down and unlocked the door of cabin number seven. There were no signs of occupation. Mr. Okyer had indeed departed, and I had, for all the good it did me apart from satisfying my curiosity, a name for the man in the taxi. By afternoon the purser had relet the cabin.

Although I had described the night attack in detail to Bernice, I had not told her everything about my encounter with the Englishman. Our conversation over the raki, for instance. I found I did not want to discuss something so private and so ephemeral. I had made a good attempt at erasing it from my mind. But it was easier for me when we finally left the ship.

We remained in Istanbul only long enough to collect mail and buy tickets. Within the week we were in Athens. For Bernice it was the beginning of her year's adventure, for me it was only a staging post, but Athens even at the height of the tourist season, clamorous with people, crowded with traffic, hot and dusty and exhausting, could still contrive to work its old enchantment, and I was glad to snatch even a few days there. The light was still the same as it had been for centuries, and the freshness at dawn, and the village life that continued behind the façade of souvenir shops and tourist tavernas.

We were staying in an apartment rented for Bernice by one of her Greek friends. It was small and at night too stifling to sleep, but it had a balcony on which to take our breakfast coffee, and one could always sleep on the roof. The friend and her husband had an apartment in the same block. One evening they took us to dine in Piraeus with another Greek couple, an American journalist and a man from the British Embassy. The American and the Englishman had known each other for years and, as the meal progressed, began capping each other's stories with great good humor. They were both immensely knowledgeable about Greece and promised to take Bernice under their wing and introduce her to anyone of interest in Athens. They knew, naturally enough, the professor of archaeology whose temporary assistant she was to be.

"He's back in Athens. A delightful man. You'll like him."

"I know," Bernice agreed. "I saw him this morning. As a matter of fact, he invited me to join a party for dinner tonight."

"You should have gone," her friend said emphatically. "Why did you not accept?"

"We had already arranged this evening—"

"We could always have arranged another evening. This is just for friends. That would have been for your job. It is very important to be on good terms with the man you are going to work for."

"It was only politeness on his part," Bernice said. "He thought I might not know anyone in Athens. He was being kind."

"Nonsense!" said the American. "He's a great party man when he gets going. Why don't we go and join him? You know his haunts, Tom."

Buoyed up by wine and enthusiasm, we suddenly decided it was imperative that we reunite Bernice with her professor. We piled into the cars and roared back to Athens.

I don't recall how many nightclubs in the Plaka we visited before we found him, I was getting a little hazy by then, but find him we did—and not only the professor.

He was seated with several friends at a round table in a small taverna with the steaming humidity of a laundry. The table, its cloth stained with spilled wine and the odd remnants of a meal, littered with glasses, coffee cups and half-empty bottles, spoke of a casual, happy party. Everyone was in shirt sleeves. In the corner, a bouzouki band, sweating vigorously, was pounding out a popular tune, and three men, arms about each other's shoulders, were weaving gently in a drunken dance.

As soon as he saw us, the professor rose to his feet, arms outstretched in welcome. Professor Andriades was a small man, brown as a nut, with shoulders slightly stooped as if he had spent too many years crouched down in the trenches of his digs. His expressive face was full of humor and intelligence. I could see that Bernice was going to enjoy her time with him.

The Greeks all knew each other. There was much embracing and laughter and pulling out of chairs. I found myself seated opposite the professor between the Englishman, Tom Shaw, and the American. Tom Shaw was tall and thin with the kind of face that looks good on a grouse moor. The American, Joe Parker, was thickset, with a high complexion, gray hair and a deadpan way of delivering his jokes.

Tom Shaw leaned back in his chair watching the dancers.

"I see Robert Denning is back," he said, gesturing towards them. "And in his usual form. Don't let him see you, Paul, or he'll latch onto the party."

The professor looked amused. "But he is with the party. Or he was. There was some slight altercation with his girl friend. They went outside to sort it out. It looks as if they didn't settle it. He came back alone. No doubt he's dancing now to forget his troubles."

"He's one of the people to keep away from," Joe Parker said half-jokingly to Bernice. "Unreliable, drinks too much and loaded with charm."

"What does he do?" I asked.

"Well, apart from being a professional bastard—"

"You are being too hard on him," Andriades said. "He's an exceptionally capable young man when he puts his mind to it. With his background, you can excuse some eccentricity."

"He's getting too old to rely on that for excuses. You're not giving him a job, are you?"

"He's coming to work on the dig for a few weeks."

"You'll be lucky if he stays two days. He'll create havoc among those earnest girl students you've got up there."

"Joe's only jealous," Tom explained to me with a serious expression, "because he's never got around to that book all journalists are going to write one day and Robert Denning has published two."

"What kind of books?"

"Oh, travel. 'Walks through deepest Anatolia.' That sort of thing."

Bernice looked curiously at the dancers. "Which one is he?"

"Have a guess."

"The one in the middle?"

"See what I mean," Joe observed. "The man never misses, even when smashed."

I had recognized him as soon as we came in. The tail of his shirt adrift from his trousers, dark hair tumbling over his forehead, a seraphic smile on his face, he was even so unmistakably the man I had sat and talked to in lamplit seclusion on the Turkish steamer.

I said to Tom Shaw: "Do you know where I could get hold of copies of his books? I'd like to read them."

"Would you?" he said. "Oh, dear!"

"I've just come from Turkey," I said.

He smiled. "I'm sorry. I didn't really mean to imply that you had been struck by a *coup de foudre* at your first sight of Mr.

Denning. I'll find a copy of one or the other of them for you."

"Thank you," I said, but he was no longer paying me any attention. A girl of striking appearance had entered the taverna and was making directly for our table. She had a full, bosomy figure encased in a flame red dress, long dark hair that curled over her shoulders and brilliant black eyes.

She went straight to Andriades. She did not waste more than a glance on any of the other guests at the table.

"Did he come back?" she said.

The professor nodded in the direction of the dancers, who by now were ambling to a stop. The girl went over to them. She put a hand on Robert Denning's sleeve and drew him away from the others. She began to talk to him.

"This should be interesting," Tom murmured.

I turned away. I took the drink that had been poured for me and sipped it slowly. I did not want to be put in the position of a voyeur. If I could have done so without comment, I would have left. A deep sadness was spreading within me and an anger at myself for my naïveté, my lack of worldliness in making so much of what had clearly been no more than an automatic reaction to any pretty girl.

"Would you have come with me?" he had asked.

And like all the others, I had replied, "Yes." I didn't want to be like all the others.

I heard his voice. "It seems we are leaving."

They had come back to the table. He stood smiling amiably at us all. "It seems a pity, just as the party's getting going. But Cleo wants to go."

With a proprietary gesture the girl fetched a jacket slung over the back of a chair and put it round his shoulders. He shrugged it off impatiently, and she caught it and held it, waiting.

"Hullo, Tom, hullo, Joe, when did you two arrive? What nefarious plots are you hatching now? Scandal and rumor, scandal and rumor, when you two get together, governments fall." He broke off. "Well, well," he said. "Well, well, well."

He was looking directly at me. I could not avoid his eyes.

"Where did you find her?" he said. "Which one of you is she with?"

"Come on, Rob," Tom said. "Don't be so greedy. Leave a few girls for us."

Cleo's patience was running short.

Paul Andriades stood up. "I want to see you tomorrow, Robert, tell you more about what we've found so far this season. There's something I'd like your opinion on. Can you get to my place by ten?"

He put his arm round Robert's shoulder and began to guide him to the door. Cleo followed, her face sullen.

Everyone relaxed, as if at the passing of a storm.

"My God," Joe said. "He certainly picks them. What a figure!"

I said: "Would Professor Andriades really ask his opinion on his work?"

"Yes," Tom said. "Robert Denning is quite knowledgeable and quite experienced."

"He ought to be," Joe said. "It's been easy enough for him."

"His father was a well-known archaeologist," Tom explained. "Joe means it was easy for him to move around in that world."

"Why don't you tell her the rest?" Joe said. "Why everyone was so sorry for him? How he's traded on it ever since?"

"Shut up, Joe," Tom said.

Professor Andriades came back. He pulled out his chair and sat down.

"I'm sorry about that," he said to me.

"It's all right," I said. "He didn't bother me."

"It was Cleo I thought might bother you. I don't think she likes competition. It was something about another woman that set off the first row." He pointed to a stain on the cloth. "She threw a wineglass at him."

"She's new, isn't she?" Tom said. "I haven't seen her before."

Andriades shrugged. "Who knows where he finds them. I think they find him. But by the way she is behaving I don't think she'll last long."

It was late when the evening ended. We got back to the apartment nearer three than two. When I awoke next morning, Bernice had already gone out. She had left a note to say she would be at the National Archaeological Museum. "Meet me there for lunch or not," she wrote, "as you feel. If it's not, see you later."

I made coffee and took it out onto the balcony. On the balcony of the flat opposite a small brown bird chirruped and hopped about a wicker cage, delighting in the morning or desperate to escape its imprisonment, according to your mood. Below, the residents' cars parked slantwise, half on, half off the sidewalk, made the street look like a scene of haphazard accident. The taxi nudging its way through its narrow confines went as carefully as if it were searching for the injured. It stopped outside our block, but no one got out.

It was my last day in Athens. I had awakened with a black depression almost too tangible to throw off. It weighed me down, pressing upon my head with a leaden weight. I pretended it was a hangover. I showered and dressed and packed my few belongings ready for the journey tomorrow. I left the flat on my way to meet Bernice.

The taxi I had seen earlier was still parked outside. As I approached, a man got out and came towards me. Robert Denning. He was dressed in a crumpled linen suit and a blue shirt and looked tired. Tired but sober.

He said: "Andriades gave me your address, but he couldn't remember the flat number. He says you're not staying in Athens long."

"I'm leaving tomorrow."

"Then I'm glad I didn't miss you."

He looked at me in silence, a slight frown creasing his forehead. He seemed uncertain now he had found me what he intended to do about it.

I said: "You have finished your travels in Turkey?"

"For the time being." He paused. "Did you tell anyone——?"

"I told my cousin about the attack on the boat. I haven't told her the man attacked was you."

"I see."

"Is that why you came to find me? To ask me to keep quiet about it?"

He said seriously: "You must know that's not why I came."

He seemed to come to some decision. He said: "Where are you going now?"

"To meet my cousin."

"Do you have to?"

"No, I don't have to."

"Then come on." He took my arm and drew me towards the taxi.

"Where are we going?"

"Anywhere. It doesn't matter. We've got to talk. We'll go to Lycabettus, get away from these streets."

The taxi driver took us as far up Lycabettus Hill as he could, and we walked the rest of the way to the top. People were coming and going up and down the steps which led to the Chapel of Saint George, and the terrace of the café near the summit was crowded; but compared with the rest of Athens, it was peaceful, and the view across the white blocks of the city to the Acropolis, golden stone against a dense blue sky, calmed my mind.

In the taxi Robert Denning had kissed me once, tentatively, then leaned back satisfied, as if we had passed some test. "That's all right," he said. "I didn't imagine it."

He closed his eyes and completed the rest of the journey in silence, his hand clasping mine. He had kept my hand in his as we climbed the hill, holding it tightly as if it were a lifeline it wouldn't be safe to let go.

In the café he was drinking brandy. I watched him warily. I told myself his good looks, the attraction between us constituted a trap I must not fall into. But at the same time my depression had vanished and I was full of a singing joy.

I said: "You've recovered from the party last night?"

He pulled a face. "I drank a lot last night because I was bored."

"Even with Cleo?"

"It may sound ridiculous," he said, "but Cleo has really nothing to do with me. I've known her only a week. I went to beg a bed from an American friend of mine. When I got there, I found he had gone away on business. He'd left me a spare key and I moved in. Ten minutes later Cleo turns up with an armful of shopping. He'd apparently sublet the flat to her for a month. That's her story anyway. I think she was just a girl friend of his who'd decided to stay on. She invited me to stay. I'd nowhere else to go, so I did. It was my own fault, but I didn't expect to arouse quite such a frenzy of desire in her ample breast. I'm probably very weak, but I find it hard to resist someone so determined to seduce me. It seemed impolite to reject her. Besides, I was missing you."

"Missing me?"

"It's extraordinary to have to admit it, but I've missed you every day, every night. I thought you might have been there to see me off the boat."

"I wanted to," I said. "I was held up until it was too late."

"Well," he said. "What are we going to do about this? I've committed myself to Andriades's dig. You are going back to England. Why go? Come to the dig with me."

I explained to him why it was not possible. In London I had an interview at the university about the interpreter's course I was to take in October. A few days after that I was booked to fly to Canada to see my mother.

"My stepfather died in April. She's not enjoying being a widow for the second time. I've promised to stay a month."

"We've met at the wrong time, haven't we?" he said. "I don't know where I shall be in a month. But have you thought how strange it is we should meet again like this? What the odds are against it?" He looked away from me across the panorama of the city. "I don't want to let you go. But I haven't the time to woo you, to convince you of my feelings. There is only one way I know of convincing you of my feelings. Let's go find a room somewhere."

He might have expected me to hesitate, to prevaricate. Instead, I said: "All right," and stood up, waiting for him to pay the bill.

If I was being a fool, I didn't care. If I simply turned out to be another name on his Don Juan's list, it didn't matter. The air, the sun, the light had intoxicated me. The brilliance of the day matched the shining carelessness of my mood. It was my last day of Mediterranean life, my last day of irresponsibility. We had met twice now by chance. How many more chances like this could I expect? I couldn't relinquish the intensity of the moment. At that moment I loved him, and something in the atmosphere, some distant pagan echoes perhaps, making themselves heard across the commercial heart of the modern city, would not let me deny it.

We found a room above a restaurant in a quiet quarter of the city. It was cool and shady, its shuttered windows opening onto a garden of tangled vines and sweet-smelling roses. The proprietor knew Robert. I did not ask how many times he might have used the room. We took wine and glasses up with us, but we did not stop to drink the wine.

He did not make me feel like a number. He made love with a longing and a passion I had never expected to experience, as if he might die tomorrow.

"I wish you weren't going to Canada," he said. "It's too far away. But perhaps, after all, it's just as well." He fell silent.

"Shall we end it here?" he said. "Do you want to?"

"No," I said. But I could see no future for us beyond this room.

"What will you do," I asked, "after Andriades's dig? Will you stay in Greece? Will you go back to Turkey?" Even as I spoke, I was thinking: Bernice will be at the dig. There will not be a complete break between us. "They say you write books. Is that what you were doing in Turkey? Getting material for a book?"

"Who's been talking to you about me?"

"Those friends of yours at the table last night. The American and the Englishman. They said that everyone used to be sorry for you. Why were they sorry for you?"

"Perhaps because my mother committed suicide when my father left her, leaving me completely on my own. I was eight years old, and I've been on my own ever since."

"Didn't your father come back to look after you?"

"It wasn't possible. He died."

"Then who did?"

"My father's solicitor became my guardian. He was a bachelor who didn't like children. In school holidays I stayed with whichever friend's parents would have me. When I was fourteen, I began to travel on my own."

"It sounds Dickensian."

"Are *you* sorry for me now?"

"Yes."

He smiled. "Come and show me how sorry you are."

"I was beginning to worry about you," Bernice said.

"I came to tell you I'm dining out," I said. "I'm meeting Robert Denning. You don't mind, do you?"

"I'd heard that he asked for your address."

"My God." I spoke with sudden irritation. "This is a gossip-ridden clique you're joining. Don't they ever mind their own business?"

"I'm sorry," Bernice said calmly. "I didn't mean to upset you. Are you sure you're wise going out with him? I'm wondering what his girl friend might do." She grinned at me. "You don't want Cleo coming after you with an ax."

I smiled back weakly. "I'm leaving tomorrow. She can have him back then."

Bernice came closer. She put a hand on my arm. "What is it, Frances?"

I said: "I've been with him all day. I don't know how I shall stand London and Canada, Bernice. I don't know how I shall bear it."

"This has all happened very suddenly, hasn't it?" she said.

"These things happen."

"I know. It's like a firework: spontaneous combustion. Those affairs are all right if you never meet again. Otherwise they tend to drag on to a messy end. It's probably lucky that you're going tomorrow. You won't get hurt. At least not so badly." She sighed and shook her head. "He's certainly living up to his reputation, isn't he! I thought they were exaggerating last night."

"Don't joke about it, will you?"

"I'm not joking." She said quietly: "What does he think about your going tomorrow? Does he want you to stay?"

"Yes and no," I said. "I think probably no. That's why I'm going."

"Well, have a drink," Bernice said practically. "Have a shower. Calm down some of that glow you came in with. Just let me know if you're not catching the plane. I don't want to go out to the airport to wave good-bye to an empty seat."

As I was under the shower, she called to me: "Paul Andriades asked us to dine by the way. The same place we met him last night. I accepted, but I'll explain about you. He'll be two guests short. He said Robert Denning was coming."

I put my head round the curtain. "I'm meeting Robert there."

Bernice shrugged. "Difficult to have a tête-à-tête with four. He must have forgotten Andriades's invitation. Still, it will be nice to have your company on your last night after all. Even," she added with a gentle smile, "for the few minutes it takes him to think up a reasonable excuse to carry you away."

I had arranged to meet Robert at nine. We arrived at the taverna a little before. Paul Andriades was already there. He was delighted I had been able to accept his invitation. It was very sad I had had such a short stay in Athens. We must make my last night memorable.

It was difficult after that sort of attention to explain that I hadn't accepted his invitation after all. Bernice gave me a sardonic glance and left me to fend for myself. I decided to leave explanations to Robert.

I was not alarmed that he was a little late: ten minutes, half an hour late. The other two were talking shop. I was content to sit and listen.

At ten o'clock Paul thought that perhaps we might eat. It was obvious Robert had been held up. He wouldn't mind if we started. He was sure to come. Paul knew that Robert very much wanted to meet me. I said nothing. Half past ten came, and then eleven. The restaurant was filling up. The musicians appeared to friendly applause and began to play. Friends of Paul arrived and joined the table, as we had done the previous night. It seemed he kept court here whenever he was in Athens.

Bernice said to me: "Do you know Robert's telephone number?"

"No."

"Do you want me to ask Paul for it?"

"No," I said. The heat and noise of the restaurant were beginning to affect me. The music was circling in my head, round and round, the insistent, repetitive beat drumming against my temples. I had eaten too little food for the wine I had drunk.

I smiled at Bernice, a little shakily no doubt.

"I know how to take a hint," I said.

She reached for my hand and squeezed it. Her face was full of concern for me. I was afraid that in a moment others might notice that concern.

"I knew I was probably being a fool," I said, "but I couldn't really believe I was. Can you understand that?"

She nodded. "Yes, of course."

I sat still, looking down at the cloth. I was visualizing the conversation in the café on Lycabettus Hill. I was remembering the long afternoon.

"I'm not a fool," I said suddenly. "Something's wrong." I stood up. "I'm going to the flat. He might be trying to reach me there." I looked at my watch. It was nearly midnight.

Bernice stood up, too. Now she was really worried about me. Paul Andriades broke off an animated conversation with a newly arrived friend and glanced up at us. With a great effort I pulled myself together.

"I don't want to break up the evening," I said. "But I still have some packing to do and an early start tomorrow."

It was a good enough excuse. Someone volunteered to look for a taxi, and we ran the gauntlet of handshakes and farewells.

"Pity Robert didn't show up," Andriades said. "He'll be sorry to have missed you."

Outside, the air seemed almost chill after the heat of the taverna. The street, little more than an alleyway off a noisier route, was full of shadows. We waited by the entrance, I seething with impatience to be gone. I felt stranded there, cut off, unable to take any positive action.

"Here's your taxi. That didn't take long." Andriades had come to the door with us.

I turned. I had been watching the other end of the street. The car was moving very slowly, a dark sedan crawling along no faster than a walking pace.

"What's the matter with him?" Andriades said. He stepped out into the road, waving his hands to attract the driver's attention. As he did so, there was movement from the shadows and a man came stumbling out into the light. He was about halfway between us and the car, a little nearer the car. He couldn't seem to walk straight; he staggered from side to side. But he had seen Andriades and half raised a hand in what might be taken for an answering wave.

"That's Robert!" I cried.

The car had stopped. The door opened, and a woman came running down the street towards the swaying man. It was Cleo.

Bernice was holding me back, her hand grasping my wrist.

"He's hopelessly drunk," she said. "You wouldn't get any sense out of him. Don't get involved."

"Let me go, Bernice."

She took her hand away. Behind us another taxi now appeared, with the benefactor who had captured it for us, grinning cheerfully in triumph.

"That was pretty quick, wasn't it?"

"Yes, indeed. Thank you so much."

He went back into the restaurant, and Bernice turned to me. "Come on."

The driver of the other car had joined Cleo. They took hold of Robert, steadying him, and began trying to lead him to the car. He broke away and, swinging wildly with both arms, caught the driver across the face.

"Oh, dear me," said Andriades sadly, "this won't do." He walked quickly forward. I left Bernice and ran after him. Andriades spoke softly to Robert. Robert put his hands on his friend's shoulders, as if for support, and stood with head bent, breathing heavily.

I said: "Robert?" He raised his head and looked at me. He looked terrible, his suit filthy, buttons ripped from it, his face white and strained as if the struggle simply to stay upright were taking all his concentration. The eyes that met mine were blank and uncomprehending. Cleo had been standing watching, as if uncertain what to do. Now she shrugged, muttered something quickly to the driver and led the way back to her car. In a moment it was backing fast down the alley towards the main road.

Bernice had followed me. "I think we should go. There's nothing we can do, and the taxi's waiting."

"Yes," Andriades said. "You go. I'll look after Robert."

I said: "I want to stay." He glanced at me in surprise, his expression changing after a moment to one of resigned understanding. He had, after all, given Robert my address.

"My dear young lady," he said, "I don't think that would be very wise. You couldn't do any good. In this state I don't think he even recognizes you. He's obviously been in a fight. No doubt he got involved in an argument in some bar on the way here. Perhaps he rang Cleo for help. It looks as if she was trying to find him before the police picked him up. I'll take him home and clean him up." He put a paternal hand on my arm. "I'm sorry about this. I'm afraid Robert is not the most reliable of men, charming though he is."

"He looks ill rather than drunk," I said.

"He looks as if he is about to pass out," Bernice said practically. "You'd better take our taxi; we'll get another." With typical efficiency she had everything organized in a moment. The driver came and helped Andriades get Robert into the taxi. Doors slammed; engine revved; they were away. It was all done so quickly it was almost like a conspiracy to keep me from him.

"Suppose he is ill," I said. "Suppose he fell or was hit and his skull's fractured. He could be dying. We should have told Paul to take him to hospital."

"He will if he thinks it necessary," Bernice said. "He'll look after him. But I wouldn't worry. He simply passed out from too much brandy. He stank of it, you've got to admit it."

"I'm feeling cold," I said. "So cold."

Bernice sighed. She linked her arm through mine. "Come on, we'll walk down to the other street and find a cab."

On the way home I said: "He had almost reached the taverna. He was coming to find me."

"And perhaps he got drunk because you're leaving. Would that be any comfort to you? Look, Frances, I'm sorry this happened, but maybe it's as well you've seen him like this. Now you know what you'd have to cope with if you did stay." She put a consoling hand on mine. "He'll probably ring to apologize before you go."

But he didn't ring. Bernice telephoned Andriades next morning at my insistence to find out what she could.

"Robert Denning must be all right," she told me. "Paul put him in his spare room. When he went to look at him this morning, he was gone."

"Did he leave him a note?"

"No, nothing. No thanks, no explanation. Just vanished. Paul's been ringing the number Robert had given him, but there's no reply. He doesn't know if it's the number of the flat Robert's staying in. He didn't give him the address."

I thought perhaps Robert might come to our apartment or, barring that, the airport. He knew which plane I was catching; he even knew which hotel I was staying in in London. He knew all my plans. I didn't even know where he was living in Athens.

I waited in the flat till the last minute, but he didn't come. He was not at the airport either. Bernice was the only one there to say good-bye. So I left Athens and set off for my new life in a state of confusion and grief and despair, and those words are not too dramatic for the way I felt.

CHAPTER 2

It was raining in London, a sad drizzle weeping down the window panes. The small hotel I had booked into in Bloomsbury was full of Swedes and Danes and Germans, all wearing mackintoshes and carrying guidebooks. I couldn't face dining there, sitting at a table on my own, pretending to read a book. I went to a pub round the corner and had sandwiches and beer and then came back and slept the sleep of exhaustion.

As I walked to my interview next day, everything seemed alien to me: the buildings, the people, the sky. The muted colors I had once loved, the soft grays, the subtle greens, seemed drab and dull, and I as lifeless and dull as my surroundings, wandering like a small lost ghost through an empty world.

The term had not yet started. Familiar rooms were deserted. There were strangers in the library and the corridors. I was too early and had to wait in an outer office, listening to the chatter of typewriters and the echoes of unknown footsteps.

When I came away, administrative details completed, forms filled, official consent received for my possible late arrival for the course from Canada, I found myself wondering what on earth I should do with my time. I knew I had allowed myself the space of these few days to find somewhere to live during the coming term, buy a few clothes possibly, see a few friends, but I seemed to lack the slightest energy necessary to do any of those things. I came to a bookshop and spent an hour there only to find when I wished to buy a book that I had very little money left and should have gone at once to my bank. I was pleased to have some purpose to my day and grew more cheerful. With money in my pocket and traveler's checks bought for Canada, I plunged into the bazaars of Oxford Street and spent with the kind of wild extravagance only those who have to be careful with money can understand.

I returned to the hotel at seven and found Robert Denning standing in the hall.

"Where have you been?" he said. "I've been waiting for you for hours."

He said it lightly, as a joke meant to disarm, but my face must have expressed so much of what I felt, bewilderment, elation, anger, that he drew me outside again into the street as if afraid of the effect of an explosion of emotion in the confined spaces of the hotel.

"What are you doing here?" I cried. He began walking rapidly along the pavement, holding my arm so tightly that he was literally pulling me along with him. I stumbled and nearly dropped packages, handbag, everything. I rebelled and stopped, forcing him to stop, too, the rage I could allow myself now that I knew he was safe, now that he was here, erupting into words.

"I've no intention of going anywhere with you. So you'd better tell me what you want here and now."

"You're very indignant. What's the matter?"

"Don't you know? Can't you remember?"

"I know I came here to find you as soon as I could."

"You were supposed to come to the taverna in Athens, but you were a little too drunk to make it."

"Ah, yes. That was unfortunate." He paused. "I understand you waited for me."

"It made no difference that I did. You didn't even recognize me."

"Things were getting rather blurred at that stage. I couldn't see very well. I recognized Paul by his voice. I do vaguely remember hearing yours."

"Were you hurt?"

"I don't think so."

"But you'd been in a fight?"

"I can't remember."

I gazed at him helplessly. Having him here was almost worse than losing him. On my own in London I would have begun to recover. After a month in Canada I would have been back on an even keel. Now his presence was going to be stamped on these streets for me. London was going to become marked for me as Athens now was. There wasn't going to be any easy escape.

"You could have telephoned me," I said. "Let me know you were all right. Said good-bye."

"It wasn't possible for me to telephone you. And I had no intention of saying good-bye."

I said weakly: "Robert, what are you doing here? You are supposed to be going on Paul Andriades's dig, aren't you?"

"I'll be back in Athens the day you fly to Canada."

"You've come to London just to see me? To apologize? To say a final farewell?"

"I've come to marry you."

I stared at him. "That's ridiculous."

"It's the only solution I can see to a ridiculous situation. Look, for God's sake, go and get rid of those parcels. We can't talk standing here. And don't run away out of any back doors. I haven't flown all this way at vast expense to have you disappear on me."

In the narrow hotel room with its neat white counterpane and its sparse modern furniture, I sat down on the bed and tried to collect my thoughts into some rational pattern. If he was serious, if the mention of marriage wasn't an elaborate joke forgotten after the next drink, what did I intend to do about it? I knew what the sensible reaction to this situation would be, what all my kind, logical friends would tell me. Admittedly there was a violent physical attraction between us. Mightn't that vanish, they would say, as quickly as it had appeared? Didn't everyone know that passion burns itself out under the strain of day-to-day living? And what kind of living would that be with Robert Denning? Everything I had heard about him, everything I had seen led to the same bleak conclusion. And to tie yourself to an attractive, feckless drunk was about the stupidest thing one could do. And yet . . . and yet . . . I didn't believe he was really like that. I didn't fool myself I could reform a man of that character, I simply did not accept that that was his character. When it came down to it, I made my mind up on instinct, there in that cold, impersonal room, and it was this instinct that I followed unvaryingly throughout all that was to come.

I went downstairs. Robert was leaning against the reception desk, talking to the porter. He smiled when he saw me and took my hand in a casually possessive gesture. The porter, smoothed into helpfulness by his charm, asked if he could find us a taxi.

"It's only round the corner," Robert said. "We'll walk."

He was like a chameleon, I thought. Unconsciously or deliberately, by means of clothes and manner he had the ability to blend into any background, to become one of any crowd. In Turkey I felt it had been deliberate; perhaps not in Greece or here. And yet, in his light gray suit and unobtrusive tie, he could, if he wished, join any bus queue and virtually disappear.

"Where are we going?" I asked.

"I'm taking you home."

"You have a home in London?"

"Oh, yes. The family establishment." There was a slight irony in his tone. "I've kept it on."

"Since you were eight?"

"Yes, since I was eight."

It looked indeed as if no one had touched it since that time. A large, gloomy mansion flat, badly in need of decoration, its rooms full of solid dark furniture, its carpets worn, its curtains heavy velvet faded in patches by the varying light. In the drawing room Robert opened one of the tall windows. "The air's stale. I haven't been here for months." Through the summer foliage of the plane trees outside I could glimpse the colonnaded façade of the British

Museum. Robert stood beside me, his arm round my shoulders. "At one time the whole block was due to come down—extension for the museum."

"What a pity."

"Perhaps. Anyway, they changed their minds." He kissed me. "But you probably wouldn't want to live here."

"Why not?" I said lightly. "I like space. And it's so convenient for the college."

He was holding me and kissing me. He went on kissing me.

I murmured: "I thought you wanted to talk."

"Later," he said. "We can talk later."

Later he showed me the kitchen and watched me while I made coffee from a jar of instant coffee that had to be hacked into pieces with a spoon.

"How long has this been here?"

"Since the last time I was here."

"I don't suppose you've got anything to eat, have you? I'm ravenous."

"I've got bacon and eggs. I bought them for my breakfast this morning. Do you want to go out to eat?" He looked at his watch. "It's quarter to ten."

I didn't want to go out. I didn't want to move. We cooked the bacon and eggs and ate it in languorous companionship, having a complete breakfast for our dinner, including toast and marmalade and tea when the coffee proved undrinkable.

Robert told me he had arrived in London at five o'clock that morning. He had had to come via Paris; all the Athens–London flights had been full. He had telephoned the hotel at what he thought was a civilized hour to find I had already left.

"By the way," he said, "I gave the hotel as your address. I didn't have another one for you."

"Gave who my address? Why did you need an address?"

"The registry office. For the license."

"The license?"

"The special certificate and license you need to get married at short notice. You'd told me your father's name and profession, and I knew your age. But the hotel was the only address I had."

"Robert, are you serious about this? You're not joking?"

"The license is in the desk in my father's study. It entitles us to be married the day after tomorrow. Come see for yourself."

I put my hand on his arm.

"The idea doesn't appeal to you? Has my exhibition the other evening put you off?"

"How much you drink and how many girl friends you have are none of my business at present," I said. "If we were married, I might consider it was."

"If I told you I wasn't drunk that evening, would you believe me?"

"Yes," I said.

"You would believe anything I told you about myself?"

"Until you proved yourself wrong."

He got up abruptly. "What I want is commitment. I want you to commit yourself to me."

"You have that commitment. You don't need to marry me to have it."

"But I want to marry you. Don't you understand? We are committed, I know that. I knew that in the first minutes we spent together on that wallowing Turkish tub. But you see, commitment to me means for life, and if it is for life, why not marry? And if marry, why not now?"

"But why the hurry?" I asked. "Why not wait until I'm back from Canada, until you're back from Greece?"

He sat down again at the table and spoke to me with a deadly seriousness that was hard to resist. If he was acting, I could not understand what his reason might be. I could not see what purpose he could be serving by lying to me.

"It is hard to explain," he said. "I've been on my own all my life. I've been a wanderer most of the time. There has never been anything for me to hold on to. There has been no center. You are now the center. Don't you understand? And I don't want to lose you. You are going away in a few days. There will be time and distance between us. Anything can happen." He repeated. "I don't want to lose you."

"Is that what you meant by the only solution to a ridiculous situation?"

"Don't you think it is? We want to be together, and we are putting continents between us."

I said: "I'll cancel the trip to Canada. I'll see my mother another time."

"No," Robert said. "Don't do that. I'm not free yet. I have some work to finish."

"You mean in Greece? With Paul?"

He didn't answer directly. He said: "When you come back in a month, I shall be free."

"Free to do what, Robert? What shall we do when you come back, if we are married?"

"We can live here while you take your course, and I'll write another book. Then we'll decide the next step together."

"I'd like to see your books."

"Come look at them then. They're also in the study. You can inspect them and the license at the same time. My credentials." He smiled ruefully. "I never thought it would be so difficult to persuade a woman to marry me." He paused. "Perhaps if you thought of it this way: if I'm married to you, you'll know I'm coming back. Drunk or sober, I'll be back."

"It would be nice to count on that."

"We'll do more than that," Robert said. "What date are you flying home? We'll go tomorrow and book a flight back from Athens on the same day. Whoever gets in first will meet the other. How's that?"

"I'd like that," I said.

"My God, how suspicious you look. I love you. I want to marry you. What's so sinister about that?"

"Nothing," I said. " I didn't expect it. That's all."

"You're a woman of strong character, aren't you?" he said. "Like a rock."

"Isn't that a good thing to be? It doesn't sound very attractive."

"I think so."

"I don't feel very strong."

"You don't know yourself yet."

"If I'm so strong," I said, "why don't you trust me?"

"What do you mean by that?" Robert asked.

"I'm not a fool," I said. "I know there is something going on beneath the surface of your life, another layer to everything you do. Everything you've said to me betrays it. Even the way you make love."

He said: "The way you make love tells me you love me."

"Now you are avoiding the question."

"Frances, of course I trust you," he said. "I'm going to trust you with my life, aren't I? I mean, with the rest of my life. Now are you going to marry me or not?"

"All right," I said. "I may be the fool everyone will tell me I am, but I'll marry you."

"Good. Let's go in the other room and have a drink on it."

He had called it his father's study, and the impact of his father's personality could still be felt there, as it could throughout the rest of the apartment. It seemed to me that Robert had changed nothing. Either because he cared so little or because he cared too much.

It was the best-proportioned room in the flat, and the best-preserved. The plaster moldings of the ceiling were uncracked; the Persian rugs glowed almost luminously in the soft light. The books lining the walls lent depth and color to the room. There was a Victorian iron fireplace and a marble mantelpiece cluttered with papers. A large oak desk was placed at an angle before one of the two windows. There were comfortable leather sofas and armchairs reminiscent of a man's club. In fact, the whole study had an air of cherished, self-indulgent, male seclusion.

On a low table beside the desk I noticed a chessboard with the chessmen set out on it as if a game were in progress. I didn't know much about chess, but it seemed as if black were in a stronger position. There were more white pieces than black off the board.

"You're in the middle of a game?" I asked.

Robert was engaged in getting glasses and a bottle of whisky from a cupboard by the fireplace. He glanced round.

"It's been going on for months," he said. "I play with an old friend in Istanbul. When we've got time, we send each other cards with our next move on them. Do you play chess?"

I shook my head. "It looks as if it's your turn." I had picked up a postcard that lay beside the board. On the message space was written "K-R5" and nothing else. It had been posted to Robert's London address a week ago from Istanbul. Automatically, as one does, I turned the card over. There was a photograph on the other side of a towering cliff against a deep blue sky.

"That's very impressive," I said. "Where's that?"

Robert came and took the card out of my hand. "That's the fortress of Van," he said. "In eastern Turkey. You didn't get that far?"

"No. Perhaps I should next time."

"Yes. And perhaps not." He opened a drawer in the desk and dropped the card into it, on top of a handful of others. "At least, not on your own. Wait until I can take you."

"Why? Isn't it safe?"

"The East is a sensitive area. They have the Russian and Iranian frontiers to worry about. They get a little edgy about people wandering about on their own, being inquisitive."

"I see. And you're right. I am inquisitive. I'm sorry to have been making free with your private correspondence."

"That's all right," Robert said. "What's mine will very shortly be yours anyway. Isn't that what they say at weddings?"

"Not registry office weddings, I believe."

"Well, never mind. Make yourself free with this instead." He handed me a glass of whisky. "Here's to us."

"Yes," I said. "To us."

"It should be champagne. I'll get some tomorrow. And I must confirm the time of the wedding. I tentatively booked it for four o'clock. Every other time was taken. It's the thing to do, marry, you see. Very popular."

"You were very sure of yourself, weren't you, to book a wedding without a bride?"

"No harm in being prepared." He smiled. "I'm a great one for advance planning."

"I would never have guessed that," I said. "Not on the evidence."

He put his glass down. "You wanted to see my books. Here you are, here's one of them."

It appeared to be an account of a journey he had made along the Black Sea coast and through the Pontic Mountains. I asked if I could take it with me when I went to Canada.

"Of course. You'll find it dull, I'm afraid. It hadn't really got a purpose to it, except to make me a little money when I was broke."

"Did you make any money?"

"About enough to finance the next trip."

"Paul Andriades told me you knew a lot about archaeology. Have you written about that?"

"I'm not expert enough. Besides, I've never stayed with any dig long enough. It can take years to examine and evaluate a site. I haven't the patience the dedicated archaeologist needs. I want my results more quickly."

I said: "That I can believe. What was your other book about?"

"Oh, undergraduate stuff. The same sort of thing, anecdotes, gossip, a little potted history. I wrote it after I climbed up Ararat with a couple of Turkish friends."

"Mount Ararat? Did you find any relics of the Ark?"

He laughed. "No."

"Ararat is in that sensitive eastern zone you were telling me about. Isn't it right on the border with Russia?"

"With Russia and Iran."

"I would have thought that was one place you couldn't go wandering about freely."

"You have to get permission," Robert said. "But my two friends vouched for me, which helped. They were army officers. And things weren't quite so tense that year."

"Can I take a copy of that book, too?"

"Yes, there's one in that shelf over there. Only don't leave them in Canada. I haven't got all that many, and they're out of print."

A narrow glass-fronted bookcase stood between the two windows. I opened the glass door and took out Robert's book. As I moved it, I saw a glimmer of gold in the dark space behind.

I realized that none of the books on that particular shelf touched the back of it. They had all been pulled out a little, leaving a narrow space behind.

I looked inquiringly at Robert.

"Oh, yes, I'd forgotten," he said. He came over to the bookcase, and I stood aside as he removed two more books. Then he reached into the space and brought out a small golden statue.

"When I'm here, I keep it on my desk," he said. "But when I'm going to be away for any period, I hide it in there. Not that I expect it to be stolen. The lady who comes in occasionally to keep the dust down is a pillar of respectability, but accidents can happen. I wouldn't want anything to happen to it, for it to be lost or damaged. It's a little too precious to me, in a sentimental way, to take any risks. It was my father's. He found it."

It was the statue of a bull, no more than three inches high. It was made of solid gold, inlaid with silver in a decorative linear pattern. For such a small object it had tremendous vitality; there was menace in the thrust of the head and the bold curl of the tail, a sense of weight and thickness in the body. Robert gave it to me to hold. I ran my finger along the curving back.

"What is it?" I said. "Where did it come from?"

"My father believed it came from a royal Urartian tomb, but

he never got the chance to prove it. As to what it is." He shrugged. "An ornament, a votive offering. Most probably an ornamental figure from a throne or a footstool. They used to decorate their furniture rather elaborately with gold and silver and ivory. But I don't think anything quite like this had been found in any of the other excavated tombs or temples. That, rather than its beauty, was its importance to my father."

I sat down, cradling the bull in my lap. "Tell me about it. About him."

"How much do you know about Urartu?" Robert said.

"Nothing. I've never heard of it. Is it something to do with Ur? One of those Mesopotamian kingdoms?"

"If you and your cousin Bernice weren't such Hellenists and had read a little history about Turkey itself, rather than about the Greeks in Turkey, you would know it was an ancient Anatolian kingdom, which existed from about the thirteenth to the seventh century B.C. and was quite powerful in its day. You know that photograph of the rock of Van you were looking at? That was the capital of the Urartian state. The core of it was all the region round Lake Van, spreading north over what is now the Russian border and south into Syria. At one time they reached the Mediterranean, but I don't believe they held that much territory for long. They were a mountain people. They used to build great fortresses on hills or mountainsides, with walled cities beneath. You can find their ruins all over eastern Turkey. And half the cities haven't been excavated yet or even located. The people remain something of a mystery even now, they left so few records, a handful of inscriptions, that's all. For a long time most of what we knew of them came from the Assyrians. You know the great bronze gates in the British Museum, the gates from Balawat? One of the scenes shows the Assyrian king Shalmaneser defeating a tribal federation of Urartians. They lost that time, but they did pretty well after that. They went under when they began to be attacked from the north as well as the south. They survived as vassals of Assyria until Assyria itself was conquered. Then they vanished from history."

"Isn't that where the old Armenia used to be?" I said. "Round Ararat?"

"Yes. Geographically the Armenians replaced the Urartians."

"Not a very wise thing to do as it turned out. That must be rather a haunted region. First the Urartians disappear. Then a few centuries later, look what happens to the Armenians."

Robert refilled his whisky glass. "I don't think I'd chat too freely about the Armenians if ever you're in Van," he remarked. "It can still be a sensitive subject. Stick to the Urartians."

The telephone rang. It was so unexpected, the sound so loud in the quiet room, that I felt immediately apprehensive, as if threatened by it. It rang again. It went on ringing. Robert brought over his whisky and sat down beside me.

"Do you want another drink?" he asked.

"Aren't you going to answer that?"

He shook his head. "Let it ring. It will only be a wrong number. Nobody knows I'm here."

It seemed to go on for a long time, though I suppose it was no more than thirty seconds. The steady ringing tone had the same effect on me as someone unwanted banging on my front door: a slight sense of guilt at not letting him in; a slight sense of fear at his insistence. At length it stopped.

"I think I would like another drink," I said.

Robert fetched it, then settled down again comfortably beside me. He picked up the bull and turned it round in his hand.

"When you look at this workmanship, it seems extraordinary that it was made by an Iron Age man."

"Did they use a lot of gold?" I asked.

"They made jewelry with it, necklaces, buttons, that sort of thing. And, as I said, decorated their furniture with it. They used a great deal of bronze, for helmets, weapons, bowls, ornaments, decorations. And iron, too, of course, for weapons, and earthenware for storage jars, cooking pots, and so on."

"You know a lot about this," I said.

I put my hand over his, and he turned his palm upwards, intertwining our fingers.

"Not very much," he said. "A little. Things my father told me. He had decided to make the unraveling of the mystery of Urartu his lifework. It began as academic interest; it became an obsession. He spent months every year out there, at first assisting Turkish or British archaeologists, later organizing his own team. He held a readership in archaeology and used to take his students out with him. He got on well with them. As a young child I can remember there always used to be young men and women constantly in and out of the flat."

"And your mother?"

"My mother was a musician. She was not the slightest bit interested in my father's work, but she adored him. She was a jealous, very emotional woman. She was jealous of his work, his colleagues, his students, the hours he spent locked away in here, in this study. I can remember the great rows they had, shouting and screaming and banging of doors. When they were here together, there was always quarreling. My mother often went on tours, my father abroad, so they were frequently away at the same time. I think that's why I was sent away to school so young." He paused. "Which is as well," he went on, "since it meant I missed the great drama when he left her. He had threatened to leave her before, but this time there was no possibility of his returning. So"—he lifted his shoulders in a sad, resigned gesture—"she went down the road to the tube station, bought a ticket to the next station on the line and threw herself under the first train that came in."

"Robert, I'm sorry."

"It's all right, it's a long time ago now, and even then she had become a rather unreal, distant figure to me. Her possessive love for my father was so great she really didn't have much to spare for me."

"And you told me your father couldn't come back to look after you."

"No. It all happened rather quickly. The headmaster called me into his room to tell me about my mother's accidental death. They called it an accident, even though everyone knew it was suicide. He said my father had asked for me to remain at the school until he could make arrangements for me. It was near the end of term. I spent that holiday with the headmaster's family. A weird time. Halfway through the holiday he had to take me to one side yet again. This time it was to tell me my father had died of some unspecified fever in Turkey and his solicitor had been appointed as my guardian. The first thing I asked that gentleman when I saw him was what was going to happen to this apartment. He had enough sense to see how much I needed it, as a kind of emotional security. So we kept it. And here we are."

"No wonder everyone thought of you as a tragic figure," I said. "It was true."

"Yes," Robert said, and grinned. "And didn't I play up to it. However, I was pretty miserable for a while. I didn't miss my mother very much, but I missed my father. This"—he held up the bull—"was the last thing we talked about before he went away."

"Did he tell you where he found it?"

"It was pure chance. They had been excavating a temple on an acropolis north of Van. The dig had been closed down for the year; my father was due back in England. Before he came back, he went wandering off on his own, reconnoitering he called it, looking at the lay of the land, planning the next stage in his great lost-cities treasure hunt. He went east towards Ararat. One evening he was staying in the headman's house in a small village. Half the village, men and boys, were squatting round, come in to see the stranger, and he began asking questions as he always did, not expecting any results, about ancient blocks of stone that might have been used to build or patch up houses, about caves in the hillside that might have been tomb openings, about objects dug up in the fields. And at this one man got up and rushed out into the night, coming back with a small object in his hands. His father, he said, had seen it lying on the hill and picked it up and brought it home, and it had been left where he put it, on a windowsill, ever since. It was the bronze head of a griffin set on a long snakelike neck. My father recognized it at once. Among the most distinctive Urartian manufactures were bronze caldrons supported on iron tripods decorated with human or animal heads. They have been found in many sites and also as far away as Athens and Cyprus. The griffin was one of the most popular animals used. He had no doubt that the villager's griffin came from one of these caldrons.

"Next morning he got the man to show him where it had been found. He took him to a long, steeply rising hill about three miles from the village. On the lower flank it was pitted with ravines and gullies and great rocks that had tumbled and smashed. The land around showed evidence of the same upheaval. My father asked the peasant if he knew when the region had had its last really destructive earthquake. He shook his head. There had been tremors, but nothing big, not in his lifetime or in his father's. Beyond that he didn't know. My father would check the records when he got back, but he was hopeful that the earthquake that shattered the hillside had been centuries ago, that it had lain undisturbed ever since and that whatever was hidden beneath the debris was still there, waiting for him. The villager pointed out where the griffin had been found, among a group of large stones. When my father examined them, he saw clear signs that they had been shaped and cut by man. He grew convinced that they were slabs from the roof of a rock tomb. These rock tombs were cut out of the hillside below a temple or a fortress. They usually had three compartments: an antechamber, a room for offerings and the tomb chamber itself where the bodies lay, either in sarcophagi or directly on the ground. Grave goods have been found distributed throughout all three chambers. The griffin could have come from the first room, and it was possible that that was the only one the earthquake had completely destroyed. The actual tomb chamber might still be intact, buried beneath the rubble.

"Where there was one tomb there would almost certainly be others. And now the shape of the hill itself began to excite him. The top was like the citadel mound at Karmir Blur, one of the most complete cities ever found. He was convinced he was on the threshold of a great discovery; a fortress, a temple, even a great city might lie before him. He got the villager to help him move aside some of the rocks and stones and searched all round them. He told me he felt that if only he could find one more piece of evidence, something to confirm what both his instinct and his professional training told him, the first indication of the entrance to another chamber, broken earthenware, a spearhead, anything, it would be enough.

"He found nothing. At last, reluctantly, he turned to go. As he did so, disturbed by their efforts, there was a sudden avalanche of small stones and rubble into a gully at his feet, and lying there, golden and gleaming in the sunlight, was the bull. He knew then, without doubt, that he had found his treasure.

"He spent three days at the hill, but he made no further attempt to find the tomb. He did not want to start something he would have to abandon in a few days. He climbed the hill, he took measurements, he took samples of stone and earth and then he returned to England with the golden bull smuggled in his pocket.

"He told me about his discovery. I believe I was the only one he did tell. He planned to go out there with a team the first chance he could. But he was committed for the following season, and I don't think he had even got as far as approaching the Turkish authorities for permission to excavate before everything ended for him."

"He wasn't there when he died then?" I asked.

"No. I was told he was in Ankara."

"Have you ever been there?" I asked. "Have you seen the hill?"

"I've never found it. My father didn't tell me exactly where it was or give me the name of the village. Remember, I was only seven. He told me the story one night, sitting on the end of my bed, making it sound like a fairy tale, like 'Sleeping Beauty,' with kings and queens and princesses and a whole city lying asleep for centuries, waiting to be awakened."

"He didn't take the bull with him when he left that last time?" I asked.

"No. When I next came back to the flat, I found it in his desk. I imagine he didn't want fellow archaeologists to see it and ask questions until he was quite ready to talk about it. He didn't want anyone getting there first and spoiling his thunder. I've been through his notes and papers, even his diaries, but there is no mention of it. One day, when I have a little more experience and a lot more money, I shall try to find his city and the man or woman, king or queen, to whom this fellow belonged. And now, since we are going away again, I'll put him back in hiding."

He opened the bookcase and put the bull back inside, replacing the books which concealed it from view.

"Thank you for showing it to me," I said.

"I'd like to give it to you as a wedding present," Robert said. "But as things are—"

"I don't want any presents," I said. "Just you."

He put his arms round me, holding me closely to him. His body against mine felt warm and familiar and right.

"We've got two more days and two more nights," he said. "Do you want to see the license?"

"Not at the moment," I said.

"What time is your plane to Canada?"

"I don't want to think about Canada," I said.

But I could think about going away now without that terrible sense of loss. Robert had been right, I thought, in wanting us to marry at once. He had been right about commitment.

In the middle of the night something woke me. Voices? Distant voices? I turned in the big bed. Robert was gone, the covers flung back. Visitors? At this hour? It was still pitch-black outside, no light coming through the half-drawn curtains. There was only a faint illumination from the hall. I reasoned that it must have been the doorbell I had heard, but I was too relaxed, too heavy with sleep to trouble much about it. I laid my head back on the pillow.

The voices came again. They sounded scratchy, distorted. I caught snatches of sentences, Robert's voice saying: "So you see, that's why I couldn't answer . . . Yes, of course it's wise . . . It won't make the slightest difference." Another man's voice replied, but a crackling sound blurred the sense. A crackling? I raised myself on one elbow and, looking round, found the answer. On the night table stood a telephone with the receiver taken off. As I lay in bed, the receiver was right beside my ear.

It was the ringing of the telephone that had awakened me. Robert had answered it, then in order not to disturb me, or in order to be private, had gone into the study to speak to the caller.

I should replace the receiver. I shouldn't eavesdrop. Robert was saying: ". . . message . . . should have plenty of time if nothing else goes wrong." The other man spoke. I heard the words "dealt with" and "careless" and something more I couldn't decipher. Then Robert's voice suddenly came over with the utmost clarity: "I've always been a bloody good liar, you know that. I missed my vocation as a con man." The other said: "Then I'll see you as arranged." "As arranged," Robert said. There was a click, then silence.

I didn't replace the receiver. If I had, Robert would know I had heard the call and would wonder if I had listened and how much I had heard. I had the feeling he would rather I knew nothing about it. I lay waiting, and after a while he slipped quietly into the bed beside me. He reached across me and put the receiver back in place. A few minutes later I heard his steady, peaceful breathing in sleep.

Next morning I mentioned that I had heard a phone ringing in the night. What was it, I asked, another wrong number?

"It was a friend of mine, John Nairn," Robert said. "The American whose flat I borrowed in Athens. He was calling from the airport. He was between planes, on his way back to Greece."

"Will you be staying at his place again?" I asked.

"Overnight probably."

"What about Cleo?"

"I have a feeling Cleo won't be there anymore."

"Did you tell your friend about us?"

"Yes. He thinks we're a pair of fools. He wishes us luck."

It sounded at that time a perfectly reasonable explanation of the call. Robert had not been the least secretive or hesitant in telling me about it. But one phrase I had overheard lingered with me: "I've always been a bloody good liar. . . ." I wanted to ask him why he'd said that, what it referred to, but I didn't want to betray the fact that I had listened to his conversation. So distrust came sidling in even before our marriage and found itself a quiet place in my mind, where later it could begin to fester.

We spent that day in practicalities, checking that the information he had provided for the marriage license was correct, confirming the time of the wedding, booking his return flight from Athens to coincide with my return from Canada. I collected most of my luggage from the hotel, leaving a token bag in the room to maintain the fiction of my residence there.

Someone had rung to ask if I was still booked in, the receptionist told me, but had not left a name. Robert asked if the caller had been a man or woman, but the girl didn't know. She hadn't been on duty at the time, and the note merely stated that there had been an inquiry.

"Don't look so worried," I said to Robert as we left the hotel. "The explanation is probably very simple."

"Let's go have a drink," Robert said. "I want to make a phone call."

"Why don't you ring from the flat?" I said. "We're so close."

He smiled charmingly. "I'm thirsty," he said.

And, I thought, I won't be in a position to overhear his conversation in a busy pub. I felt rather ashamed of that reflection. It was, after all, only inspired by my own guilt as an eavesdropper.

The pub he chose was one he must have used many times, directly opposite the entrance to the British Museum, only a short walk away from his flat. From my table in the window I watched the people come and go across the broad courtyard. Though it was after six, the gates were still open for the readers in the library. The museum itself had closed. Too late for me to go look now at the gates of Balawat. It was a long time since I had been to the museum for other than specific exhibitions, but I must have seen the gates countless times on school outings and other childhood visits. They had made no impact on me at all. Neither had the great Assyrian statues and the monolithic heads, huge dark shapes cut from dark stone, that inhabited the same hall. Taken from their palaces and temples, from the desert and the baking sun, they had lost their vitality. I had walked past them unmoved.

Robert sat down at the table beside me.

"Are you tired?" he asked me.

"No, I don't think so."

"Good. We're going to a party."

"Tonight?"

"Right now."

"Where?"

"Down in Chelsea. An old friend of mine."

"I can't go like this."

"Of course you can. You look fine."

He was out, whistling for a taxi before I could protest any further.

The three-story house was tall and narrow and, as the limousines parked outside confirmed, expensive. Our host was a tall, thin, elegant man in a pinstripe suit and a delicate aftershave. He pressed my fingers in gentle acknowledgment of Robert's introduction and waved Robert in the direction of the dry martinis.

"Let's lose him, Frances," he said. "I'd much rather talk to you on your own. Let me show you my pictures."

The party was spread through two rooms of the ground floor of the house. The women there were far better dressed than I and a good deal older. The men were older than the women and appeared to know each other very well. It did not seem the sort of party to which Robert and I would normally have been invited. In between being shown the Poussin in the hall and the Sargent in the dining room, I caught glimpses of Robert in deep conversation with an elderly man with an aquiline profile.

"And I've a rather nice Sickert in the study," my host was saying. "I wouldn't want you to miss that."

The study was a small room and seemed brilliantly lit after the subdued indirect lighting of the rest of the house. After a few moments he switched off the brightest of the lamps. "It is rather dazzling, isn't it? I'm afraid I need more light these days for close work. The penalties of age."

He looked fifty but could have been older, I supposed. He had one of those long, handsome English faces which rarely change. His smile was bland and social, and he carried the conversation without the necessity of my uttering a word. As he pointed out the technical qualities of the Sickert, I wondered why he was spending so much time on me. He hadn't mentioned my forthcoming marriage, and I got the impression he didn't know about it. So if Robert hadn't told him that, what had he told him about me to merit such attention?

All I knew of him was the little Robert had told me in the taxi, that his name was Victor Ransome and that he was at the Foreign Office.

"Who is the man Robert was talking to?" I asked.

"I'm afraid I didn't notice," Ransome said.

"Late sixties. Rather distinguished."

He smiled. "That could describe quite a few of my guests. Perhaps it was Edmund Chance. He was a friend of Robert's father."

"Did you know his father?"

"Before my time," Ransome said. "I see you've finished your

drink. Come along and I'll get you another."

In the crowded rooms there was no sign of Robert or his companion. I was handed a fresh glass and introduced to Victor's wife, a woman as plain as he was good-looking, a fact which made me wonder, rather uncharitably, if she was the source of the wealth that surrounded us. She smiled at me in as vague a manner as her husband and asked me if I didn't find London very hard to get about these days. Five minutes later Robert appeared and rescued me. We were back out on the embankment in another two. He took me by the hand, and we dodged through the traffic to the opposite pavement. On the other side of the river, the trees of Battersea Park looked thickly massed like a forest awaiting exploration. To the right and left of us the graceful lines of the Albert and Chelsea bridges were blurred by the slow-crawling procession of homeward-bound commuters.

Robert leaned against the parapet and gazed down at the sluggish Thames.

"What was all that about?" I asked.

"Didn't you enjoy it?"

"Not very much. Why did we go?"

"I wanted to see someone."

"Edmund Chance?"

He glanced up. "Yes. He acted as my agent for the earlier books. I wanted to talk to him before returning to Greece, to discuss an idea for the next one."

"Did you know he was going to be there?"

"Yes, of course. When I rang him from the pub, he was on his way to Victor's. It was my only chance to see him."

"I would have liked to meet him," I said.

"I would have introduced you if Victor hadn't whisked you away so promptly."

"I thought you had asked Mr. Ransome to keep me amused while you had your little chat."

Robert laughed. "I'm afraid Victor's propensities are well

known. After twenty years with Lady Evelyn, any remotely attractive and reasonably young woman is inclined to sweep him off his feet."

"Is that why we rushed out of there as fast as we rushed in?"

"Edmund had to go, and I'm hungry. Aren't you?"

I laughed. I couldn't help it, he looked so boyishly ingenuous.

"When we're married," I said, "I think I should be well advised to trust you just about as far as Lady Evelyn should trust her Victor."

"Oh, go on," he said. "Show your beautiful legs and get us a taxi. It's the only way we'll get one to stop in this traffic."

That evening I talked to him again about the golden bull.

"If it's solid gold, it must be worth a great deal, apart from its historical value. Don't you ever worry about burglars?"

He shrugged. "There's nothing at the flat to tempt burglars. It's hardly a wealthy neighborhood. They're more likely to go after the tourists in the hotels. Easier and more rewarding."

"But if someone had seen the bull—" I persisted.

"No one knows about it," Robert said. "No one's seen it. You are the only person I've ever shown it to."

"What about your cleaning woman?" I said. "If you keep the bull on your desk, she must have seen it."

"Do you know what you're doing?" Robert said. "You're acting like a married woman and getting protective about me."

"I'm getting protective about the bull," I said. "I don't believe you have a proper sense of property. I'm supplying it for you."

"A sense of property," Robert said, "perhaps not. But possession, yes. You'll find I'm a very possessive man."

It was late when we returned to the flat. We opened the door to darkness and silence, a waiting, expectant silence as of people hiding, people listening. Even when we put on the lights, they did not seem to disperse the shadows. The open doors of empty rooms worried me. I shut them quickly, one after the other.

"What's the matter?" Robert said.

He had noticed nothing because there was, of course, nothing to notice. My imagination was quite capable of turning the most familiar surroundings into threats. Without my awareness it had been brooding over the tragic, unhappy woman who had lived here and conjuring up ghosts for me to frighten myself with.

"Nothing's the matter," I said. "I've decided to have a little attack of bridal nerves."

"That's very touching," Robert said. "It means you're taking it seriously."

"Of course I'm taking it seriously! Aren't you?"

"There, there!" He put his arms about me as if comforting a child. "What is it? Don't you like this place? Don't worry, we don't need to live here."

"You couldn't sell it," I said. "It means so much to you. It's your home."

"I'm not eight years old anymore. I don't need it. It's convenient, that's all. But it belongs to a past I'm quite ready to draw a line through and forget. We'll start somewhere new, you and I."

But I wondered when we went into the study that was still so much his father's, when I thought of the golden bull that was the tangible reminder to Robert of his father's obsession, a constant goad to him to complete his father's unfinished business and fulfill another man's dream, whether we could escape so easily from that particular ghost of the past.

We were married the following afternoon at four o'clock. We had forgotten about the necessity for witnesses, and two girls kindly came down from the office at the registry to act for us. It was an odd time of day for a wedding, too late for a celebration lunch, too early for dinner. We took a taxi back to the apartment and had champagne and iced cake for a celebration tea. Summer had returned, and the sun flooded through the tall windows and made golden patterns across the floor. Robert fetched the bull and stood it beside our version of the wedding cake.

"A votive offering," he said, "to bring us luck."

During the morning we had collected my case from the hotel and I had paid the bill. We had packed our cases ready for our separation next day. They stood together in the hall, waiting only for the addition of our wedding clothes. Robert had worn his gray suit, and I a summer dress. He had bought me a nosegay of flowers in colors that matched my dress, and I pressed them in a book and took them to Canada with me like a sentimental Victorian.

I promised myself I wouldn't cry when we parted, but I did all the same. Robert said he wouldn't write. He would be too far from civilization to make it a practical proposition, and anyway, he never wrote letters. I asked him to wait with me at the airport until the last possible minute. When it came, he pressed my hand and left, without looking back.

I slept for most of the flight, and when not sleeping, I sat in a state of limbo, physically limp and emotionally drained. I felt as if I'd been melted in a fire to a state of soft, pliable vulnerability, all my defenses burned away. In some ways I didn't like the effect that love had on me. I was no longer independent and carefree. I was involved, enmeshed, committed, just as completely as Robert had wanted me to be. I had lost my freedom.

I didn't tell my mother about my marriage straightaway. I was shocked by the change I found in her. I had left her brisk, efficient, almost too self-sufficient. I found her overweight, nervous, diffident. She wanted to talk, and I let her. I let her feed on me. I hadn't been before to the house in the hills overlooking Vancouver. They had moved into it only a few months before my stepfather died. The view over the sea and city and mountains was beautiful, but perhaps too overwhelming. It rained sometimes, too, that first week, a fine mist sweeping in from the ocean, veiling hard outlines, deadening sound, isolating us in our loneliness. Vancouver seemed so very far away from Europe, more than an ocean, a continent. Plain, forest, mountain; the thread connecting me with Robert was stretched so far.

One day my mother began to cry gently without sound, her face crumpling like a child's. I knelt beside her chair and put my arms around her. After a while she wiped her eyes and blew her nose and put on the semblance of a smile.

"I don't like being a widow again," she said. "I feel it is too late to start my life a third time. I don't know what to do."

"Do you want to stay here?"

"I don't know."

We sat in silence, she gazing out of the window and I sitting at her feet, wondering if and when I should tell her. At least, I thought, it might shock her into some reaction. So I told her.

At first I thought she hadn't taken it in, she looked at me so blankly. Then she said, with all her old humor: "Well, that puts paid to my bright idea of moving in with you." And smiled and hugged me. "Why didn't you cable me? I'd have flown over for the wedding. How strange you are. Tell me all about him."

She didn't appear surprised at my impulsiveness. "First thoughts are often the best. I married your father after knowing him only a few weeks. It must run in the family."

She seemed revitalized. There was an extension of family, growth to offset death, something for her to look forward to, grandchildren perhaps and, if not that, visits, happiness, life. She became imbued with a new energy. She decided to redecorate the house and alter it. She decided to make bed-sitters out of two of the bedrooms and let them to students. She wanted to go to the cinema, to take me round the shops, to show me the sights. The heavy burden of her growing dependence on me, which had so worried me in the first few days, vanished in an hour.

When I came to leave, I would have been able to do so without guilt if it had not been for that last glimpse of her at the airport. As she turned to leave, something about the stoop of her shoulders, the quick turning away of her head made me wonder if it had all been acting, if I might really be leaving her in a worse state than before. But if it was acting, it was because she wanted me to believe it, because she was determined to lift the burden from me herself. If I had still been single, she might have let it rest on me a little longer, perhaps for a year even. Once she knew I was married, she knew she was on her own. But whatever the truth, whether acting or genuine, the result was the same. She had released me, and I had to accept the gift, and without guilt, or all the effort she had made would be worth nothing.

The flight back seemed longer than the flight there, and the nearer we got to England, the less I thought of my mother and the more of Robert. I had read both his books while I was in Canada. He had an easy facility in writing; he evoked scenes and situations with great economy. He managed to tell much about the country and little about himself. I was interested to note that even in the narrative of his journey to Ararat he wrote very little about the kingdom of Urartu as if he didn't want to inspire too much interest in his readers, as if this were something to be kept private.

I had had to go to the public libraries to find out more about the kingdom. One thing I did discover was that Karmir Blur, the great city he had mentioned, lay in Soviet territory. The new frontier ran through ancient Urartu. There was a photograph of the frontier region in the second book, a valley near Ani, bleak, treeless, desolate.

I had heard nothing from Robert, but I did receive a long

letter from Bernice soon after I arrived in Canada in reply to one of mine announcing my news. She had seen Robert. He had come into Paul Andriades's Athens office "positively fizzing with high spirits." They had all gone out to dinner to celebrate our marriage, and next day he and Paul had gone off to the dig. Paul found it more useful to have her based in Athens at present, but she would be going up to the excavations from time to time.

"In case you are still worrying," she continued, "Cleo appears to have left the scene. I saw her the other day, strangely enough, getting into a car with a man who looked exactly like the Turk who took our taxi that day by the temple. Of course it couldn't have been him. How many Turks does one find in Greece? About as many as Greeks in Turkey. She didn't look too pleased in any case. By the way, does your marriage mean you are giving up the idea of the interpreter's course? Are you coming to Athens to join Robert? It would be wonderful to have you here. Give my love to your mother. . . ."

I liked the idea of Robert fizzing with high spirits. I was beginning to feel that way myself, though I had broken our arrangement in one respect. I had discovered that if I kept to my original flight plans, I would be arriving in London on a Sunday. By the time I reached the center of London most of the shops would be shut. It would be very difficult to find any-where to buy food or wine or the simplest household supplies. I wanted the flat to be ready for Robert, to be alive and wel-coming, so I changed my flight for a day earlier.

We landed on time on a brilliant early fall day. London had never seemed so beautiful to me. I felt as if I'd been on proba-tion in some select prison and had now been told I could go home. On the way to the apartment I stopped to buy, as well as food, a huge bouquet of flowers, yellow and white, to lighten the gloom of the place. I found bowls and vases and filled the rooms with blossoms and pulled wide the curtains and opened the windows and walked through the whole length of the rambling flat, staking my claim on it like a cat marking out its territory.

For supper I made scrambled eggs and ate them in front of the ancient black and white television set Robert had not bothered to change. The picture leaped sporadically like the jerking of an old film, and after a while I gave up the attempt to watch any program, had a bath and went to bed, sinking luxuriously into sleep, after so much travel, so much strain.

I had forgotten my ghosts, the echoes of lost voices I had seemed to catch, the snatches of quarrels long over. I awoke suddenly in the pitch-black of night knowing I had heard them again. This time there was no Robert speaking on the telephone, no open receiver crackling by my ear. There was just an intensely electrifying sense of presence, of something alive that should not be there. Before I could stop myself, I called out, "Robert?," thinking he might, like me, have returned early. There was no answer; the silence, if anything, became more dense. I slipped out of bed without putting on the bedside light. I walked on bare feet towards the bedroom door. My outstretched hands touched it before I was ready. I paused, collecting myself, trying to remember the exact layout of the flat. I had not shut the bedroom door completely when I came to bed. I could open it without noise. As I looked down the long corridor, there seemed to be for a moment a glimmer of light from the direction of the study.

"Imagination?" I said to myself. "Or reality?" My heart was racing inside my breast like an engine out of control; my instincts were all geared for flight. If my unconscious mind had anything to do with it, there was danger here—

Intruders in the flat, burglars who thought we were away. Or rather who knew Robert was away and knew nothing of me. How many people could know that I was here? Unless they had watched me enter the flat, no one.

They thought they were safe. The light shone again, swinging in an arc. Did they know about the bull; was that why they had come? I mustn't confront them; I must get help. The phone by the bed. I must find my way back to the phone by the bed and ring the police.

I put my hands out to find the frame of the door and touched flesh. Warm, living flesh. I screamed, knowing it was a hand, a man's hand; screaming as it thrust me to one side, as a light blinded my eyes, screaming as the blow came, more shattering than ever I could have imagined it, sending me down through spinning, dazzling, aching splinters of light into a pit of darkness.

CHAPTER 3

"How are you feeling? No, don't bother to answer. I can guess. You've got a lump the size of a pigeon's egg."

I was lying on the bed with a blanket thrown over me. My head was throbbing like a thousand road drills, and there was a totally unknown man standing at the bedside.

I struggled to raise myself. Another man entered the room. To my immense relief, he was wearing the uniform of a police constable.

"Has she come round, sir?" He looked down at me. "Don't worry, madam, a doctor's on the way."

"How did you get in?" I whispered. "Who called you?"

"This gentleman called us." Someone shouted a name outside the room, and he turned on his heel. "Doctor won't be long," he said.

I looked at the stranger. "How many more people are here?"

"Only Detective Sergeant Williams. He's in charge. I expect you're wondering who I am."

"I thought you were the one who hit me," I said.

"I suppose you would. That hadn't occurred to me. That makes us quits. You frightened the life out of me. I thought you were dead. I'm a friend of Robert's, by the way. My name's John Nairn."

He wasn't as tall as Robert but was powerfully built with an open, pleasant face and tightly curling hair springing from a broad forehead. His voice was soft and attractive with an accent more English than American.

I said: "I thought you were in Athens."

"I come and go a lot. Look, do you think you should be talking? You're supposed to rest till the doctor comes. You must have been out at least fifteen minutes."

"It was you who found me? How did you come to be here? Did you see the men?"

"Men? There was more than one then?"

"There was one with a flashlight in the study. And the one who was waiting for me." I remembered the touch of his hand beneath my fingers. "There might have been more, even. I don't know."

"You're shivering," Nairn said. "You've probably got delayed shock. I think you should rest now. I'll leave you."

"Please," I said. "I want to know what happened. Did they take much?"

"I don't think they took anything. It looks as if first you disturbed them, then I did, and they gave up and ran. It was such a shock finding you. I hadn't expected anyone to be here, particularly not a beautiful woman lying prone in the hallway. Rob had told me you were in Canada."

"You've seen Robert?"

"He stayed with me his first night in Athens. I haven't seen him since. We often use each other's apartments, you know. When he heard I might be coming to London, he gave me a spare key. Told me the place would be empty."

"It would have been, but I came back a day early. It's lucky for me he did give you the key. He's due back himself tomorrow or, rather, today, I suppose it is now."

"Is he? I didn't know that. By the way, I'll clear out once the doctor's been." He paused. "Unless you'd like me to stay around the rest of the night? I think someone ought to be with you."

"I don't want to turn you out in the middle of the night, but there's no need for you to stay unless you want to."

"It's my pleasure," Nairn said.

The police doctor arrived, a bluff, matter-of-fact man who had seen too many victims of violence to make much of my crack on the head. He rattled off a series of questions, my name, where I was, what I'd been doing yesterday, how much I remembered of the attack. At the end of his examination he told me I was lucky, no doubt was blessed with a good thick skull and was suffering from mild concussion, which should clear up in a week. The headache would begin to go in a couple of days. I was to stay in bed for the whole of that day and rest as much as possible afterwards. I was to get in touch with my own doctor if I began to feel worse. He wrote out a prescription for pain-killers, touched my shoulder in a fatherly way and departed as briskly as he had arrived.

After the doctor, the police. Detective Sergeant Williams was a quiet man with a regulation raincoat and a laconic manner. Since there wasn't very much I could tell him, the interview was short. He confirmed that as far as they could tell, nothing had been disturbed in any of the rooms. John Nairn must have arrived a few minutes after I'd been knocked out. The intruders would have heard his key in the lock, hidden from him and slipped out while he was coping with me. There was no sign of forcible entry. It looked as if they'd come in through the front door. Didn't I normally bolt it? I said it hadn't occurred to me to bolt it. He shook his head sadly and asked me to get in touch if I found anything missing.

Once they had gone, I became obsessed with the need to go through the flat myself, to see if it really was untouched. I got off the bed gingerly and pulled on my dressing gown. At my first step I was nearly overcome by a wave of nausea. I sank down on the edge of the bed and waited until it passed. Then I began again. I got as far as the kitchen. John Nairn was seated at the kitchen table, nursing a glass of scotch. He looked alarmed when he saw me. "Hey! You shouldn't be up. You should be resting."

"I'm all right. Can I have some of that?"

"You can't have alcohol with a head injury. What you want is tea, hot, sweet tea. Isn't that what the English always give you for shock?"

"I don't think I could manage to lift the kettle."

He pulled a chair out for me. "Come on. Sit down. I'll make the tea."

I watched him as he moved in a casually competent way about the kitchen, finding milk, cup, tea, teapot with ease.

"You're very domesticated," I said.

He laughed. "*Force majeure*. I happened to get married to a liberated lady who thought putting a pan on a stove degrading for one of her talents. There's a limit to the number of times I like eating out. So I learned to cook."

"Lucky lady. Are you still married to her?"

"No."

He poured the tea. I didn't usually take sugar in my tea, but he piled it in and I drank it and it tasted like nectar. The threat of sickness retreated.

"It's very good," I said. "Most Americans make tea too weak."

"I haven't known Robert all these years for nothing," he said. "He does drink other things than the hard stuff occasionally . . " He paused and looked away.

"But not often?" I said.

He turned back. He was embarrassed by his faux pas. "Well, you know Robert."

"Yes," I said. "You've been friends for a long time then."

"I met him about ten years ago, bumming around Greece. By the way, I haven't given you best wishes on your marriage. That was quite a surprise. I never saw Rob as the marrying kind. But now that I've met you I can understand it."

"That's very gallant of you since you've only seen me looking like this."

"You look pretty good to me. Pale but interesting, isn't that what they say?"

There was a soothing quality about John Nairn. His quiet

voice, his calm manner, his presence gave an impression of reliability and strength that would make most women, I imagined, feel cherished and protected. They were just the qualities needed by anyone feeling as vulnerable as I was at that moment.

"Any idea what they were after, Frances?" he said. "The men who attacked you?"

I said: "No," automatically, and waited for him to ask me about the golden bull. He was one of Robert's oldest friends. If Robert hadn't told him about the bull, it certainly wasn't up to me to do so.

He didn't mention the bull. He said: "I suppose they found out the apartment was empty and took a chance on picking up something of value. They must have had a shock when they discovered you were here."

"You don't think they'll come back?"

"No. You can forget them. Why don't you go back to bed and get some sleep?"

"What time is it?"

He looked at his watch. "Three o'clock."

"You were late getting in from Athens, weren't you? I hadn't realized it was as late as that."

"There was a strike somewhere along the line. We had to circle for about two hours before we could land."

"I wonder if that means Robert will be late tomorrow."

"What time's he due?"

"Midmorning. I've got to check the time. I've got the flight number in my diary. I hope he's not delayed. I hate hanging round airports."

"You don't mean you're thinking of going out to the airport to meet him?" Nairn said.

"Well, of course. He'll be expecting me. He'll think there's something wrong if I'm not there."

"He'll be damn right there's something wrong. I heard what the doctor said. Stay in bed for the day, rest as much as you can. You're in no condition to hang around crowded airports."

"I'll be all right. I'm much better already. That tea's revived me."

I smiled at him to show him how well I felt. I didn't tell him that the slightest movement of my head made me dizzy.

"I wanted to have a quick look round," I said. "That's why I got up. To satisfy myself that nothing's been taken."

"All right," he said. "Let's take a look."

He came with me, an unobtrusive presence at my elbow, protective hand steadying me when I swayed. It soon became clear that the police were right. Nothing in the flat seemed to have been touched. In the study the desk was undisturbed. The chessmen waited patiently on their board; the bookcase was unopened. I would check the golden bull later, when I was alone, but it was clear they hadn't got to it.

I felt I could sleep then. There was, after all, nothing to worry about.

I awoke next morning knowing I was going to see Robert that day. It was early, plenty of time before I set out for the airport. But as soon as I got out of bed, I knew I wasn't going to make it. The sense of well-being was illusory. At my first movement the throbbing head was back, and the weakness.

I couldn't disguise my physical state from John Nairn.

"Look," he said. "I'll go meet Robert. It's quite obvious you can't."

"I couldn't ask you to—"

"It's no great trouble. It's Sunday. There'll be very little traffic on the roads, and I've got nothing better to do."

"What exactly are you doing in London?" I asked him. "I'm afraid I don't even know what sort of work you do."

"I work for a shipping company," he said. "I'm based in Greece, but I move around a lot. I've come over for some meetings. But they don't start till tomorrow. So relax. Look after yourself. I'll explain to Robert."

He continued to act like a guardian angel all that morning. He found out the nearest pharmacy remaining open on a Sunday and collected the tablets the doctor had prescribed for me. He went to the newsstand for the Sunday papers. He made us coffee. He checked the flight time.

By the time he left for the airport the pain-killers were beginning to work. I was too restless to go back to bed, so I took the Sunday papers into the study and spread them and myself out on one of the sofas. It was strange, but after a while I began to get the feeling that something was not quite right with the room. The brilliant yellow flowers I had arranged in a deep white bowl were on the desk where I had left them, but not quite where I'd left them. I had placed them at an angle to catch the light from the window. Now they were solidly in the center. The police might have moved them, but why should they? They had been checking that nothing had been disturbed, not disturbing things themselves. On the other hand, if you had wanted to open the top desk drawer, the flowers could have been in your way.

I got up and looked more carefully round the study. The chessmen were all slightly out of their squares as if the table on which they stood had been lifted bodily out of the way and then replaced. And the desk chair, had that really been so neatly tucked in as it was now? I was touched by spider fingers of fear. Even though the men had been gone so long, their presence still shadowed the room. The soiled imprint of their hands was everywhere. I was sick at heart even before I opened the glass doors of the bookcase. I took all the books from the shelf and laid them on the desk so I could be quite sure. There was no mistake. The golden bull was gone.

I was out of the study when the phone call came. I nearly missed it. I had not been able to decide what to do. To tell the police would be to break Robert's confidence. Not to tell them might mean the bull's being lost for good, melted down most probably for the intrinsic value of the gold. Robert would be here soon. He would have to make the decision. Perhaps the time lost would make little difference; the men had had the bull in their possession for twelve hours already.

As far as I could tell, they had taken nothing else. But then I knew very little of what Robert might have locked away in the drawers of his desk. I tentatively tried the top drawer. It opened easily. Inside was a jumble of papers, bills, receipts, old checkbook stubs, torn scraps of notes tangled up with pens, Scotch tape and a spilled carton of paper clips. The next drawer was the one into which he had tossed the postcard from his chess-playing friend in Istanbul. The thieves had been through this one as well; it was in as much of a mess as the other. I stacked the chess cards in a neat pile and riffled through them. The last one was missing. I couldn't see any reason for it to have been stolen. Perhaps Robert had transferred the move onto the board and thrown the card away. It was odd, though, when he appeared to have kept the rest. I closed that drawer and tried the others. They were locked, and there seemed to have been no attempt to force them open. Perhaps that was when I interrupted them. Too late, I now knew.

I felt desperately sad for Robert and so angry I couldn't bear to stay in one place. I went to the kitchen and made some tea. Then I got out the vacuum and began sweeping and cleaning with vicious attack, banging against skirting boards and door-frames as if they were the heads of my enemies, only stopping when my own head began to protest. It was then I heard the telephone. I had no idea how long it had been ringing. There was an impatience about it as if it might stop at any moment. I ran back to the study and grabbed the receiver. John Nairn's voice came over the line to me.

"Frances? Rob must have missed the plane. He wasn't on it."

I sank down onto a chair. "Are you sure?"

"Quite sure. I was there in good time. I saw everyone who came off."

"No message for me?"

"I thought of that. I've checked. There's nothing. Look, there's a plane due in from another airline in an hour. I'll wait for that."

"Thank you. That's very kind of you."

"I've got nothing better to do," he repeated. "It's just as well you didn't come along. How are you feeling?"

"Much better."

"Good. You'd better stay by the phone. Robert might phone."

But it wasn't Robert who rang an hour later. It was Nairn. Robert hadn't been on that plane either.

I wasn't worried at that stage, just disappointed, and that was offset by the fact that the delay was giving me more time to recover from the blow to my head.

Nairn returned about eight o'clock with no news. He had intended moving out to a hotel that night, but he asked if I would like him to stay.

"I thought you might be a little nervous."

"I shall be all right," I assured him. "I'm going to bed early. And there's a phone by the bed."

"Nevertheless, I think I should stay. I don't think Rob would want you to be alone."

I suppose I was grateful; but by then my excess of energy was rebounding on me, and I was too tired to care one way or the other. All I wanted to do was sleep. I didn't feel capable of entertaining anyone. John Nairn, however, was the least troublesome guest one could have. Presumably he had found sheets and blankets the previous night and made up the spare bed for himself. I had done nothing for him. And now he didn't even require feeding. He said he'd had something to eat at the airport.

By next morning there was still no message from Robert. There was little point in going to the airport. Instead, I stayed by the phone.

Nairn packed his bag and went off to his meeting. He told me he'd be in touch later. He was at the front door at seven with a frozen pizza and a bottle of wine. He could tell by my face that there was no news.

"Any more flights tonight?"

"No direct ones. If he changed planes, he could still be here."

"Well." He paused. "I'll wait with you. All right?"

I stood aside to let him in.

"Hell," he said in the middle of his pizza. "There's something not right here. Look, I'm free tomorrow morning. I'll make some phone calls. See what I can find out."

If we were married, Robert had said, I'd know he was coming back, drunk or sober. I repeated that to myself, and it helped a little; but I hadn't been with him long enough to have the confidence I needed. And John Nairn's words, kind though they were meant to be, didn't help.

"Do you think there's been an accident?" I asked him.

"We'll find that out tomorrow."

"He might have been held up on the archaeological site."

"That's possible."

And he might have changed his mind about this impulsive marriage of his and decided to disappear quietly. Beneath his surface of reassurance I felt Nairn would not be surprised by this explanation, and neither would anyone else who knew Robert.

That night, when John Nairn, at my insistence, had left, I rang Bernice. Her voice came loud and clear across the miles.

"Hello, darling, how *are* you. How wonderful to hear from you. How's marriage?"

I said without preliminaries: "Have you seen Robert in the past few days?"

"Oh." Her voice changed, and I realized how false had been her exuberant greetings. "I was hoping he was with you."

"Tell me what you know, Bernice, please."

"He went to the dig with Paul Andriades, as I wrote to

you. He was there a week, and then he left, vanished in the middle of the night. No one has seen him since."

"What do you mean 'vanished'? He must have had some sort of transport. Did he take a jeep, or what?"

"He was there at dinner one night. Next morning he was missing. His gear was gone, but no truck or car. Either he walked out or someone collected him. We assumed he was missing you and had left for England or Canada."

"And no one saw fit to make any inquiries?"

"They all knew what Robert was like," Bernice said apologetically.

"Unreliable, you mean," I said.

"Paul got in touch with me," Bernice said. "Asked me if I could find out anything in Athens. I got those men from the embassies to check around, you remember, the ones we had dinner with? They couldn't trace him."

"So you were worried?" I said.

"I was worried for you," Bernice said simply. "I was half hoping to find out he'd been run over by a bus. At least that would have been an acceptable explanation. When you rang just now, I was hoping against hope Robert was with you."

"He was supposed to arrive on a plane from Athens on Sunday," I said. "There's been no sign of him, no message."

"What are you going to do?" Bernice said.

"Try to make sure he hasn't been in an accident and then sit tight here and wait for him. I don't see what else I can do." And yet even as I spoke, I knew I could never sit still day after day, waiting. I would have to take some sort of action, for my own sake.

"Have you been to the Greek police?" I asked.

"Tom Shaw, the Englishman, handled all that for me. There has been no report of an accident involving Robert. He got the address of John Nairn's flat from Joe Parker and went round there. There was a new tenant who'd never heard of Robert. John Nairn was away."

"I know," I said. "He's turned up here. He's been helping me."

"There you are then," Bernice said helplessly. "What else can we do?"

"If I come out there," I said, "can you put me up?"

"Of course, I can," Bernice said. "But it's not as desperate as that yet, is it?"

"I don't know," I said. "I really don't know."

On Tuesday afternoon, Detective Sergeant Williams called on me. He expected my husband to have checked through the contents of the flat by now and to have made a list of anything missing. I told him my husband had been delayed. He asked how I was. I told him I was quite recovered. He asked if I had remembered anything else about the night of the burglary or about possible stolen property. Perhaps my answers were too pat, my denials unconvincing. He brought out my typed statement and took me through it sentence by sentence. Then he sighed and asked to look round the flat once more.

I wondered if he had information I knew nothing about. Perhaps he was simply a good detective. He clearly had an instinct that everything was not as it should be. Watching him prowling round the study, lifting and replacing pieces on the chessboard as if they could convey something to him, I was tempted to tell him about the golden bull, but with Robert himself missing, the loss of the bull had become relatively unimportant.

I held within me now a constant nagging fear. It kept urging me that something was wrong, something was wrong. Robert was ill or injured or threatened. He needed my help; he was relying on my help. "You're a woman of strong character," he had said. Now was the time to prove it. Now I had to be strong.

I put aside all the implications that had come across in Bernice's call, that Robert had simply walked out on me, either deliberately or because he'd gone off on a drinking bout somewhere. In order to be of any use, I had to remain clearheaded and rational and unemotional, but I was going to listen to my instinct as well as my brains. If I were guided solely by logic, I would accept everyone else's version of Robert's disappearance and do nothing.

I got out the telephone directory and looked up Victor Ransome's number. I might as well try every possible contact. As I dialed, I imagined the phone ringing in that well-lit study with the Sickert on the wall. I was lucky. It was after six, and he was at home. He was surprised to hear from me, and seemed even more so when I asked him for Edmund Chance's telephone number. I could tell he wanted to ask why I needed it but was too polite to put the question direct. He said he hadn't realized I knew him.

I volunteered a story: "I've a message for him from Robert, and I've foolishly mislaid his number." I had looked that up, too, but the number was unlisted.

"One moment, I'll get my address book." He read out the number to me, and I took it down.

"How is Robert?" he asked.

"He's very well. He's in Greece."

"Ah, on the trail of material for another book, eh? Well, we must meet when he gets back. Tell him to give me a ring."

It seemed clear Robert hadn't been in touch with him.

I hadn't quite decided what I was going to say to Edmund Chance, but I was sure something would come to me. All I really wanted to know was if he had heard from Robert, if he had any idea where he might be. The subject of Robert's new book, for instance, could be a clue. But Edmund Chance was either out for the evening or away. I tried three times and had no reply.

John Nairn came to see me at seven. I was now so used to his solid comforting presence, I would have been disappointed if he had not come. I trusted him, and although I didn't realize it at that time, I was beginning to take him for granted.

He told me he had spoken to a colleague in Athens, who had then spent the day going over much the same ground that Tom Shaw had already covered: police, hospitals, Robert's drinking companions, his favorite restaurants, his friends. He had drawn a blank everywhere.

"If he's in Athens," John said, "he's keeping out of sight."

"If I've heard nothing by tomorrow morning," I said, "I'm going out there."

He looked doubtful. "Are you sure that's wise?"

"My head's nearly recovered," I said. "Even the bump's going down."

"I didn't mean that. I meant—what can you do there that we haven't already tried? I think it would be a waste of your time and money."

"You're probably right, but I can't simply sit and wait."

"Didn't Rob tell me you were starting some sort of course at the university?"

"That doesn't begin for another week," I said. "I've plenty of time."

Nairn shook his head. "I don't like it."

"I'm sorry you disapprove," I said. "But I'm still going."

He suddenly smiled. "I expect I would do the same thing in the circumstances."

We were drinking coffee in the kitchen, sitting opposite each other in very much the way Robert and I had done. Thinking of Robert, I was for one flashing moment filled with a sense of unreality, as if he had been a figment of my imagination and the only truth was contained here, in this other man sitting at the worn kitchen table, drinking his coffee, smiling at me.

He said: "I hope you can look after yourself. I rather doubt it."

"I'm very competent."

"Perhaps. Don't go wandering around in the dark, will you?"

All night I had lain awake in the dark, trying to make sense of what was happening, trying to hold on. I said lightly: "You think those burglars will follow me to Athens?"

"I wish I could come with you," Nairn said. "I feel responsible for you."

"Because you were the one who rescued me?"

"Because Rob's not here and someone has to look after you."

"You're standing in for your friend?"

"You could put it like that."

"I wonder if he knows," I said, "how good a friend you are."

"Don't embarrass me with praise," he said. "I just happened to be here."

I asked him how long he was going to be in London.

"I'm not sure. Another few days."

"Would you consider moving in here?" I said. "I'd like to think there was someone here if Robert did turn up or telephone."

"Don't worry," Nairn said. "I'll hold the fort."

That was the arrangement we made. Next day I flew to Athens.

Bernice met me at the airport with Paul Andriades.

"It's the only time Paul's got free today," she said. "I thought you could talk to him driving back."

She was looking well, tanned a golden, glowing brown. I felt like a bedraggled sparrow beside her. Paul Andriades patted my hand in sympathy, rather in the way you console the bereaved. At that moment I almost regretted coming.

They led me out to the car.

"You're very pale," Bernice said. "Have you been ill?"

I told them about the attack upon me and immediately regretted that, too. Bernice's maternal instincts, already aroused by my "abandonment," as she saw it, by Robert, were released in full flood, and I had great difficulty in persuading them that I should not be put to bed at once on arrival at the flat.

As we approached the city, as Lycabettus and the Acropolis rose to ' greet us, I began to relax. I hadn't realized how hot it still was here in late September. The streets were full of summer. The dazzling whiteness of the buildings, the women's bright dresses, the noises and hustle of traffic affected me like an electric shock, jerking me back to life. The quiet and gloom of the Bloomsbury flat, the anxious loneliness of my vigil of the past few days had lowered and depressed me more than I knew. Now optimism and hope rushed at me from the vitality of Athens. I smiled at Bernice.

"It's nice to be back," I said.

"We're glad to see you," Paul said. "But I doubt if we can help you. However, let me tell you what I do know."

Robert had driven up to the excavations with Paul the day after his arrival in Athens. He hadn't said how long he was staying, but he gave the impression that he intended to be there for a month. He settled into the team at once and worked hard.

"He seemed very happy," Paul said. "Full of life and energy and exuberant high spirits, almost too much so. There was an explosive quality about him, as if any minute he might, well— explode! It affected the whole camp, and not for the best. There began to grow a kind of tension, an expectancy, as if we were all waiting for something."

"For the unexploded bomb to go off?" I suggested.

"That's exactly it," Paul said. "Then one night he seemed quieter, more serious. He came and had a long talk with me about the excavations, about our findings and my evaluation of them. When we parted, he said he was going straight to bed. Next morning he was gone."

"He didn't tell anyone he was going?" I asked.

"He spoke to no one that night except me, and he told me nothing. I was astonished when I realized he had gone. I would have organized a search for him, in case he had taken a walk in the night and accidentally injured himself, in a fall perhaps, but he had taken all his things, so it was clearly deliberate."

"Had he brought much with him?" I asked.

He shrugged. "He had a rucksack, and it wasn't filled. A change of clothing, books, not much else."

"Can you think of any reason why he should go off like that without telling you?" I said. "And you don't need to hide anything. If there was a girl involved—"

"My dear Frances, he wasn't interested in the girls. Of course, he joked with them and teased them a little, but the only girl he talked to me about was you. He was very happy about his marriage, I know that."

"Thank you for that," I said. I paused. "It's in the north, isn't it, your excavation? A fourth-century palace, Bernice told me."

"There are always problems of dating, but the evidence is accumulating, yes."

"The caution of the professional," Bernice put in with a smile. There was such an affectionately intimate note in her voice that I was distracted from my own self-centeredness to wonder briefly about their relationship.

"Did Robert ever talk to you about his father's work?" I asked Andriades.

"Not very often."

"I was wondering"—I hesitated—"if there could have been anything comparable between the excavations his father was involved in and yours."

Paul took time to consider his answer to this.

"All excavations share certain basic techniques," he said at length. "But apart from this—" He broke off.

"I know that Robert wants to complete his father's work one day," I said. "He wants to gain more experience in field work. I believe that's why he came to you. I wondered if during that last talk with him you mentioned other sites that might have had more relevance to him."

"You mean he packed his bag and went off to another site, without saying anything to me, because it might provide more of the kind of experience he wanted?"

"Would you think that too unlikely?"

He laughed. "Nothing is impossible with Robert. But I don't

think it was archaeology that was on his mind. There was something else, something more exciting."

I said: "Are you going back to the dig soon?"

"I'm going straightaway," Paul said, "once I've dropped you and Bernice."

"Can I come with you?" I asked.

He exchanged glances with Bernice.

I said: "Two different people have tried to trace Robert in Athens without success. Don't you think it might be better to start from the place he disappeared?"

"I doubt if you will find out anything helpful," Paul said. "But you're welcome to come. And to be perfectly frank, it would be more convenient for me. I could do with Bernice at the site. It's not always very pleasant out there, by the way. It can still get pretty hot. Do you think, with this recent injury—?"

"I'm quite recovered," I said. "Don't worry about me. And it couldn't be much hotter than Turkey."

He nodded. "OK. We'll all go. I've got to collect someone first, a colleague who's coming to visit us for a day or two. I'll drop you at the flat, Bernice, and pick you up again in half an hour."

We had a cup of coffee in the flat while Bernice gathered up her things.

"You're enjoying the job?" I asked her.

"It's fascinating," she said. "He's a good man to work for. He doesn't believe in keeping things to himself. He discusses everything with everybody. Every night over dinner the whole team talks over the day's problems, the day's finds, the next problem to tackle. I've been up there several times. It's a valuable education just listening to him talk."

"And he's a nice man, too," I said with a smile.

"Yes." She paused, looking across at me.

That was a stiff little speech Bernice had made to me. There was a constraint between us that had not been there before. The metaphor of an illness returned to me. Bernice was treating me with the care accorded to an invalid, someone not wholly responsible for her actions, and the sickness she believed I was suffering from was a blind infatuation with Robert.

"I wish this hadn't happened to you," she said. "When I met Robert again, I liked him very much. He was an easy man to like. I just wish you hadn't married him."

"I wish you wouldn't talk about him in the past tense," I said. "He's not dead, and he hasn't walked out on me. It isn't as simple as that."

"How do you know?" Bernice said.

"Because I know him," I said. I spoke with more conviction than I felt.

There was little discussion about Robert on the journey north. The presence of a stranger precluded it. Paul's visiting colleague was a German professor on his way through from a conference. He was in his sixties, courteous, smiling, at ease. He sat in the front passenger seat next to Andriades and talked archaeology with him for the seven hours it took us to get to the site.

"Do you get many visitors?" I asked Bernice.

"Quite a few. A couple of journalists came about a month ago. They'd heard rumors of important finds. I think they were a little disappointed to discover they consisted of six feet of wall and a flight of steps!"

"Was Robert there then?" I asked.

She understood the significance of my question at once. "Yes, he was. You think they might have had something to do with his disappearance?"

"I don't know," I said honestly. "But any contacts he made that week—"

Bernice looked at me with quickening interest. Until I arrived in Athens, until I had stubbornly stated my faith in him, I don't think it had occurred to her there might be any other solution to Robert's disappearance than the obvious one they had all presumed.

"Something he learned from them made him leave, you mean? Something unexpected?"

"Yes, it could be that," I said. Or something expected. Some message. Hadn't Robert mentioned a message in the telephone call I had overheard that night? And then something about there being plenty of time if nothing else went wrong. Plenty of time for what? Robert had been talking to John Nairn. I must ask Nairn what it meant. But wouldn't he already have told me if that conversation had had any relevance?

"Perhaps I could talk to the journalists when I get back to Athens," I said. "If you've got their names."

"I can look them up for you."

"You're feeling quite well?" Paul asked me. "I'm not driving too fast for you?" I reassured him.

With a long drive ahead of us, he had taken the toll highway for speed. We swept through the plain of Boeotia to the coast, turning inland past Thermopylae, to Lamia. It took me some time to reconcile myself to the brilliant light, to those tantalizing glimpses of the Aegean, to the summery holiday spirit that invaded even this carload of earnest historians. Adventure, I thought, any risk would seem nothing but adventure in this atmosphere; I felt the anticipation of it myself. An eagerness, an excitement, wasn't that how Paul had described Robert's mood?

We stopped for lunch at the roadside, a brief picnic since Paul couldn't bear to waste time. Nevertheless, it was growing dark, and I was feeling the effects of the long day's travel through the heat as we approached the burning plain of Thessaly.

At Larissa we left behind the smooth-surfaced main roads, turning off into secondary roads that grew narrower and less well maintained until we were bumping along something little better than a cart track. We passed a silent village, a clutch of houses huddled round a well. Our headlights caught the frightened eyes of an animal, the crumbling pattern of a wall, and then we were through.

"Our nearest point to civilization," Paul remarked without irony. "It's not far now."

When he stopped, we seemed to be in the middle of a field. I smelled the earth as I stepped wearily from the car. The air was already cool. Bernice touched my arm. "This way." She led me round the back of the car, and I saw the low shapes of buildings and the soft gleam of oil lamps.

This was the second year at the site. The sheds put up in the first season had been left for the second. There were three of them, long tin-roofed huts used for the cleaning, sorting and recording of finds, for storage, for a site office for Paul. The team slept and ate in tents. There were eight of them when I was there, three permanent assistants who stayed for the season, five student volunteers who had come for periods of from a fortnight to two months. Numbers had varied from eight to fifteen throughout the summer.

"I don't like working with a larger team than that," Paul explained. "You cannot control the work so well. We do get local workers when we need them, when we were opening up the site last year, for instance, and a few men still come in from the village to help with moving earth and so on; but mostly there have been just this small number. I prefer to go slowly, with everything under my close direction, everything"—he closed his fist tightly and smiled—"in my hand."

We were in the dining tent, eating a welcome meal of lamb stew. There was wine on the table and hunks of now-stale bread. The lamps threw flickering shadows across the canvas walls. His volunteers, who had eaten before we arrived, were grouped around the table, sweaters over shirts against the night air, talking quietly. Paul introduced them to us. Of the three men, one was a surveyor, one a photographer and the third the indoor assistant in charge of all the material taken from the trenches. The five students were all girls: two American, two Greek, one French. They smiled and shook hands and avoided my eyes. The fact that I was Robert's wife seemed an embarrassment. They turned with hardly disguised relief to the German professor.

Paul refilled his wineglass. "All right, Christos, let's have the reports on the last couple of days."

They began to talk shop, the long discussions over dinner Bernice had told me about. I listened for a while, then took the flashlight she had given me and slipped away unnoticed. I was sharing a tent with Bernice. She had said she would show me the tent Robert had used next morning. She didn't think it would tell me anything; he had had it to himself, so there were no witnesses to the time he had left that last night.

I wrapped myself in blankets and tried to sleep. The silence, the darkness were oppressive. I began to wonder what on earth I was doing out here in this wilderness, what I thought I was going to achieve. Was I just comforting myself with a semblance of action? None of those nice, hardworking people in the dining tent was going to be of any use to me. They were totally removed from the dangerous, wayward world that Robert seemed to inhabit. There was an innocent unworldliness about them. No wonder his presence had alarmed them, like a tiger among goats.

I awoke at first light and walked out into a breathtakingly beautiful morning. The sun was gentle, the air limpid. Its clarity telescoped distance, bringing folds and twists and cliffs of rock in astonishing detail to the eye. The plain was guarded by mountains. To the north, the majestic range of Olympus filled the horizon; to the west and east the wooded slopes of foothills were visible, and the massif of Pindus barred access to the sea. I had gained the impression the previous night that the site was in a barren region, but now I saw there were trees here, too, poplar and plane trees lining the banks of a stream, nearly dried out by the long summer but with still a narrow flow of brackish water between flat stretches of baked red mud.

The excavations covered an area of some three acres on the southern side of the stream. To the untrained eye it was at first glance as unimpressive and confused as any modern construction site in its most elementary stages, but as I looked closer at the deeply cut trenches with their exposed layers of wall, the sunken steps, the raised platforms, the shadowy imprint of the vanished buildings began to emerge.

"They're working on the storage rooms at the moment." Paul Andriades had come to join me. "Perhaps you can see the tops of the vast storage jars over there. We're leaving them in place until we've cleared the whole section, photographed it and so on. I think it will probably be the last piece of work this year. We'll be closing down in a few weeks. Here." He handed me a mug of coffee. "I saw you wandering round, looking rather lost. Perhaps this will help."

"Thank you." The coffee was strong and very hot. I cupped both hands round the mug as I sipped it. "You're up early."

"We start early. Best time of the day for our work. Are you interested in archaeology?"

"I know very little about it."

"Here, let me show you something." He jumped down five feet or so into a trench below us. He turned back and held out his hand to help me. "Come on!" His enthusiasm was infectious. I set the mug of coffee down on a stone plinth and joined him. A few yards along the trench he stopped. "Now, what do you see?"

Rising above the trench at this point was part of a wall, made of great blocks of stone. It continued down into the earth, the face of the stones visible where the soil had been cleared away. Beneath the first line of wall was a layer of earth. Below that, more stone.

"I see a wall," I said.

He laughed. "Well done. But if you look a little closer, you will see that the soil here is discolored, and the stones below, here and here, are blackened."

I put my hand out and touched the scorched stones. They filled me with a kind of uneasy awe.

"Blackened by fire?" I said.

"Exactly. The first building here was destroyed and burned, and a second, grander edifice built on its remains."

"Do you know who built it?"

"I have theories based on historical facts, but not enough proof yet to substantiate them. The Aleuadae family were in power here, all round Larissa, before the region was conquered by Philip of Macedon, but as to who built the second palace, whether it was Philip himself perhaps or one of his generals—" He shrugged. "Now you see why it takes so long. There can be no guesses in this business. One piece of evidence on another, like a detective, that's my job."

I had seen Andriades only relaxing before, in the taverna in Athens. I liked him better out here. Like most men, he was at his most attractive when absorbed in his work.

"Have you found anything to indicate it could have belonged to a king?" I asked.

"Some gold ornaments, necklaces, earrings. I sent the most precious to Bernice in Athens. Everything is being packed as it's recorded, now, ready for the move. Go have a look in the sheds, if you're interested."

"Paul—"

"Yes," he said quietly. "I know. This isn't helping you very much about Robert."

"May I tell you something in confidence?"

"Of course."

"When I was attacked in the flat in London, something was stolen. No one knows about it. I haven't told the police. It belonged to Robert's father. He found it in Turkey. He smuggled it out of the country. Robert told me I was the only person he had shown it to. He kept it hidden."

"You mean an object from an archaeological site?"

"Yes. That was why I asked you if Robert had talked to you about his father's work."

"Only in general terms, and then not often. You didn't tell the police about the theft because it had been smuggled out of Turkey?"

"And because Robert had made such a secret thing of it. I expected him back any minute. I was going to leave the decision to him. Now I'm wondering if it could be more than the isolated incident I thought it, if it could be in any way linked with his disappearance."

"You think the burglars knew where it was, or did they find it by chance?" Paul said.

"I think they must have known where it was," I said.

"So the next question after that is how they came by that information," Paul said.

"Of course"—he hesitated—"there is the possibility that Robert told someone unintentionally, when he'd had a little too much drink."

"I don't think so," I said. "He wasn't obsessed by it; it wasn't something he was brooding about all the time. It was precious to him because of his father, one of his last memories of him."

Paul said: "You know about his father?"

"Yes, Robert told me."

"I wondered," he said. "I wasn't sure you knew."

"Do you think I should tell the police?"

"Was it very valuable?"

"Oh, Paul," I said, "I might as well tell you, having told you this much. It's a small golden bull. Robert's father found it on a hill in eastern Turkey. He thought it came from a Urartian tomb somewhere in the hill. He was going back to find the tomb, but he never got the chance. Robert hopes to find the place one day and excavate it."

"Ah," Paul said, "now I understand your questions about my last conversation with Robert. I can be of no help to you. He gave no indication of his plans. One point worries me, though. Your robbery in London came almost three weeks after Robert disappeared. I hope there's no connection."

I stared at him. "You mean someone forced the information from him? That he's being kept a prisoner or been killed?"

He put his hand on my arm. "No, Frances, of course I don't. Archaeologists don't behave in such a melodramatic way just to be first in the field with a new discovery. And I don't think ordinary criminals would go to such extraordinary lengths for one single object. As for kidnapping, with Robert using the bull as a ransom, the very idea is ridiculous. We don't have such bandits in Greece. This isn't Sardinia, after all. No, my advice to you is to go back to London, tell the police about the theft, let them look for the bull in the normal way, and then wait there in London for Robert. I believe there is a perfectly simple explanation for his disappearance. After all, he didn't expect you to be back from Canada until a few days ago. You are the important person to him. Why should he tell any of the rest of us what he was up to? He never has before. Go back and wait. There'll be a message from him soon."

It was good advice, and my common sense told me to follow it. People did not behave in such melodramatic ways. And yet the very place where we were standing belied that truth. Centuries before, men had fought and died on this very spot. They were still fighting and dying all over the world. Violence was commonplace. I had been touched by it. Robert, on the boat in Turkey, had already been involved in it. He was not immune. My worst fears for him could yet prove true.

In the dining tent Bernice was seated at the bare table, sorting through a box of cards. She looked up with that slightly concerned glance I was becoming used to.

"There you are. I wondered where you'd got to."

"Paul's been showing me the excavations. He brought me some coffee, but I'm afraid I let it get cold. Is there any more?"

There was an earthenware jug beside her. She put a hand on its curved brown side to judge its warmth. "Try some of this. It still feels hot."

She filled up my half-empty mug. "There's dried milk somewhere."

"Don't bother. I like it black." I pulled a chair out and sat down.

"Well," Bernice said, "have you learned anything?"

"About archaeology, yes. About Robert, no."

"I'm sorry," she said. "I knew it would be a waste of time."

"I haven't started yet. How many of the people here now were here when Robert was?"

"The three full-time assistants and, let me see, the two American girls, Jan and Susan. And the French girl, Monique, I believe. The Greek girls came only two weeks ago. But none of them will be able to tell you anything. If they knew anything, they'd have said so at the time."

"It might be something casual Robert said to them, which they don't realize is important. Or something they saw, something he did."

Bernice sighed. "You're certainly persistent, I'll say that for you."

"I don't understand why that surprises you."

"Let me put it this way. If your affair with Robert had remained a straightforward romantic fling, if you hadn't gone and got that piece of official paper which calls you married, would you be so determined to find him? Wouldn't you accept the situation for what it is?"

"Perhaps that's why he married me," I said lightly. "To make sure he did have someone to come after him and find him. One doesn't let a husband go as casually as a lover. And you don't know what the real situation is any more than I do. Robert told me he had unfinished business to complete. It was going to take a month. Perhaps it is simply taking a little longer."

"What kind of business?"

"I don't know. I thought he meant his arrangement to work on the site here with Paul for a month, but it's clearly not that."

Bernice was silent for a moment. Then she said: "I don't want you to be hurt, you know, any more than you have been. That's all it is."

"I know," I said.

She smiled, more cheerfully, more like her normal, uncomplicated self. "Come on. I'll show you the tent Robert used, not that it will tell you anything. Wretched man, I could cheerfully murder him. He causes nothing but trouble wherever he goes. You should hear Tom Shaw on the subject."

She was right. Robert's tent didn't have a great deal to offer in the way of clues to his disappearance, except that it stood at the back of the small encampment, close to the rough track that was the sole road to the outside world. It would have made it easy for him to slip away from the site without being seen.

One of the American girls was walking along the path between the tents as we made our way back to the working area. She said, "Hi!" rather shyly, ducking her head to one side as if instinctively trying to avoid being looked at.

Bernice said: "Hello, Susan."

I said: "Can I come and talk to you later?"

She said: "Sure. I'll—I'll be around."

She was small and slight, with brown hair pulled back from her face in a ponytail. She wore a T-shirt, very short shorts and canvas shoes. She looked about twelve years old.

As we walked on, Bernice said: "Now why should she blush at the sight of us? She's never done that before."

"How can you tell with that deep tan?"

"She's upset about something," Bernice said.

"Good," I said. "Let's hope it's a helpful something."

I didn't catch up with Susan, however, until quite late in the afternoon. In the meantime, I talked to most of the other people on the site. They were all, in spite of my uncertain reception the night before, apparently concerned and anxious to be helpful and, from my point of view, quite unrewarding.

Robert was good company, the surveyor, Nicholas, said, and a good archaeologist, but he got the impression Robert wasn't really serious about the work. In what way? I asked.

"Always joking," Nicholas said. "Always laughing, making people laugh. He was not a serious person."

"Did he leave the camp very much?"

"As far as I know, he didn't leave it at all. Every night he was there in the dining tent, talking till all hours."

"Were you surprised when he left?" I asked.

"No, not really. I got the impression he was a person of impulse. Looking back on it, I think he was using us, this place, to pass the time while waiting for something."

They all came up with much the same story. They had all liked Robert; none of them was very surprised when he left; they had all with hindsight felt that he was waiting for something. This nervous tension of his had infected them all, as Paul Andriades had said. They seemed relieved that he had gone.

It was to Nicholas, bespectacled, dedicated, too unimaginative even to think of lying to save me pain, to whom I put that fairly delicate question: "Was he drinking a lot while he was here?"

He even looked surprised to be asked such a thing. "No, a little wine at meals perhaps. Why do you ask?"

I shrugged, trying to look indifferent to my own question. "It might have shown that he was anxious—"

Nicholas shook his head. "He was the least anxious man I have met. I would have said nothing would worry him. Was there something he should be anxious about?"

So Robert's excitable mood hadn't been due to drink, nor, I was sure, had his disappearance. I had never believed that to be the explanation, but I was glad to get this kind of confirmation.

The two Greek girls had been working in the clearing hut when I first visited it. When I glanced in later, they had gone, and Susan stood alone by the sink, carefully washing a tray of soil-grimed objects.

"Hello," I said. "Can I help?"

She looked up and away again in the same diffident manner she had shown before.

"If they're very fragile," I said, "perhaps I'd better not."

"You can help if you like," she said. "They're shards of pottery. They take them back and fit them together. These aren't a particularly interesting bunch. There's no decoration on them."

She handed me a soft brush, and I joined her at the sink. I

chose a large piece of earthenware as being less likely to break on me and began cleaning it, copying the American girl's careful actions. As she finished each fragment, she placed it on a tray on the other side of the sink.

"What happens to them after this?" I asked.

She nodded behind us, to the three long tables that had been placed parallel to each other down the length of the hut.

"When the objects are dry, they're put in the appropriate trays on the bagging table, according to material: pottery, bone, iron, marble and so on. Then every piece is marked and recorded on the other tables and finally packed in boxes and crates for removal to Athens."

"The site is closing down soon, Paul Andriades told me."

"Yes, most of us have got places we have to be by the end of October."

"You're going back to America?"

"Yes. I've got another year at college, and then I want to work for my master's degree." She picked up a scrap of material hardly bigger than her thumbnail and began cleaning it with slow, deft movements. She had very delicate hands. All her features were small and delicate. She didn't really look strong enough for the hard field work out in the trenches.

"I'm not looking forward to leaving," she said. "I'd rather stay here."

"Perhaps you'll come back next year."

"Oh, sure, I hope so." Then she said, with her head down and so quietly I hardly heard her: "Any news of Robert?"

"Not yet."

She glanced at me and then, when I met her gaze, looked quickly away again. She had not yet once looked me directly in the face.

"Have you been married to Robert long?" she asked.

"No, not long."

There was a pause, a hesitation drawn out for nearly a minute in which I could almost feel her gathering up her resolution to speak, to tell me something which in that moment I most definitely did not want to hear. "He'll create havoc among those earnest girl students you've got up there," Joe Parker had said to Paul.

She said at last: "I didn't know he was married, you know."

"No," I said. "I don't suppose you did." I felt a cold shiver of misery, like an inward sigh. Not diffidence, her manner, but guilt confronting Robert's wife; was that the answer? Oh, Rob, no, I thought, not so soon, not so quickly gone from your mind.

"If I'd thought it would make any difference, I'd have spoken up at once," she said. "I didn't realize they thought he'd had an accident and that he hadn't told anyone where he was going."

"Do you know where he went?" I asked.

She shook her head. "No, I don't. Oh, it's all so silly. I feel like such an idiot."

"Won't you tell me what you do know?" I said. "Whatever it is."

She put down her work and wiped her hands on a towel. For the first time she looked at me. "It isn't what you think. I made a fool of myself, that's all. Then I was too embarrassed to say anything. I didn't even tell Jan. I pretended I didn't go, and after that I couldn't very well change my story."

"Jan is the other American here, is that right? Red hair. Your friend?"

"Yes. We came over here together. I'm not so sure she is my friend now. We've kind of broken up over this."

"You said you pretended you didn't go. Go where?"

"I'll try to explain. It's pretty simple really. But it's embarrassing telling you. I'd decided to keep quiet, and then, when you turned up last night, I thought it might be serious, his disappearance, and the small bit of information I had might help."

"Yes," I said. "Thank you. Anything might help."

She turned away again and began fiddling with the objects on the drying tray, arranging them into some kind of order.

"You know Robert is very attractive," she began hesitantly,

"and a lot of fun. All the girls liked him, but I happened to be working with him in one of the trenches out there, so I spent more time with him. He used to talk quite a lot, sometimes seriously about what we were doing; sometimes he'd make jokes, or tease me, you know, about being small and not looking my age. So I suppose I got the impression he was more interested in me than the others. Jan didn't think so. She said he thought of me as a kid. I thought she was jealous; most men usually prefer her to me."

I remembered the redhead only vaguely from last night. A thin, rather foxy face. I hadn't seen her yet today. I'd been told she'd gone into the village with the truck.

"Well, twice during that week Robert went to the village to pick up the mail. They bring it up from Larissa once a day, and with all the interest there is in these excavations, there's usually quite a lot. The second time he went I was taking a walk by the river, trying to keep cool. He pulled up and told me to jump in, said he'd buy me a drink. There's a kind of café in the village," she explained, "one grubby room full of old men. He bought me some sweet, sticky drink and an ouzo for himself, and we drank them, sitting on a wall outside."

So Robert had left the encampment. Perhaps Nicholas didn't count trips to the village as leaving it.

"Was there any mail for Robert, do you know?" I asked Susan. "When you collected it, did you see him take any letters for himself?"

"I don't think so," she said. "I don't remember seeing him with any letters. They came in a bag. He just slung it in the back of the truck."

She fell silent. I'd distracted her, broken the thread of her thoughts. I prompted her. "And after the trip to the village?"

"Yes," she said. "This is where the stupid part starts. The next day, the day he actually left, I didn't see Robert at all. Not until the evening anyway. He spent a lot of time with Paul Andriades, I think. He talked to him at dinner. He didn't pay any real attention to me. It was as if he'd forgotten my existence until Jan brought me the note."

"Ah," I said. "The jealous Jan."

"I didn't realize it was a trick, you see," Susan said, "because I'd never seen his writing. I didn't know Jan's either, as it happened. We'd met on the trip over. And she seemed so offhand about it I didn't suspect a thing. Just tossed me the envelope with my name scrawled on it, said she'd found it in our tent. She didn't even wait to see me open it. She told me afterwards she hadn't meant to upset me, it was just a joke, and since I'd seen through it, no harm was done. You see, when she owned up, I told her I had recognized her writing and hadn't gone." She looked at me with sad blue eyes. "It sounds pretty childish, doesn't it? I thought it was cruel at the time. She wanted me to wait out there like a fool. She thought once I believed he'd stood me up, I wouldn't have anything more to do with him and she'd have a chance. It didn't occur to either of us he might be leaving."

"What exactly did the note say?" I asked.

She blushed. "A lot of silly stuff, like a love letter. And if I felt the same, would I meet him at one o'clock that night under the trees where the path ran by the river? That was the coincidence that convinced me he meant it. It was where he'd picked me up the day before."

"So you went," I said.

She took a deep breath. "Yes."

"Didn't Jan stay awake to see what happened?"

"I think she meant to, but the kind of life we live out here, all the hard work and fresh air—" She laughed, sounding for the first time like the untroubled girl she must have been before Robert came. "Well, it's pretty hard staying awake till ten, let alone one. She was fast asleep when I left the tent, I'm sure of that."

"You had no trouble staying awake," I said.

"No," she said.

"No. Neither would I have had," I said.

She didn't know how to take that. She hesitated, and I thought I had put her off again, but then she said: "It was a full moon, a beautiful night. I didn't need to use my flashlight."

"And what did you see?" I asked.

"Nothing for a while. I went to the place we were supposed to meet and waited there. After twenty minutes I began to wonder if I'd got the wrong spot. I still didn't doubt the note. I thought I was at fault. So I began to walk along the riverbank. There's a bend a little farther along, with a clump of trees. It was then I saw Robert. He was walking along the path, ahead of me. I was going to call out when he turned off and disappeared into the trees. I ran after him, but as I got to the trees, I heard voices. Robert's and another man's. I went on, but carefully, because I was beginning to realize the note was a phony. Robert had come out to meet someone all right, but it wasn't me. I was right into the trees before I saw the truck. It had been pulled off the road into the shadows. Robert was standing by the door, talking to someone inside, the driver."

"Did you see him?" I said.

"No. If I'd gone any closer, Robert might have seen me. I didn't want that. But I heard his voice. He said to Robert: 'OK. Let's go.' He was an American."

"And then?"

"Robert walked around to the other door, opened it and got in. I saw he was carrying a rucksack, but I didn't know that was all the luggage he'd brought to the dig. I thought he'd be back. He closed the door, and they drove off."

"On the road to Larissa?"

"I suppose so. The road only goes to the village, and I think the only good road from the village ends up in Larissa; but I don't know the region well enough to say."

"And then you went back to the camp?" I asked.

"That's right. I went to bed, and the next morning I pretended nothing had happened. I showed Jan the note and said someone was playing malicious tricks, and she admitted she'd done it. It was a shock, I must say."

"You didn't think of telling anyone, Paul perhaps, when you found out Robert hadn't come back?"

"People didn't seem terribly surprised that he'd gone. No one spoke to me about an accident or hinted there was any mystery. I thought Paul Andriades must know all about it, and the reason I didn't was that Jan was right and Robert had only thought of me as one of the team, a kid, no one of importance to him. It's only been these last few days that anyone has mentioned his name again or mentioned that he had actually disappeared. Then it seemed too late to say anything. I wasn't going to give Jan the satisfaction of knowing I'd taken her note seriously after all; that I'd believed all the nonsense she'd put in it. And I'd told everyone I'd been asleep all that night. I couldn't go back on that without telling the whole story, without seeming to be a complete fool."

"Oh, dear," I said at the end of all this.

"I told you it was a stupid business."

I smiled at her. "I'm glad you've told me. Don't worry about it."

"I'm glad I've told you, too," Susan said. "Does it help?"

"Yes, of course it helps."

"I suppose you'll tell everyone now."

"I'll make sure Jan doesn't hear about it," I said. "It's none of her business."

"Thanks." Then she added: "You don't have to worry either, you know. I'm over it now, and anyway, it was mostly imagination on my part."

That "mostly" was a nice touch.

"It's all right," I said. "I know how attractive Robert can be."

"He's a nice guy," Susan said. "I hope you find him soon."

"So do I," I said.

At the door of the hut, on my way out, I stopped. "You spoke of the interest the excavation has aroused. Have there been a lot of visitors while you've been here?"

"Quite a few. They've been a bit of a nuisance to Paul at times, stopping him from working. They've mostly been other archaeologists, like the German professor who came up with you last night, but there have been one or two journalists. There was a bit of a rush before I came here, I gather. That was when the rumors first got out that the site might be connected with Philip of Macedon. They were hoping for another palace like Pella, but we haven't found any mosaics yet. With nothing exotic to show for all this work, their interest died away."

"You're becoming a cynic," I said.

She grinned. "Maybe. And that might not be a bad thing, don't you agree?"

I went straight from there to Paul. He was working with Bernice in the hut he had made his office.

"Well," he said, looking up at me. "News, obviously. What have you found out?"

"Robert left here that night in a truck driven by an American. It had clearly been arranged beforehand."

"Now how did you find that out?"

"One of the girls saw him leave."

"Susan, I bet," Bernice said. "I knew she was hiding something."

"If she knew this, why on earth didn't she tell us?" Paul said.

"Oh," I said vaguely. "Reasons—boyfriends."

"Did she know who the American was?"

"No. And she couldn't describe him; she didn't see him. Have you any ideas?"

"John Nairn perhaps," Paul said. "He's a good friend of Robert's, and he's American."

"No," I said. "It's not him. He came to the flat in London, and he's still there. He didn't even know Robert had disappeared."

"Well, then—" Paul turned to Bernice. She shrugged.

"Don't look at me. I don't know Robert's friends."

"Where could he go from here," I asked, "if he didn't go back to Athens?"

Bernice got up and produced a folding map of Greece from one of the shelves. She spread it out on the table. She looked up at me with a slightly quizzical expression. "If he didn't go south, he could have gone west and ended up in Albania; northwest would have brought him to Yugoslavia; northeast and he'd have come to Bulgaria and Turkey. Or he could have taken a boat from the east coast to one of the Aegean islands. You've got quite a choice."

"This road going north along the coast," I said, "is that a good one?"

"Continuation of the highway we came on," Paul said. "It goes as far as Thessaloniki. It's a fast route."

"You don't know why or where he could have gone," Bernice said. "Admit it."

"You're right," I said. "I don't know. But I'm guessing he didn't go back to Athens. I'm guessing he arranged to come here in the first place because it was a good jumping-off place for the next leg of his journey."

"That makes sense," Paul said. "Thinking about it, I couldn't see any reason for him to come up here just for a week, unless perhaps he was keeping out of the way."

"Keeping out of the way of what?" Bernice asked in surprise.

"Paul has a theory that Robert didn't plan to disappear," I said. "That something unexpected made him pack up and go so suddenly."

"That's what you were saying on the way up," Bernice said. "You thought those journalists might have had something to do with it."

"Or he could have got a message through the post," I said. "He fetched it twice during that week, I'm told."

Paul leaned forward in his chair. He addressed me with the

precision of a tutor instructing a pupil. "It seems to me we've got two possibilities. The first is that Robert came here, as he said, to work for a month gaining the kind of experience of a dig he wanted, until it was time to rejoin you in London. But something happened that week that changed his plans, some threat, some message. Whatever it was, he felt he had to get out fast."

It was very hot in the shed. The heat had been gently baking its wooden frame all day. The door had been left open for ventilation, but there was no breeze. Outside, the heat haze shimmered and danced above the empty plain. The mountains had retreated, their outlines blurred.

Bernice said quietly: "Why should he be threatened?"

Paul didn't reply. He looked across at me as if I should know the answer to that question.

I was suddenly tired, tired of Robert's silence, of my own anxieties, of the confusion in my mind.

I got up and walked across the room. Books, papers lined the few shelves. I ran my finger along them. Everything so ordered, so neat; like Paul's mind, like his world.

"Perhaps he wasn't threatened," Paul said at last. "Perhaps it was all planned."

"The second alternative," I said.

"Yes. The one you believe. Which means that all along Robert was acting according to a plan he made before he ever came to Greece, that he intended from the start to spend no more than a week here, that his departure by truck was arranged, that wherever he is now, whatever he's doing is part of that plan."

And it all fitted: his behavior in London, his talk of a message, of unfinished business, his air of excitement, of anticipation that had been noticed by everyone, his secret departure by truck.

"Do you really believe that?" Bernice said to me.

"Yes," I said.

"In which case, why didn't he tell you? Why didn't he give you any warning? Why haven't you heard from him?"

They were questions I didn't want to answer. There were two

possibilities to that, too: one, that he had never intended to come back to me; the other, that he had been prevented from doing so.

I pretended my choice was certain, but it wasn't, not after that ambiguous conversation with Susan.

"Because he's run into trouble," I said. "Because something's gone wrong."

A shadow fell across the entrance of the hut, a voice said: "Something gone wrong? Not one of the trenches collapsed, I hope, Paul? I've driven all this way to inspect them."

Tall, elegant in appearance, cool in manner, one of those smooth faces you soon forget. I wasn't expecting to see him, and so for a moment I didn't recognize him, until Paul got up, arms out in welcome. "My dear Tom, this is a delightful surprise! Come in, come in. Why didn't you let me know you were coming?"

"How?" Tom Shaw said with a smile. "By carrier pigeon?" His glance embraced the room, rested on me. "No, I'm sorry, I didn't have time to write. I only knew yesterday that I'd be coming anywhere near you. I'm on my way to Thessaloniki. A little official business. I couldn't resist making a detour to see you. Can you find a corner of a tent for me tonight?"

He was ushered in and found a chair, and Bernice went off to find the nearest equivalent to a long, cool drink that they had. In the small interval of silence he said softly to me: "Does your presence here mean good news or bad about Robert?"

"It means no news at all," I said.

"I'm sorry." He spoke kindly, but I had the impression that despite his efforts on my behalf to trace Robert in Athens, he was not greatly interested in me or my problems. At dinner he more or less admitted it. Paul, still occupied with his German professor, had placed Tom next to me. I thanked him for his help in looking for Robert. He waved my gratitude aside.

"You know, you disappointed me," he said. "I didn't think you would fall quite so readily for Robert's notorious charm. Though, of course, there were signs of it at your first meeting in that taverna, weren't there, now I come to think of it."

His glance was speculative. "What are you doing here?"

I tried to put defenses up against his probing, watchful gaze. I think I already sensed that intentionally or not he was going to hurt me. I made my tone light. "Looking for clues. This is the last place he was seen, after all."

"I should have thought the clues were obvious. Once we had dealt with the possibility of accident, illness or arrest, that is. They lie in his previous behavior. I understand they've had plenty of visitors to the site, including the odd journalist. That makes it obvious what happened, doesn't it? After all, this isn't the first time he's run off when someone turned up who could make the connection between him and his father."

He put an olive into his mouth. He saw my puzzled expression.

"I thought you knew about his father," he said. "Paul said Robert had told you."

"I know he was an archaeologist," I said. "I know he died when Robert was eight, very soon after Robert's mother had committed suicide."

I was wondering if he was talking about the golden bull, if there were people who knew the secret of that hill in Anatolia that Robert believed belonged only to himself. That was why it came as a greater shock when Tom spoke; it was a blow so entirely unexpected.

"Robert's father is not dead," he said. "I'm sorry, I thought you knew. He's alive and well and living in Russia, where he has been enjoying an honored retirement for the past twenty-five years. Robert changed his name to his mother's maiden name, but some people still find out. Are you sure you've never heard of him? Maurice Arden, one of the more successful defectors of the fifties, the traitor who got away, just in time."

CHAPTER 4

I was not sure how long I had been alone, wandering along the barren riverbank, beneath the dusty trees. The others would not miss me. I had left them still seated round the dining table, drinking and talking, speculating about men vanished into dust centuries ago with an immediacy that made the loss of one living man seem unimportant. I had walked without any sense of purpose or direction, and now I had come to the place where the truck had waited for Robert. Its tracks were still visible in the earth. The last place anyone had seen Robert.

The dying light gave the grove a sinister aspect. The small leaves shivered in the faintest tremor of a breeze, rattling dryly like paper crumpled in the hand. A site for an oracle, an altar to a rustic god. Trees full of trapped spirits, a landscape full of ghosts; Robert as haunted as the place, running away from his own ghosts—

Until now the name of Maurice Arden had meant little to me. I was not even born when he fled to Russia, a few hours ahead of the police. It was all past history to me, the notorious spies and traitors of that time, their faces the faces of the actors who portrayed them on television, their lives the stuff of fiction. They belonged to a world so radically different from my own, a tight, enclosed, self-absorbed world of interlocking relationships and outworn theories, of convictions that, if sincerely held now, made them seem naïve, and if not, intensified the self-regarding treachery of their actions.

And they were all growing old. Maurice Arden must be sixty

at least. He had been devoted to Robert. How much had he missed him? Had he ever been in touch, or had the story of his death in Ankara, the story Robert had told me, been a deliberate attempt to protect, for a while at least, his young son from the truth and save his own face? Had the solicitor who became Robert's guardian been instructed to give him that version alone, and if so, how long had it been before Robert learned the truth? It had had the ring of conviction when Robert had told it to me. I did not want to believe it was Robert's sole invention, constructed to deceive me. There were a lot of things I did not want to believe about Robert.

A twig cracked behind me. I swung round and saw Paul Andriades standing at the edge of the trees, watching me. He came slowly forward.

"Bernice wondered where you were," he said. "I volunteered to find you."

"You shouldn't have left your guests."

"My guests are perfectly happy. I'm sorry about what has happened. I thought Robert had told you about his father."

"He should have told me, shouldn't he?" I think it was that that had disturbed me most, driving me away from the company, from Tom Shaw's curious, slightly pitying gaze, from Bernice's frank concern. If Robert couldn't tell me about something so fundamental in his life, if he couldn't trust me with that, what else had he hidden from me? And who else? I thought of our first evening together in London, the ringing telephone left unanswered—because I was there?—the later call he took while he thought I slept, the unexpected visit to Victor Ransome's house, his long talk with Edmund Chance. What had been his real purpose in coming to London? Why had he married me? Had I seen or known something dangerous to him? The incident on the Turkish boat, for instance? "I've always been a bloody good liar," he had said. "I missed my vocation as a con man."

Or was I letting my imagination run away with me? Was everything as straightforward and uncomplicated as the explanations Robert had given me for his actions? He had followed me to London because he loved me and did not want to lose me. He had not told me about his father because, as Tom Shaw had implied, he was too ashamed of the connection. He thought I would not marry him if I knew. And when two journalists visiting the camp saw him and recognized him, perhaps tried to interview him about his father, he picked up his things and ran. Could it really be as simple as that?

"Do you think Robert is as unstable and neurotic as Tom Shaw believes?" I asked Paul.

"I think he had a very unhappy childhood which has colored his later life," he replied.

"A diplomatic answer meaning yes," I said. "I suppose his father's defection was the final blow for his mother, the real reason for her suicide, but that doesn't make her any more emotionally stable. Not a very happy inheritance for him."

"Now don't you start feeling sorry for him," Paul said. "I should think that's the very reason he didn't tell you the whole truth. He didn't want your pity. He wanted things between you to begin on a fresh, clean basis, with no hang-ups from the past."

"And yet he's gone," I said, "because of the past."

Paul admitted it. "It looks like it."

"Could someone drive me back to Athens tomorrow?" I said.

"You're going back? I think perhaps that's wise."

"There's nothing else to be done here, and my course in London starts next week."

"You must give me your address in case I hear any news. Will you be at Robert's flat?"

"Only to see John Nairn, if he's still there, and in the remote chance that there's a message from Robert. Then I'll find somewhere else to live."

"How will Robert find you if he comes back?" Paul said. I noted that "if" spoken so spontaneously. "If" he comes back, not "when."

"He can find me through the university," I said.

Paul nodded. "I'm sorry."

"Don't start being sorry for me," I said, "or I shall burst into tears. It's going to be bad enough facing Bernice. She never trusted Robert."

Paul smiled and, taking my hand, tucked it through his arm. "We shall go face her together." We began to walk back towards the camp.

I think what depressed me more than anything at that moment was Paul's complete acceptance of my idea. He believed that Robert had left me. Perhaps he would come back one day, perhaps not. It was behavior typical of the man they knew. They were only sorry for me for having believed him to be otherwise.

I did not wish to talk to anyone else that night. I left Paul when we reached the tent I was sharing with Bernice and began to pack my things. A few minutes later Bernice came in. She sat down on her camp bed and watched me for a while in silence. When she did speak, it was clear Paul had warned her of my intentions.

"Would you like me to come back with you?"

I looked up. "To Athens or to London?"

"If you really need me in London—"

I smiled at her. "It's all right. I'm not going to take you away from your work or Paul. Now there is a reliable man." I put up a hand to stop her speaking. "Don't tell me how sorry you are for me because I don't want to hear it."

"I was going to ask you about Maurice Arden," she said mildly. "I don't know very much about it, but I don't see that an archaeologist could have had much to offer the Russians."

"He apparently had quite a lot to offer them when he was in the intelligence service during the war. And he remained in the service for about a year after the war before he took up his university post. But Tom Shaw said his main job seems to have been recruiting. Robert told me the flat was an open house for students, and not only students of archaeology, I gather. It was one of the students Arden approached who finally gave him away.

He happened to have an uncle in the intelligence service himself. He went straight to him with the information, and they began linking everything up. Somehow Arden got wind of it and got away. He turned up in Moscow to a hero's welcome."

"And his wife killed herself and Robert was left to cope," Bernice said. "I feel a great deal more sympathy with him, knowing all that."

"I think that kind of sympathy was what he was trying to avoid getting from me," I said.

"That makes sense."

"Yes." I sighed. "It's all very reasonable, isn't it?"

Bernice hesitated. "I'd like to say how sorry I am, even though you don't want to hear it."

"I know," I said. "But you understand why I want to get away."

"Paul's arranging for a car. Christos can drive you. He can take some of the artifacts down to Athens at the same time. By the way, I suppose it's of no interest to you now, but I did look up the names of the two journalists who visited the site while Robert was here. I suppose if you got in touch with them, they could confirm that they had recognized him as Maurice Arden's son, or perhaps they even came up to interview him, knowing he was here."

"Were they Greek? Could I see them in Athens on my way through?"

"As a matter of fact, they were German, one from a news magazine, the other from a press agency. I've written their names down for you." She handed a sheet of paper across to me. I sat down on the bed and looked at the two names written on the paper in Bernice's clear, neat writing. The first name was B. Ullman. The second had me staring at it first with disbelief and then with a growing excitement: N. Okyer.

It seemed to me extraordinary that it had meant nothing to Bernice until I remembered that I had said nothing to her about the presence of the Turk in the cabin opposite ours on the boat to Istanbul or that I had discovered his name from the purser. Nor had I told her that the man involved in the fight on board had been Robert.

"Okyer," I said. "That's not a German name; that's Turkish."

"That's not very likely, surely," Bernice said. "A Turkish journalist in Greece?"

"Where did you get the name?"

"There's a record kept of all visitors in a book in the office. They sign it themselves."

"So Mr. Okyer signed his own name?"

"Yes, I suppose so."

"You couldn't have made a mistake copying it out?"

"No. What is all this?"

"Did you see the two journalists?"

"No, I was still in Athens at that time."

"Did Paul?"

"Yes, of course."

I got off the bed. "I must go see him—"

"Now, wait a minute," Bernice said. "What is all this about? Why should this journalist, even if he is Turkish, make all this difference? There are a lot of Turks working in Germany after all. But in either case I don't see what there is to get excited about."

I sat down again. "Bernice, you remember the man who took our taxi on the road in Turkey and left us stranded. His name was Okyer." And I told her how I knew and what had happened on the boat and how Okyer kept crossing Robert's path in a way too frequent to be coincidental. A sequence of events was forming in my mind, a mysterious yet logical pattern.

"Do you remember writing to me that you'd seen a man very like the passenger in the taxi getting into a car with Cleo? I think that was the same man. And I don't think Robert left here so suddenly and secretly because someone had recognized him as Arden's son. I think he left because Okyer had tracked him here, to what was more or less a hiding place for Robert. I think he represented a threat to Robert. And now that we know Cleo knows Okyer, I think we can assume she is involved, too. I think Robert got out of Turkey and came to Athens because he had nearly been killed there, and I think Okyer had something to do with that. And, Bernice, I don't believe Robert was drunk that night in Athens; I think he was drugged. Do you remember how Cleo and the driver grabbed him and how he hit out at them? He was trying to escape from them."

Robert had practically told me that himself. "If I told you I wasn't drunk that evening, would you believe me?" he had asked.

"What about the shot we heard at the temple?" Bernice said. "Are you telling me that Okyer fired it, that Robert was up there somewhere, one of the riders of the horses I saw there?"

"It could well be," I said. "Doesn't it fit in with everything else? Okyer was at the temple; he was on the boat. He turns up in Athens, pretty annoyed with Cleo because she'd made a mess of things. He gets word of where Robert might be and comes up here to the site to check. He finds him but can't do anything right away because of all the people around, and that night Robert gets out. His leaving has nothing to do with his father or with me. He had to go to save his life."

"But why should this Turk want to kill him or kidnap him or whatever it is you think is his plan?" Bernice said. "You say it's nothing to do with his being Maurice Arden's son."

"Well, perhaps it is, indirectly," I said. "We know Arden is in Russia, but it is not inconceivable that he got a message to Robert, perhaps about the location of a lost city he believed he had found in Anatolia. I know Robert did get a message about something, and we also know someone is very interested in that city."

I looked at Bernice's bewildered face and told her about the golden bull, what it might represent and what had happened to it. Since the burglary showed the Urartian tomb was no longer a secret, it now seemed right that Robert's friends should know as much about it as his enemies.

"You're going to tell me next that it was Okyer who hit you over the head," Bernice said.

"We don't know that it wasn't," I said.

She gave a sigh that was half laughter, half exasperation. "I can't take all this in. Someone stole a golden bull that comes from a hill in Turkey that might conceal a city. Why? It wouldn't help them to find it, would it?"

"It might. If they knew the village Maurice Arden had been staying in that week, they could show the headman the golden bull and say, 'The man who found this gave it to me and asks you to show me where he found it.' And there they would be with first claim on whatever lies hidden there. It is the only evidence anyone has that the tomb exists and that Robert's father had been the one to find it."

"No genuine archaeologist would be involved in anything like that," Bernice said.

"What about modern grave robbers?" I said. "Suppose there are tombs there filled with as many riches, say, as Tutankhamen's tomb? Suppose they think Robert knows the location and they want him to tell them where it is?"

"I thought you said they were trying to kill him?" Bernice said.

"I don't know, Bernice, I don't know. I'm only guessing at all this, trying to find an explanation that fits. And the more it fits, the less I like it. I don't really know why these people have been following him, why they seem to want him, dead or alive, why the golden bull was stolen, but of one thing I am certain: when Robert left here, he was heading north for Turkey, and I'm going after him."

I was suddenly overwhelmed by the terrible thought of what his long silence might really mean.

"If they've killed him," I said, "I want to know it, and I want to know why."

Paul's description of the second of the two journalists fitted

Okyer. Paul protested that after a month his recollections were not exact, but he did remember Okyer because he thought at the time that he looked more like a boxer than a journalist. The journalists had arrived together but left separately. They had come from Thessaloniki, and Ullman had gone on towards the Yugoslav border, while Okyer had begged a lift in a car going to Larissa to pick up supplies. Paul assumed he was making his way to Athens. They had arrived quite early in the morning and left before lunch. He didn't recall either of them talking to Robert. "But that doesn't mean they didn't," he concluded. "I wasn't with them all the time."

We were back in the office hut, Paul seated at the table he used as his desk, Bernice standing near him. Tom Shaw had come wandering in after us and taken a chair to a corner of the room, where he sat with it tipped backwards against the wall, listening quietly to everything that went on.

"Why don't you sit down?" Paul asked me.

"I'm too restless."

"Try to talk her out of it, Paul," Bernice said. "She's got this mad idea of going off to Turkey after Robert."

"If he was running away from a Turk," Paul said, "why go to Turkey? Wouldn't he try to disappear somewhere in Greece?"

"Exactly," Tom Shaw interrupted. "I quite agree. I still think my thesis is correct. He got in a cold funk about being damned with his father's name once more and simply ran for cover. He'll turn up in a week or so."

I ignored him, turning back to Paul. "He was waiting here until the time came to move," I said. "He had received a message and had been given a date—to meet someone or be somewhere, I don't know. You said yourself you got the impression he was waiting for something. This site was the quiet, safe place he had chosen to wait. Then Okyer turned up, and it was no longer safe. So Robert goes, earlier perhaps than he intended, but he'd still go in the same direction, towards this meeting in Turkey. It all began there, and it's going to end there, I know it.

Before I left for Canada, he told me the business he was involved in would be over in a month. Now it's well over the month. It's just taking longer than he thought. Perhaps something has gone wrong. Perhaps Okyer did catch up with him. I've got to find out."

"Where will you start?" Paul said. "Where will you go?"

"She's no idea where to begin," Bernice said. "It's ridiculous."

"I'd go to the ancient Urartian heartland," I said. "I'd follow the clues Robert left me. I'd start at Van and go on from there."

"You can't do that," Paul said. "It's not safe to travel in that area alone, particularly for a woman. Haven't you been reading the papers? Strikes, riots, terrorist attacks, they've practically got a civil war out there. You're going to find martial law in most of the territory you want to cross, and the nearer you get to the eastern frontiers, the more difficult it's going to be to move about the country."

"I shall go to Istanbul first," I said. "I shall find out what I can from there."

I swung round to Tom. "Or could you help me? Could you find out if any British subject has been in trouble during the past few weeks? Arrested, injured, attacked—"

Tom shrugged. "That's hardly my field. I'm not concerned with Turkey. However—" He gave me a half smile. "I'll certainly make inquiries when I get back to Athens. But I have to go to Thessaloniki first. I'm sorry."

"Don't bother," I said. I was beginning to get angry. They were supposed to be my friends or, if not mine, then Robert's. But nobody wanted to help. Nobody wanted to believe in any explanation of his absence other than the one most calculated to damage his reputation—and to cause them the least trouble. Robert was a charming fellow; but he was a coward and a drunk, and whatever had happened to him was entirely his own fault.

"I'll make the necessary inquiries," I said. "Istanbul first, then Ankara. I can do that by phone."

"No use trying to telephone Ankara from Istanbul," Tom said. "Internal communications are practically at a standstill."

"I have discovered," I said, "in my short life as a traveler that nothing is quite as bad as it is reported. Will you take me with you to Thessaloniki?"

Tom was startled by my direct attack. "You want to come with me?"

"If you don't mind. It's only about three hundred miles from there to the border. I can make arrangements for transport in Thessaloniki."

Bernice gave a protesting cry. "Frances, don't do it! Or if you must, for God's sake, take someone with you. Paul's told you it's not safe. You might get yourself killed."

They accepted my decision in the end. I suppose they recognized the obstinacy that not even I had known was in my character. Tom Shaw no doubt preferred to call it plain stupidity, while Bernice thought me blindly obsessed by Robert and Paul considered my reactions understandable but ill-advised.

I left the camp next day with Tom Shaw, having borrowed some money from Bernice. Money, I realized, was going to be a difficulty. The trip to Turkey with Bernice had taken what spare cash I had had. I had left only enough to keep me for the next year, and I had dipped into that to pay for my ticket to Greece. I could cable my mother for money, but I didn't want to worry her with requests coming from Greece or Turkey when she thought I was safely settled in London. As for Robert, I had no idea what his financial position was, but in any case I couldn't touch his bank account. There had been no time for us to arrange anything like that. I decided to spend what I had and let the future take care of itself. In Thessaloniki I would cable my bank and arrange a transfer of funds to Istanbul.

Before I left the camp, I sat down and wrote a letter to my department head at the university, explaining that for domestic reasons I would be a late arrival for the course. I also informed him of my marriage, something I had neglected to do. He would probably conclude that that was the domestic reason for my absence.

As I sealed and stamped the letter, I felt in a strange way as if I were cutting my ties with England. I realized I had set no limit in my own mind to my search. I was acting as if I might never return.

It was 130 miles from the site to Thessaloniki, and I didn't relax until we had left the plain and were through the 6-mile defile of the Vale of Tempe and in sight of the marshy coast. The road through the vale was good; the light was green and sylvan after the strong leonine glare of the plain, the air fresh and cool after the heat; the climb up the slopes of Mount Ossa looking down on the milky waters of the river, its banks thickly guarded by plane and poplar, by willow, oak and wild fig trees, was beautiful; but I was nervous, oppressed by the narrowness of the gorge, by the towering rock, by Olympus raising a threatening head to the north.

"You're very silent," Tom said. "What's the matter? Changed your mind already?"

"Was anyone ever trapped in here?" I asked.

Tom laughed. "Plenty, I should imagine. It was always the vital pass between north and south, the one outlet to the sea. And if you're susceptible to ghosts, you could choose from Xerxes, Alexander, Pompey in defeat after Pharsala, not to mention the Crusaders. But it really belongs to Apollo. It was here, you know, that Daphne was turned into a laurel tree to escape his passionate advances. Not terribly lucky with his love life, poor Apollo." He paused. "But you're running towards your Apollo, aren't you, not fleeing from him?"

I looked at him. "Is that really how you think of me?"

"It's difficult to know," he said. "You're very young, aren't you? And the young are always romantic. Robert can play the romantic figure par excellence."

"You wonder why I married him," I said. "Don't you also wonder why he married me?"

"Frankly, yes. Not because anyone in his right mind wouldn't if he had the chance," he added gallantly. "But Robert, I would have thought, hadn't got the sense. Or the stability."

"You think he's sensible for marrying me and I'm foolish for marrying him."

"That about sums it up, wouldn't you say?"

"I don't think I'm going to say anything more at all for a while," I said.

He smiled; his manner imperceptibly changed: friendlier, a little less patronizing. "We're nearly out of the gorge. You'll be able to breathe again. It's odd, I only get claustrophobia in lifts."

We had set out early and met little traffic on the road. We reached Thessaloniki at ten. We drove in from the west, through straggling suburbs, past the railway station, into the commercial heart of the city. Tom found a place to park and switched off the engine. On the other side of the square a new building was going up. There was a rhythmic thudding of machinery, a clattering of drills, the shouts of workmen calling to each other. White dust choked the site and drifted across to us.

"I don't think I've ever been in this city without feeling I've arrived in the aftermath of some great disaster," Tom said. "What they're not putting up, they're pulling down. It's a little calmer and more picturesque in the old town, but unfortunately that's not where our business is." He nodded in the direction of a four-story brick building that looked almost antique in comparison with its neighbors. "That bank should be able to cope with your financial arrangements. I happen to know they speak very fair English in there. Always easier to deal with money in your own tongue, I find. As for hiring a car and a driver, I've got an idea about that. Meet me back here in an hour."

"You're being very helpful," I said. "Thank you."

"If you can't beat 'em, join 'em," he said. "I don't suppose we'd be able to stop you now."

They say that Thessaloniki, set in the curving arm of the sheltering bay, the sea before it, the mountains behind, and the majestic mass of Olympus sixty miles to the west, has one of the most beautiful settings in the world, but I was given little time to appreciate it. When I got back to the car, Tom was already there.

"All arranged?" he said.

"Yes," I said doubtfully. "I hope so."

"There speaks the seasoned traveler. Don't worry. They're as reliable as any. Now if you don't mind, I'm going to take a quick whiz round the town."

"All right," I said. "If that's what you want to do."

"I'll tell you the reason later," he said.

He went fast, even by the standards of Greek traffic, rocketing down modern avenues and up steep, narrow alleys, past raw concrete blocks and squat Byzantine churches, beneath the balconies of wooden houses looking more Turkish than Greek, round ancient ramparts, through gardens and finally along the spacious promenade that runs from the White Tower to the docks. He pulled up at last outside the Mediterranean Hotel.

"Thank you for the tour," I said breathlessly. "Was that all-inclusive, or does it cost extra?"

He was looking in his mirror. His face was taut with concentration. After a moment he relaxed.

"Well, that settles that," he said. "We seem to have picked up a tail. I noticed it on the run into the city, but I thought it was just chance. However, anyone who sticks to us through that last little performance of mine must be anxious not to lose us. Now what do you suppose they're up to?"

I looked behind, but I couldn't distinguish one parked car from another. "Where are they?"

"About five cars back. Black car. Two men inside."

"What do they look like?"

"Hard to get a good look at them. Dark, sallow. Could be anyone. Do you want to walk past, see if you recognize them?"

"No!" I shrank back.

"You think they might kidnap you?" he asked. It was hard to

tell from his expression if it was a serious question.

I sat up. "I'll go look at them," I said.

"Good girl." He stretched across and opened my door.

I walked slowly back along the sidewalk. One, two, three cars . . . As I approached, both doors of the black car suddenly opened and the two men got out. The driver came round to the pavement. They stood looking at me, waiting. When I stopped, they began coming towards me. I turned and ran back to the car. I jumped in and slammed the door.

"Perhaps they were going to kidnap you," Tom said.

The men had gone back to the car. After a moment they drove past us, picking up speed, and roared away towards the docks. They hadn't looked at us as they passed.

"I've never seen either of them before," I said to Tom.

He sighed gently. "I think the thing to do," he said, "is to go have a large pot of European coffee in the hotel over there, with cream, and perhaps some thin toast, butter, jam. They might even have marmalade. I rather rushed my breakfast this morning."

In the hotel I went to wash. I looked at myself in the mirror and admitted I felt frightened. What had struck me about the two men on the sidewalk was the complete lack of expression on their faces, like two Mafia thugs in a second-rate film. No doubt they would explain there was nothing personal about it; they were just doing their job as they shot you full of holes. But what had they got to do with me? Then I remembered the telephone call to the hotel in Bloomsbury inquiring whether I was still registered there. Did they have something to do with that? Had I been followed all the time, on the plane, to the site? What exactly had Robert got me into when he married me?

Over the breakfast table, with the hot, courage-restoring coffee, we discussed what I should do.

"Do you want to go back?" Tom said.

"No, of course not."

"Well, one thing's for certain. You can't travel the odd four hundred miles to Istanbul on your own."

"I wouldn't be on my own."

"I wouldn't rely on a hired driver in a crisis. He's likely to abandon you if any trouble arises. On the other hand, if you tell him you're on the way to a lover, pursued by your angry husband's henchmen, he might get into the spirit of the thing."

"We don't know," I said, "if they're still going to follow me."

"They seemed pretty anxious to keep up with us. I don't suppose they are far away now. It's likely we'll meet them again on the road."

"We?" I said.

Tom carefully buttered another slice of toast. "I've decided to drive you to Istanbul myself," he said.

"What about your business here?"

"A day won't make much difference. I've already spoken to the people concerned explaining my delay. I should feel responsible if I let you go on your own and you disappeared on the way." He smiled at me. "We really don't want to lose you, you know."

"You didn't feel that way about Robert."

"Oh, Robert can look after himself!"

There seemed little point in hanging around Thessaloniki. The sooner we got past the border, the happier Tom said he would feel. I didn't share his assumption that any followers would turn back at the frontier.

As it happened, in the first hour we saw no one who could be called a tail.

"Either your confrontation really did put them off, or we've managed to lose them," Tom said.

"Would it put them off?"

"If they were relying on secrecy, yes, it could alarm them to discover we were aware of them. Have you any idea why they were following you?"

"Because I might lead them to Robert?"

He nodded. "Possibly. In which case they don't know where he is any more than we do, which should encourage you. As for who they are"—he shook his head—"an international team of grave robbers, hard to accept, you know."

"Perhaps they were going to kidnap me." I paused. "At any rate, they've made you change your mind about the reasons for Robert's disappearance."

"My dear girl, I'm too old a hand to change my opinions as easily as that. I'm keeping an open mind."

"It might all be a complete mistake," I said. "Those men might have taken me for someone else."

"Don't let's get too complicated," Tom said. "It's enough of a crossword puzzle as it is. You know, back there there's a town where the inhabitants dance on hot coals once a year. I've a feeling before this affair is over, we're going to be quite adept at that ourselves."

The road was narrow, mountainous and twisting. When it leveled out, Tom suggested I drive for a while. With the limited experience of someone who didn't own a car, I was to be grateful later for this practice run.

At Asprovalta we stopped to fill the gas tank. Tom walked to the edge of the road and looked back down the way we had come. A truck rumbled past, leaving a stench of diesel. There was no sign of the black car.

In another hour the road began to climb in a series of hairpin bends and Tom took over again.

"Not that I don't think you're a safe driver," he remarked. "But I think I'll be faster on the corners."

Past Kavalla, with its tobacco-scented air, the landscape became flat and marshy.

"Not my favorite kind of countryside," Tom remarked. "Full of malaria until it was drained. Ah—"

"What is it?"

"They must have gone ahead and waited for us at Kavalla. There are two routes to it from Thessaloniki. They couldn't be sure which one we'd take, but they knew if we were heading for

Turkey, we'd pass through here. Now let's see how serious they are." He put his foot down.

Glancing back, I saw the ominous shape of the black car quite a long way behind. The men didn't attempt to overtake us. Other traffic came between us, but all the time, as we ran through the flat lands by the sea, climbed past mountain villages and towns that grew more Turkish than Greek with every mile, and across a seemingly endless plain, they were there, a black shadow, an anonymous threat on the horizon, ever present, ever distant. Then at Alexandroupolis they disappeared.

"There you are," Tom said. "They were seeing us off the premises. I told you they'd turn back at the frontier. When I get back to Athens, I shall try to find out who those fellows are."

We crossed safely into Turkey in a line of trucks and coaches without incident or even very much delay. The next part of the journey is blurred in my mind because of what happened later, but I remember that the relief of losing the black car left a sense almost of anticlimax, as if our travels should have ended there at the frontier. The 150-odd miles we still had to go to Istanbul seemed an added burden.

"Why don't you try to sleep?" Tom said. "You've nothing to worry about now."

I offered to drive, but he said he wasn't tired. Sometime during the next half hour I drifted off to sleep. When I awoke, it was to find the car stationary. Tom had driven it away from the main road and parked it in a slight dip, masked by bushes. He smiled at me. "I'm just going to stretch my legs. I shan't be long."

It was nearly nightfall. The brief dusk was upon us. Alone in the car, I felt it closing in on me, like mist. The outline of a low hill was already merging imperceptibly with the horizon, and the shapes of objects closer to me, a pile of rocks by the curve in the road, the bushes, a lone tree, were blending, softening, fading even as I watched them.

It was growing cold, a chill in the air and a chill of disquiet settling over me. I did not like to be in isolated places at this time of day. I liked to be in a town, surrounded by warmth and light and voices. It was too quiet here. But not completely silent. There were small disturbing sounds, the rustling movements of small animals embarking on their nocturnal life, of birds settling to sleep.

I got out of the car and leaned against the door, waiting for Tom. I could hear nothing from the main road, no noise of traffic. I wondered how far we were from it, how far indeed we had driven while I slept. I realized I had no idea where we were.

And still Tom did not return. He had been gone for ten minutes. I walked up and down beside the car, becoming more uneasy with every second. Another five minutes passed, and unease was sliding quietly into a fearful apprehension. The place, the time, the strains of the long day were telling on me. Irrational though it was, I was beginning to feel as if I'd been abandoned here, like a child left behind at a picnic. I called Tom's name, once, twice. There was no response. At last, reluctantly, feeling rather foolish, I went to look for him.

I found him thirty yards from the car. He was on his knees, struggling to rise.

"You're ill!"

He put his hand out towards me and grasped mine so tightly that he left it bruised. I put my other arm round him to help him get up. There was a sticky patch on his back, the jacket torn.

I said: "What happened?"

He said: "Stabbed. Didn't see who. Came up from behind. Get to the car."

He had to lean all his weight on me to make it. When we reached the car, it was too dark to see his face clearly. I opened the rear door and helped him into the back seat. I switched on the interior light. The pallor of his face frightened me.

"I must get you to a doctor. Where's the nearest town, forward or back? I don't know where we are."

"Listen." He seized my hand. "Doctor no use. I know. Don't stop, mustn't stop. Don't stop for anything. Get to Istanbul. Ring embassy. Tell them didn't rob me. Not thieves. More important . . ."

I said: "I'll stop at the first police station; you must have help."

"No!" He shook his head weakly. "No use for me, too dangerous for you. Don't stop." His face twisted into the semblance of a smile. "Sorry. Stupid. Own fault. Didn't take it seriously enough." Then he coughed and his mouth filled with blood and he died, there on the back seat of the car, still holding my hand.

I don't think I have ever felt so alone as I did at that moment. I couldn't believe it had happened. The suddenness, the unexpectedness of it stunned me. But as I stared incredulously at those waxen features, that stare fixed in death, I was filled with a growing sense of anger mixed with a terrible guilt. It was because of me that Tom Shaw was dead. I had drawn him into my affairs, against his will, on behalf of a man he despised. He had been kind to me, he had gone out of his way to help me, to protect me, and this had been the result.

I forced myself to action. I closed his eyes. I fetched a car rug from the trunk and covered him with it. One long hand with its carefully manicured nails and an elaborate signet ring on the little finger slipped almost lazily from concealment. I lifted it up and placed it back across his body. It was then that real shock swept over me, and I was struck by an overwhelming, paralyzing panic. Whoever had killed Tom would want to kill me. For some reason I didn't yet know, they wanted to stop me from reaching Istanbul. It was no longer something to speculate about; it was deep and dangerous, and I was out of my depth in it all, and I had to learn to swim fast or drown.

I got into the driver's seat, turned the car and drove what seemed a half mile or so back to the main road. I found myself thinking, why didn't they kill me then, at the car, when I was alone, or when I went in search of Tom? They had gone by the time I found Tom, but why had they gone? What did they want?

I don't think I doubted for an instant that it was the men who had been following us who had killed Tom. There were always stories of people on lonely country roads being attacked and robbed. Bernice and I had been warned of it. But Tom's murderer had made no attempt to fake a robbery. A swift, silent, if not entirely clean, kill and then away. And if I had had any doubts as to their identity, they would have been eradicated in the next few minutes. For they were waiting for me a mile or so up the Istanbul road.

Perhaps it wasn't the same car. Perhaps it wasn't black. It could have been black; it could have been any dark color. It was a black shape that slid into position behind me and stayed there mile after mile, and that was enough for me. The panic came back, and I had to fight it down with noise. I put on the radio as loud as it would go and, with tears of shock and grief rolling down my cheeks, roared my way through the night to the accompaniment of the drumming and piping of *davul* and *zurna* and the shrill shrieking of assorted popular songs.

At one stage I caught up with an army convoy, ten trucks filled with young troops, lumbering along on the crown of the road in a billow of dust and exhaust. I passed the last two and slipped in behind the third and for ten miles drove to a chorus of shouts and whistles as safe as a cat in a basket. When they turned off, we had already reached the tatty conglomeration of holiday houses and shacks strung along the Sea of Marmara all the way to the city, and there were enough lights and traffic to make me feel safer and to wonder what I was going to do when I got to Istanbul.

I tried to think of all the options. The British consulate would be shut. I could ring the consul privately; but that would mean parking the car and looking for a telephone, and that would make me too vulnerable. I could look for a police station; but the city was an impossible place to find your way around even if you knew where you were going, and I was afraid of the dangers of hesitation and the difficulties of discussing my situation with the equivalent of a British desk sergeant. I could check into a hotel and telephone the British Embassy at Ankara from my room, but then what would I do about Tom and the car?

I had to be honest with myself and confess I was too frightened to attempt any of these chores because they involved my being out in a public situation too long for safety. However, apart from attempting to drive straight on to Ankara, which would be physically impossible without rest, it seemed I would have to choose one of them.

And then I remembered Madame Ağaoğlu.

My handbag was lying on the passenger seat next to me. I took a hand off the wheel and pulled it closer to me. I opened the flap and delved inside for my wallet. There was one section where I kept cards and shop bills and the odd pieces of paper one collects from here and there. I emptied them all out on the seat and went through them one by one, holding them up in front of me, slipping them back as I discarded them. I was thinking of the darkened boat, the night I had first met Robert, churning slowly along the Turkish coast, and of Madame Ağaoğlu, plump and seductive in her silk nightdress, full of kindness and generosity to the feverish Bernice, taking charge of us, handing over medicine, urging me to come and see her when I was next in Turkey, handing me her card with her address in Istanbul. . . . And there it was, engraved in a curling black script as round and decorated as herself.

The address was unfamiliar to me, but since we were coming to the outskirts of the city, I took a risk and stopped at a garage and shop complex large enough and well lighted enough to protect me. I was nearly out of gas, and it gave me a chance, while the tank was being filled, to buy a street map of Istanbul from the souvenir shop. I noticed thankfully as I walked back past the car that the harsh lights threw the rear seat in shadow; not even I could be sure what that long bundle wrapped in the tartan blanket might be. But I only glanced at it; I couldn't bear to let my mind dwell on it or I might break down.

A large tour bus had followed me into the garage, effectively blocking any other vehicle from coming close to me. Not that I could see my pursuers, but I knew they were still there. Passing through the lighted streets of a village some miles back, I had caught a glimpse of them in the rear mirror. Now I took the opportunity of asking the bus driver, in my halting Turkish, the best way of reaching the district where Madame Ağaoğlu lived. He seemed quite impressed by the address. It was apparently a fashionable suburb on the European side of the Bosporus. He told me to follow him until he turned off for the Bosporus bridge and then continue along the coast road. He marked it on the map with a ball-point pen and made getting there seem quite easy. I drew aside to let him pass and then, tucked as tightly as I could behind him, entered the Topkapi gates in my own kind of convoy.

Nothing ever being as simple as it first appears, the last stage of my journey was more nerve-racking than any other part of it. We had met the evening traffic, but I had felt safe tailing my friendly bus driver through the noise and confusion of Istanbul. When he turned off on the road to the Bosporus bridge, horn hooting in farewell, I was alarmed to realize how frightened I still was. To go on alone along that narrow road by the sea with its lights and its restaurants and its gardens full of people, so normal, so casual, so ordinary, was almost more of an ordeal for me than those first moments driving away from the place where Tom had been murdered. I was so tired, so worried, and I couldn't find the damned house. I found the district easily enough and then fretted that I had gone too far. I had to stop and ask the way twice before I found anyone who could identify the place, and then there it was, hanging high on the hill, with a view of the Bosporus and lights streaming from every window. At least, I thought thankfully, someone was at home.

The wrought-iron gates were open. I drove up the steep drive through a garden flooded with the scent of roses and carnations and parked among the five or six other cars in front of the house.

It seemed to be a yali of the old kind, used as a summer residence by the wealthy merchants of the nineteenth century, spacious yet delicate-looking, built of wood that had weathered into a soft silver gray, with a long arcade facing the garden and fragile balconies above. There were soft sounds of music from within, and as I waited for someone to answer my knock on the door, a spotlight from one of the ferries plowing up the Bosporus swung in a fine arc across the hill and caught me for a second in its beam, pinning me in its blade of light like a butterfly on a board, fatally exposing me to any watcher down below.

My judgment of Madame Ağaoğlu as a woman who would take the most unlikely events in her stride proved to be justified. I had arrived in the middle of a dinner party, disheveled, slightly hysterical, with a diplomat's corpse on the back seat of a travel-stained car and no very coherent explanation of what I was doing there. Fetched from her guests by a perplexed butler, she swept to the rescue, glowing with jewelry and good health, and took complete charge of me. An hour or so later I was ensconced in a guest room, bathed, fed, wrapped in one of Madame's dressing gowns, waiting for the phone call to come through from the British Embassy in Ankara.

The room was high and square and lavishly furnished, with tall windows opening onto balconies. It wrapped itself around you with the softness of its materials and the plethora of its detail, from the carved and decorated furniture to the intricate patterns of the embroidered coverlet on the bed. Satin cushions were scattered across wickerwork armchairs and modern chaise longue alike. The silk curtains moved gently in the evening breeze; the shades of the lamps gave off a rosy glow. It was as luxuriantly warm and welcoming as its mistress.

Madame Ağaoğlu sat in an armchair by the window, smoking a cigarette.

"Please don't feel you must stay," I said. "Your guests—"

"They have gone." She raised a hand. "It was nothing to do

with you. It was time for them to be going."

I said: "I'm so sorry about all this, but I could think of nowhere else to go."

"I would have been offended if you had not come here. My husband agrees."

I had met Halim Ağaoğlu very briefly. Short, dark, as plump as his wife and immensely dignified, he had treated me with the greatest courtesy and tact, considering that at first, at any rate, he had not the slightest idea what the untimely commotion caused by an unknown English girl could possibly be about.

I had made my story as uncomplicated as I could. I thought I would keep the more detailed explanations for the embassy. I said that Tom Shaw was a friend who had been driving me to Istanbul. He had been attacked on the road and killed. Before he died, he had told me to continue straight on to Istanbul and ring the British Embassy. I didn't know if the fact that he was himself an official of the embassy at Athens had anything to do with his death. He had not been on official business at the time.

Madame Ağaoğlu looked across at me and puffed gently at her cigarette. "You tell me you have married since we met. Is your husband in Turkey?"

"I can't get in touch with him," I said, "but he is somewhere in Turkey."

"He is traveling, you mean. On business?"

"Yes," I said. I paused and at that moment decided on the basis of my reception from the Ağaoğlus to speak more freely than I had planned. I suppose I was desperate. I had to seize the slightest chance of constructive help, and from the glimpse I had had of her husband and her guests, he would have plenty of influential contacts.

"I am very worried about my husband," I said. "He is the reason I have come to Turkey. He was due back in London over a week ago. He seems to have completely disappeared."

"You have had inquiries made here?"

"He was supposed to have been returning from Athens. It is only in the last day or so I have had reason to believe he might be in Turkey. I was on my way here to begin inquiries."

"Ah—" She considered me thoughtfully. "My country is not a very good place for foreigners to be in at the moment, I am sorry to say, especially if they are away from the more civilized centers. In some regions there is anti-American feeling whipped up by agitators. I know your husband is not American, but simple country people cannot tell an Englishman from an American. Would you like my husband to make inquiries for you?"

"I should be very grateful."

"It is nothing. He knows many people in the police and so on. It may speed things up. Perhaps your husband has had an accident and is in some country hospital. It will all be reported somewhere." She produced a sheet of embossed notepaper from a bureau by the door and handed it to me with a pen. "Write down his name and the direction in which you think he may have been traveling, and we will get someone on it right away."

I put down Robert's name and beside it "Istanbul—Ankara—Van," wondering all the time I was writing if in doing this I could possibly be betraying him. But I had to start somewhere. I had to trust someone.

I handed the paper back to Madame Ağaoğlu. She folded it neatly and said: "While you are waiting for news, you must stay here." She waved away my protests. "Why go to a hotel? What point is there when we have so much room? Now you have had a great shock and you must rest. Your car is in the garage, and the police have been notified about the body of your friend. I will call you as soon as Ankara can be reached. There is always delay on the lines nowadays. These are difficult times, my dear. We must pray they will not become even more anarchic and dangerous."

I said as she was leaving: "I thought—I had the impression I might have been followed here—by the same men . . ."

She looked back at me. "You think the people who murdered your friend now want to murder you? You saw them? You could give evidence against them?"

When I did not reply, she took my silence for assent.

"Then you must certainly stay here. Here you can be protected. Don't worry. We shall soon find out if anyone watches the house, and we shall know how to deal with them. Good night, my dear. Try to rest until the call comes."

As it happened, I was asleep when the telephone call to Ankara finally came through and it was Halim Ağaoğlu who gave the first report of what had happened to the night duty officer at the embassy.

I had been unable to stay awake in spite of all my determination. Kindness and warmth undid more resolutions than hardship. I awoke in the early hours of the morning to a pale, clear dawn over the Bosporus and an at first uncomprehending sense of despair. When recollection came to me, I felt no more cheerful but calmer, for I had been dreaming of Robert, intricate, intense dreams of loss and search, and I woke believing he was dead until I remembered Tom. I had seen his eyes blankly gazing at me from his dead face. . . .

In my suitcase I carried one of Robert's books on Turkey, the one with his photograph on the jacket. I got up and fetched it and sat on the edge of the bed, looking down at the face portrayed there, younger, smoother, more innocent than the man I had married: an undergraduate face with posed head, casual toss of tumbled hair, would-be sophistication in the glance . . .

"Robert," I said aloud, "Robert," as if speaking his name could bring some relief from the aching need I felt for him.

There was a tap at the door, and Madame Ağaoğlu entered, followed by a manservant carrying a tray of tea.

"Put it down there." She waited until he had left the room. "My dear Frances, I did not wake you last night, you looked too exhausted. My husband spoke to the embassy. They are sending someone down straight away. He should be here soon."

"Thank you. I'll get dressed at once."

"No need for quite such haste. Wait until you have had your tea." She poured tea into a cup and brought it to me. "And I am sure you will be glad to know inquiries are already being made about your husband. Is this he?" She picked up the book. "Robert Denning. I see it is. May I borrow this? It would be helpful to have photographs of him."

I had a sudden shiver of alarm. I needed help in searching for him, but I felt instinctively that photographs of Robert, dispersed into goodness knew how many hands, could be dangerous. I had to find him with the least publicity, the least noise.

"It is too dark. I don't think it would reproduce well. And he looks different now. He wrote the book some years ago."

"He was very handsome then," Madame Ağaoğlu said. "I imagine he has grown even better-looking. Experience adds character. And what is his business? He is a writer?"

"Yes," I said. For what else was he? I realized I didn't know how Robert made his living, how he paid for the flat, his journeys to and from Greece and Turkey. Perhaps his father had left him a private income.

My ignorance of my husband's affairs was a matter I didn't particularly want exposed, but it was difficult to keep it from someone as friendly and open as Madame Ağaoğlu. She had an ingenuous kind of curiosity at which it was impossible to take offense, especially considering the kindness she had already twice shown me. Fortunately her questions were frustrated by the arrival of the official from the British Embassy in Ankara.

Anthony Stephens was a young man much in the same mold as Tom Shaw. He was so polite and solicitous of me in our interview that it took me quite some time to realize that he thought of me as Tom Shaw's girl friend and that we had been going off on a mild spree together when Tom was killed. I tried to explain.

"This was only the second time I'd met Mr. Shaw."

Stephens's right eyebrow rose in a fractional display of disbelief. "He was driving you from Greece to Istanbul. Was he going on leave?"

"No. He intended returning the next day. He had business in Thessaloniki."

In the silence that ensued after this I felt impelled to explain, to justify poor Tom's interest in me, that he knew my husband.

"Ah, yes, Mrs. Denning. Your husband being Robert Denning. He is staying here with you?"

"Perhaps you know him," I said. "He has spent quite a lot of time in Turkey."

"I don't recall meeting him." He repeated: "Is he here?"

"No," I said. "He is not."

"He is in Turkey, however?"

I didn't reply directly. I said: "Mr. Shaw wanted the embassy to know that he wasn't robbed. His attackers weren't thieves. His murder had another motive."

"And what motive might that be?"

I paused. "Mr. Stephens, would it be possible for me to talk to someone more senior?"

"Certainly, if you care to come back to Ankara with me."

"I can't come immediately. I'll come later."

"Very well. And this is all you can tell me about this incident?"

I looked into his bland blue eyes and said: "You've never heard of Robert Denning?"

"No."

"So you have received no reports of an accident to him or anything like that?"

"Not to my knowledge. Such reports wouldn't necessarily come to me. Do you want me to find out?"

"You don't ask me if he is missing or what he is doing in Turkey."

"Obviously he is missing or you wouldn't want us to look for him. And you've made it plain someone in the embassy will know all about him. By the way, how long has he been missing?"

"For more than a month."

"And Mr. Shaw, as an old friend, was going to help you find him?"

"Mr. Shaw was going straight back to Greece. I was hoping the people at the embassy would help me to find him."

"Why didn't you tell me this immediately, Mrs. Denning?"

"I wanted to see if you already knew about my husband's situation, if he had been in touch with you about his plans."

"You make it sound very intriguing."

"I don't mean to be mysterious. I simply want help."

"But discreetly. No fanfares."

"Yes, that's right."

"Why, Mrs. Denning? I wonder what you imagine your husband can be up to."

"When you discover what he is up to, I believe you'll find the motive for Mr. Shaw's murder."

"Ah . . ." He looked at me in silence for a moment. Then he said: "If Mr. Shaw's murder is linked up with your husband's activities, the motive could have been to prevent your arrival in Turkey."

"Yes," I said. "That had occurred to me."

"You said the murderers followed you to Istanbul."

"I said two men in a car followed me. I don't know who they were."

"Do you think they know you are here, in this house?"

"Probably. I made myself rather conspicuous looking for it."

"Mmm . . ." He began gathering his things together. "Do you intend staying here for the next day or so?"

"Yes."

"Good. I think someone more senior may very well come to see you, Mrs. Denning." He shook hands. "It's been a pleasure meeting you. I'm sorry you've had such a nasty experience. I hope we can clear it up for you. Don't worry about Tom Shaw or his car. I've taken charge of both."

He paused, looking through the windows of the small reception room we had been given for our interview. "Beautiful spot, isn't it? The Bosporus is the best part of Istanbul. I should stay in the garden if I were you. Don't go wandering off too far. Enjoy the view and the roses." He smiled. "Good-bye. Perhaps we'll meet again."

"Perhaps. Good-bye, Mr. Stephens."

He left, taking, with Tom Shaw's car, my only independent means of transport. That didn't trouble me too much at that stage. I was only too happy to follow Madame Ağaoğlu's instructions to spend the day resting. I suppose I was suffering from reaction, but once Tom Shaw's body had been taken away, I succumbed to an immense lethargy which left me with only enough energy to sit for hours on a chair in the arcade watching the slow procession of traffic up and down the glittering Bosporus.

In the afternoon I stirred myself to write to Bernice. I told her what had happened and where I was and asked her to pass on the news to Paul Andriades. I imagined the alarm with which she would receive the letter. By that time I would probably have left the Ağaoğlus' house, and that perhaps would be just as well. I didn't want Bernice rushing after me or trying to persuade me to go home. While I rested, my inner resolution had hardened. If I had ever considered giving up, I couldn't do so now, for I felt that would mean betraying Tom as well as Robert.

At dinner Halim Agaoglu told me the results so far of his investigations on my behalf.

"I have been in touch with friends in the police. There is no record of your husband's entry into Turkey, but then there wouldn't necessarily be one. You think he entered from Greece?"

"Yes."

"It needn't have been by the Ipsala crossing. He could have slipped across by boat, landed in the south. There are plenty of small bays along that coast. Would you say he wanted to avoid attention?"

"Quite probably."

"You don't think he is involved in anything illegal? Drugs, for instance."

"I am sure he is not," I said.

"Forgive me for asking. It was the first reaction of the police. They are going to check along the route you indicated. But if he came from the south, that would be another matter. I shall suggest to them they make inquiries along the southern route as well."

"Thank you," I said. "I appreciate very much what you are doing."

"It is nothing," he said. "It is my pleasure. Will your embassy also be checking?"

"I hope so. I have asked them to."

"Then I shall let them know what we are doing," he said. "I wouldn't want us to be at cross-purposes."

I couldn't stop wondering, as I realized the ramifications involved in my requests for assistance, if Robert would be pleased or furious at my actions; whether I was helping him or threatening to ruin whatever enterprise he was engaged in. I clung to the belief that if he was not in trouble, I would have heard from him. Before I went any further, I wanted to confirm that there had been no message from him and asked Madame Ağaoğlu if I could make a telephone call to England. She installed me in the reception room where I had talked to Anthony Stephens and left me alone.

I must have picked the right moment in the day, for there was relatively little delay in getting through to London. The delay was in waiting for someone to answer the ringing telephone in the Bloomsbury flat. I had to beg the operator to keep trying the number. I didn't want to accept that John Nairn might have gone and that there might be a letter waiting there for me from Robert, one that would remain unopened and unread.

At long last the receiver was lifted. I heard the operator tell me I was through, and I heard, faintly, a man's voice. For a second I thought it was Robert. My heart gave a great leap of excitement. Then the line cleared, and John Nairn was asking briskly who it was, and I realized it was the slight distortion that had made their voices sound alike.

He was amazed to find I was in Turkey. "What on earth are you doing there?"

"It would take too long to explain."

His voice had softened when he heard my name. He had just come in, he said. He had heard the phone ringing as he opened the front door. If he'd sounded abrupt, it was because he couldn't think who could be ringing him from Turkey. "Have you found Robert?"

"No," I admitted, knowing then that there could be no message.

"Neither have I," Nairn said. "There have been no letters, no calls, no sight or sound of him, and if he turns up tomorrow, it will be too late. I'm leaving."

"Oh . . ." I let out a breath.

"Don't worry," he said. "I'll leave a note in case he does come. If you give me an address or phone number where he can reach you—"

I gave him the Ağaoğlus' address and telephone number.

He said: "Perhaps you'll tell me what all this is about one day."

"I hope I'll be able to."

"You sound rather low. Has something happened?"

I said: "A friend of mine has been murdered."

"Good God! Where did that happen?"

"On the road, between here and the Greek frontier."

"Are you all right?"

"Yes, I'm fine."

"I don't like the sound of this. Can't you leave the search for Robert to others and come home?"

"Do you think I'd be any safer in London?" I said.

"I don't blame you for saying that," Nairn said, "but those burglars won't come back, I'm sure of it. I've had a message from the detective, Sergeant Williams, by the way, also wanting to know if you had any news of your husband. Since nothing was stolen, I don't quite know why he is being so persistent. Do you?"

It seemed unbelievable that it was only two days since I'd left London. The theft of the golden bull seemed to have taken place in another world.

"I expect Sergeant Williams is simply following the proper routine," I said. "If he calls again before you leave, tell him I don't know when I shall be back. I don't think I could come back alone to that flat. Not yet anyway."

"I wish you weren't alone where you are," he said.

"There are people here—"

"I meant someone concerned for you, someone to look after you." He paused. "I wish I'd come with you. You know I've missed finding you here when I came in at night." There was an odd silence I felt unable to break. Then Nairn said: "I am sorry about Robert, you know that."

"Yes," I said.

He said good-bye, very quietly, and rang off.

The following morning I had an interview with a Turkish policeman. He was a man of over six feet, with bright, intelligent eyes, and he frightened me a little as if there were something I was concealing I should feel guilty about. Halim Ağaoğlu stayed with me throughout, seated in a chair in a dark corner of the room, contributing nothing but his presence. The embassy was aware, I was told, that such a meeting would be taking place. As it happened, the policeman asked very little. We spoke in German, which we found easier than his English or my Turkish. The main query seemed to be why, after the attack on Tom Shaw, I had not stopped at the first opportunity to get help, but he seemed to accept that Tom's instructions and my own fears prevented that. He appeared doubtful about the existence of my pursuers. At the request of Halim Bey, he informed me, a policeman had been keeping an eye on the house but had seen no sign of any suspicious characters. I didn't point out that the men would hardly stay in sight once they had seen the policeman there.

All that day I grew more restless. I began to feel, in spite of the kindness of my hosts, trapped in that charming house. I seemed to have handed over all responsibility for finding Robert to others, which might appear to be sensible but which worried me and left me uneasy. I knew in my heart that this wasn't a simple matter of a missing person, yet that was the way it would be treated, as if Robert were a tourist gone astray from a bus tour, instead of an erratic, eccentric and experienced man who was very much concerned in his own mysterious business.

My apprehension grew when Madame Ağaoğlu, hushed and conspiratorial, came to tell me another visitor had arrived from the embassy. "Your husband has distinguished friends," she said. "I hope he has good news for you."

She showed me into the same small room and closed the door. The man standing by the window turned to face me. A distinguished figure indeed, as Madame Ağaoğlu had said, with his aquiline features and erect bearing. I recognized him at once, though the only time I had seen him before had been a glimpse of him talking to Robert in Victor Ransome's house in Chelsea.

"Well, Mrs. Denning," said Edmund Chance, "this is a fine kettle of fish you've landed us in. What exactly do you intend to do about it?"

CHAPTER 5

The shock of seeing the so-English figure of Edmund Chance standing aloofly in a crowded Turkish salon was blended with relief. I felt that now that he was openly involved in this affair the mystery would soon be over. Nothing had been more difficult to bear than the uncertainty. Here, clearly, was the man with the answers. His actual remarks passed over my head. My first reaction to the incongruity, the complete unexpectedness of his appearance, was to laugh.

"You find this amusing, Mrs. Denning?" he said, his manner as disapproving as his tone.

"Some of it, yes, I do. I hope you're not going to be pompous, Mr. Chance. It's a little too serious for that, isn't it? Why don't you sit down and tell me what Robert's literary agent is doing in Turkey? Have you been guiding him along the most commercial lines of research? Or have you, perhaps, nothing whatever to do with books at all?"

He sat down with great deliberation, the spindly, decorated chair looking hardly staunch enough to bear his weight.

He said: "Did Robert tell you I was his agent?"

"Yes. I suppose it was the most plausible thing that came into his head. I didn't quite believe him even then."

"This was at the party in Chelsea?"

"Yes."

"I didn't realize you'd seen me."

"Well, Mr. Ransome did do his level best to keep me out of the way. Are you going to tell me why, and what has happened to Robert, and what exactly you meant by saying I have landed you in, what was it—a pretty kettle of fish?"

He took out a flat gold cigarette case, opened it and offered it to me. I shook my head. He took out a cigarette and lit it with a gold lighter. He took his time. Everything he did was carried out with the same unhurried calculation. He gave me the impression he was watching and weighing my reactions all the time. My main reaction was impatience, which no doubt he was counting on. Impatient people tend to be careless, and I had quickly grasped the fact that he was as suspicious of me as I was of him.

"May I ask why you came here," he said at last, "and not to an hotel?"

"I was afraid of being murdered."

"Ah, yes, the two men in the car. They seem to have disappeared."

"I hope they have. They were very real at the time."

"No doubt. We have the evidence of Tom Shaw's body, haven't we? What reason do you think they had for killing him?"

"I don't know, Mr. Chance, do you?"

"Stabbed from behind. Not a great deal of strength needed if you take the victim by surprise. You heard nothing?"

"No. I presume you're not suggesting I stabbed him?"

"And so," he continued, ignoring me, "overcome by this dreadful tragedy and fearful for your life, you came straight here, to the Ağaoğlus." He drew on his cigarette. "Old friends, are they?"

"Mr. Chance, if you're here in an official capacity from the embassy, you will already have read my statement to Anthony Stephens. When are you going to tell me about Robert?"

"For some reason, Anthony neglected to ask you about the Ağaoğlus. May I repeat my question: are they old friends?"

"I had never met Halim Agaoglu before. I met Madame Ağaoğlu on a boat going from Marmaris to Istanbul. The same boat, incidentally, on which I met Robert."

He glanced sharply at me. "I thought you met Robert in Athens."

"No. As a matter of fact, he had two men attacking him with a knife that night. But he was luckier than Tom Shaw. He managed to fight them off. He told me the motive was robbery, but it wasn't, was it? Any more than it was for the attack on Tom."

He was silent, considering me through a veil of tobacco smoke. From outside I heard the hooting of a steamer and the soft murmurings of bees among the roses. Sunlight slanted across the richly patterned rugs. Chance gave the faintest of sighs, like a devoted father whose daughter has disappointed him.

"You've been making a great deal of noise," he said. "Policemen at the London flat, flying visits to Greece, questions, questions, you even rang Victor Ransome, I hear, and then finally bringing in, of all people, someone like Tom Shaw, getting him murdered and ending up here—" His gesture encompassed the room, the house, the foreignness of the household I had sought shelter in. Oh, how well he managed to imply with that gesture what a nuisance I was being, how badly I had let the side down with my unrestrained behavior, my hysterical determination to find a lost husband no matter how many people I got murdered on the way.

I made a big effort to be patient. I didn't want him to know, or anyone to know for that matter, how deeply frightened I was, of the situation I was in, of the people like him I was getting involved with. And I was frightened of Edmund Chance. It is not difficult to recognize ruthlessness when you meet it. He was a pretty impressive character, indeed, for a newly fledged language graduate with not much experience of the world to have to cope with. I knew my only defense was to appear more worldly than I was. If he but knew it, he only had to huff and puff a bit harder and my walls might very well cave in. Except for the bond tying me to Robert. Chance was going to have to put up some very strong arguments to make me abandon my search for Robert and achieve his intended mission of dismissing me back to England.

He made no bones about it. He said: "You know it would be

safer for you and better for Robert if you caught the first plane back to England."

I said: "You tell me what I'm interrupting and I'll go."

"I'm afraid it is not possible to divulge certain aspects of the situation." He caught my look and changed to a gruffly paternal note. "I know it's been very hard for you. Believe me, my dear, I do understand—"

I said: "Our marriage was a surprise to you."

"I admit it. A complete surprise."

"And naturally, not welcome."

"Let us say, not convenient at that particular time."

"Were you watching me, hoping I'd go away?" I took a chance and added: "Was it one of your people who checked the hotel in Bloomsbury to see if I was still there?"

He nodded. "We thought you would follow the pattern of most of Robert's girls. It quite amazed us to find he had taken out a marriage license."

"Robert knew it must have been you," I said. "He rang you at once to find out what was going on. And you told him to come see you at Victor Ransome's house."

"That's correct. But you've got the wrong emphasis. It was I who wanted to find out what Robert was up to. And I don't simply mean his marriage. By the way, you might be interested in this." He took a photograph from an inner pocket and handed it to me. A not very flattering shot of me taken against the background of Ransome's study. I recognized the wallpaper.

"To help you check up on me?" I asked.

He nodded. I handed it back to him. "You know you're going to have to tell me something, Mr. Chance. I'm not leaving until I know where Robert is, what he's doing and when I can expect to see him again. And that's not just a sentimental request. I've already been struck on the head, chased and frightened out of my wits. I'm not too happy about leaving this room, let alone this house, and certainly not until I know who or what it is that is threatening me."

"I have a feeling that it is you who are threatening me, Mrs. Denning. With more noise."

"You think I might go to the press. Young wife searches for missing honeymoon husband. That sort of thing?"

I smiled, and surprisingly he smiled back.

"We're not quite such ogres as you think," he said, "but you must admit Tom Shaw's death and your fleeing to the protection of this house are a trifle suspicious."

"I'm on your side, you know," I said. "That is, if your side is Robert's."

"I think you can safely assume that," he said.

"Then you can tell me where he is."

"I was hoping you'd tell me," Chance said. "I'm afraid I haven't the slightest idea."

I suppose I had suspected, ever since Tom Shaw had let slip the truth about Robert's father, that it would come back to Maurice Arden. Pacing up and down the room, pausing occasionally to look from the window down the terraced garden to the narrow, busy coast road and the equally busy waters of the Bosporus, Edmund Chance finally, still with a certain reluctance, told me the complicated story. His own position and his organization he left unspecified, but it was hardly difficult to guess at them. What disturbed me was the realization of how closely Robert had been involved with them and for how many years.

"Did you use his guilt at his father's treachery to catch him?" I said.

"I trust it was a little more subtle than that," Chance said. "As for Arden's treachery, well, that was real enough, but we had, in my opinion at least, successfully turned him before we allowed him to leave. Do you know what I mean by that?"

"You made him a double agent," I said. "And do you mean that his escape to Russia was arranged by you?"

"Quite well done, wasn't it? No one suspected any collusion.

Of course, you're too young to remember it. When we trapped Maurice Arden, we gave him a choice. Prison here or a slightly more flexible kind of prison over there. We promised to look after his son, and he agreed."

"You didn't worry about his wife?"

"We couldn't tell her. We told him he could give her the choice of going with him, but that it would make life more difficult for him. It was Arden's decision not to tell her. I don't think he foresaw the suicide."

"It was hard luck on Robert," I said.

"He survived."

"So Maurice Arden has been working for you all these years."

He nodded. "Until this year, when he told us he wanted to come home. He was getting on, and he hadn't been well. He wanted to end his life in England. He wanted to see his son again before he died."

"Has Robert known the true position all this time?"

"Not when he was a child," Chance said. "That sort of knowledge would have been much too dangerous to put into a boy's hands. But since he was about eighteen, yes."

"And because of that, he worked for you."

"It may have had something to do with it," Chance admitted.

"And is his father coming home?" I asked.

"Well, there you have it," Chance said. "That is what all this rather disastrous mess is about. Quite a few people didn't think it would be a very good idea to let Arden back. Think of the confusion if the press got hold of it. There would be either a great fuss about the forgiveness of a traitor or an even greater fuss about the clever way we'd been pulling the wool over the Russians' eyes all these years. Either reaction equally unacceptable. And then there were plenty of people who didn't altogether trust Arden. His work for us had not been all that productive. Routine stuff, no great coups. It hadn't been decided either way when there was a new development. We got the tip-off that the Russians were on to him. Whether he had become careless or whether he deliberately let it happen to force our hand, we don't know. Anyway, every year for the past five years he had been working on an archaeological site in Soviet Armenia, which, as you may know, borders on Turkey. He had pursued his work in Russia. Had quite a distinguished career in his field, I understand. But this year, instead of waiting to assess the situation or to give us time to get something properly arranged, he jumped the gun. He arrived unexpectedly at the site and got word to us that he was coming over."

"So you sent Robert to fetch him?" I asked.

"Robert wouldn't let anyone else go," Chance said. "But it was a complete botch-up from start to finish. Arden didn't turn up at the rendezvous, but other not so welcome characters did. Robert had trouble getting away. Obviously a number of his contacts had been blown. One man was shot. Robert himself had a couple of narrow escapes and in the end had to get out of Turkey altogether."

It was clear I had met Robert in the middle of one of those narrow escapes. Chance's story explained so much, brought into focus so many things about Robert, the sense of danger he carried with him, the intensity of his emotions, his secrecy.

"As a result of this fiasco," Chance was continuing, "certain parties now hold Robert in less than high regard. They think he may have been in unofficial touch with Arden, may have been careless or too trusting. They think the whole operation may have been a maneuver to expose a network and stamp it out, with Arden as the stalking-horse."

"And what does Robert think?" I asked quietly.

"Ah . . . There you have it," Chance said, "the cause of the present trouble. Robert has been entirely loyal to his father, and that has posed some problems. He believed his father was still somewhere in the frontier region, although whether on the Russian or Turkish side was not yet established, and he intended to find him and get him home."

"So whatever he is up to now is without your backing?" I said.

Chance shrugged. "Unfortunately, yes. But he's got to be found. He told me in Chelsea when I was doing my best to dissuade him from any precipitate action, when I did, in fact, forbid him to do anything at all without my authority, that he had received a message from his father. I told him it was probably false, but he was prepared to take the risk. If it is a trap, then he's in great danger. Apart from his value to them in the information they could get out of him, I sense a certain vindictiveness in the attempts on him. Taking revenge on Maurice Arden through his son."

"Who is helping Robert," I said, "if you're not?"

"He has plenty of contacts in Turkey and elsewhere. He has friends who possibly may not let him down, and others who may."

I said: "And you think I'm endangering him."

Edmund Chance made a sweeping gesture that was almost theatrical. If he was intending to intimidate me, he was succeeding, not by his dramatics, but by his revelation of Robert's unprotected situation. "He'll work better alone," I told myself unconvincingly. "He'll be safer alone."

"Of course, you're endangering him," Chance boomed at me. "You are his vulnerable point. If they knew where he was, you don't think you'd be sitting safely here? They'd have picked you up on the road and be using you to blackmail Robert to give himself up. As it is, they are going to stay closer to you than leeches in the hope you'll lead them to him. And when you do, you won't have very long to say your good-byes."

"Mr. Chance, you're frightening me."

"I hope to God I am. Now will you go home?"

I said: "Why did they kill Tom Shaw?"

"I don't suppose the bullyboys responsible had the slightest idea he was a diplomat. They'd probably been told to keep you isolated, unprotected, kill your driver and see where you'd run to. If you knew Robert's whereabouts, even if he'd told you to keep away, they would be hoping terror would send you running to him."

"So that's why they followed me and didn't kill me?"

"You're getting the idea," he remarked sardonically.

There was a long pause. Chance leaned against the windowsill and lit another cigarette. I said: "You know why I'm here. Robert told me he would be back in London in a month. Do you think the fact that he is missing means that he is dead?"

Edmund Chance did an unexpected thing. He came across the room to me and put his hand on mine. He changed from accuser to comforter in an instant, making me distrust him even more.

"If he was dead," he said, "no one would be bothering about you. An odd way to reassure you, I know, but it's true."

"Thank you," I said. "But you shouldn't have abandoned him."

"If I'd abandoned him," he said gently, "what would I be doing here?"

I looked up at him. It was impossible to read any emotion in those pale, cold eyes.

"I have had no message from Robert," I said. "I would tell you if I had."

He patted my hand. "I know." He went back to his place by the window. It occurred to me there was probably someone out there, down on the road, with whom he was keeping in touch. Someone guarding his retreat, watching for strangers?

I said: "Did Robert tell you what the message from his father contained, where it was from?"

He shook his head. "No. He thought I might try to stop him if I knew. But I have a very good idea."

"So you are trying to find him?"

"Naturally, before someone else does."

"There is no point then in my formally requesting the embassy to make inquiries about him. If it was a question of accident, or illness, or arrest, as Tom Shaw put it, you'd know?"

"We would know. By the way, I hear the Ağaoğlus are making inquiries for you."

"Yes. You will want me to let you know if they have any results."

"That won't be necessary. We shall get the same information.

I just wondered why they were being so helpful. Have they met Robert?"

"No," I said. "They are being helpful out of kindness. Like most Turks, they believe in helping their friends."

"Very commendable. I wouldn't have thought Halim Ağaoğlu was so altruistic. I wouldn't confide in them too much."

"I haven't told them anything except that Robert is missing."

"Very wise." He spoke now almost absentmindedly, his thoughts clearly moving ahead to other matters. I'd been dealt with satisfactorily; the interview was over. "When will you leave?"

"I don't know," I said. "In a day or two."

That brought his attention back to me. "I wouldn't wait too long. Would you like us to book a plane ticket for you?"

"I can't afford the air fare. I'll go by train."

"You cannot possibly go all that way by train," he said in mild exasperation. "I think the department could stand the cost of your air fare."

"I'd rather it didn't," I said. "I'll make my own way back to London."

"Mrs. Denning, I hope you're not going to start being difficult."

"Not at all. I just like being independent. You'll let me know at once, won't you, about Robert?"

"Don't worry, I'll keep you informed. You're very wise in leaving the arena, as it were. If Robert should have discovered by any chance that you were in Istanbul, he might have tried to get in touch, and with you being watched, you can imagine the danger."

"Yes," I said. "I've got the message, Mr. Chance. Keep out, stay away, don't interfere."

He smiled, with the first sign of genuine feeling. "Sensible girl. I knew you'd understand."

"And also," I said, just to tease him, "keep my mouth shut about Maurice Arden?"

"I hardly need to answer that, do I?" Chance said. He shook

hands with ritualistic formality. "Good-bye, I shall look forward to seeing you in London when all this is over."

As soon as the front door had closed behind him, Madame Ağaoğlu came tripping into the room, her perfume preceding her. She was dressed for a social occasion and looked slightly flustered.

"My dear," she said, "I did not know whether to interrupt. Any news?"

"No," I said. "Nothing."

"I have some news," she continued. "I would have liked Halim's advice, but he has gone to Adana for several days. A friend of his has telephoned to say there is a young Englishman in police custody who has a story to tell that you may be interested in. If it is true, of course. He has been arrested in connection with drugs, so who knows what is real and what is his fantasy? Do you wish to talk to him?"

"He has met Robert?"

"There have been no names mentioned. But it must be a possibility or they would not have troubled to telephone. I am going into town now. Do you wish to come?"

"I'll come," I said. "Of course."

"I will take you to the place where the Englishman is, and all you do is show my card. You are expected. I assumed you'd want to talk to him."

In the car she asked: "Will you be able to find your way back to the villa?" She seemed to hang upon my answer, and there suddenly came unbidden into my mind the knowledge that she was on her way to meet a lover. That uncharacteristic air of flurry and hesitation betrayed her. How easily I could have upset everything by begging her to accompany me or by expecting to be collected at a certain time.

"I shall be perfectly all right," I said calmly. "I'll find my way back. I have been to Istanbul before."

The car was chauffeur-driven. We sat in the back, isolated by the glass screen.

I said, with perfect truth: "I do not know what I would have done without you."

"Oh, my poor dear," she said. She clasped my hands in hers. There were tears in her eyes. "I shall pray for you."

It was, although we did not know it, our farewell.

The Englishman's name was Raven, though whether that was his real name or a nickname gained on the road I never discovered. He told me he was twenty-two but looked ten years older, thin almost to emaciation, with tattered jeans and a matted woolen sweater ripe in odor. He sat hunched on a bench in a corner of the lawcourts, talking amiably to his Turkish guard and smoking thin cigarettes with stained fingers. The Turk was a peasant boy with cropped head and baggy uniform, pleased to have got such an easy job for the day.

I had shown Madame Ağaoğlu's card to several attendants before anyone would agree to accept responsibility for it. Eventually it was borne away and returned in the manicured hand of a small dapper man in a tan suit who introduced himself in fluent English as an "advocate," Nejat Güney. He was the friend of Halim Ağaoğlu who had organized this unofficial meeting.

"My dear lady, please come with me. I have but a moment. I am engaged on a case."

He spoke rapidly, moving me briskly along corridors as he talked. He had arranged for the young man to be brought here since he himself had to be here and it would not have been suitable for a well-brought-up young lady to have gone to a police station or, worse, to the jail.

"I can let you have ten minutes with him," he said. "Then he must go back. You may find what he has to say is of no use to you, but"—he shrugged—"who knows? In these matters it is often a question of seizing at straws."

I agreed that it was and thanked him for his help. He shrugged again. "It is little enough. I would say the young man is quite unreliable, you know. If he thinks it will help his case to make up a story, he will do so. Don't place too much credence in him. He is a wanderer, a vagabond. You know, I can never understand why young men with the benefit of education choose to wander around aimlessly like wild gypsies. Some even have money sent to them from abroad to continue in this life. Others sell their blood to hospitals or, like this chap, peddle drugs. It is a great nuisance for us, and it is not good for the Western image."

"There aren't so many of them now, are there?" I asked. "With all the international trouble, haven't most of them gone home?"

He gave his most expressive shrug so far, his spruce shoulders nearly touching his ears. "They get stranded. The young man says his passport was stolen and the consul will not give him another because he cannot identify himself. It is clear he sold the passport and has been nowhere near the consulate."

"Has the consul seen him?" I asked.

"No doubt, no doubt, but there is no need to mention this visit to the consul. It is quite informal. Here we are."

As we approached the bench, the Turkish guard lumbered to his feet, prodding at the boy to do the same. Güney unlocked a door beside them and waved us inside. It seemed to be some kind of waiting room with upright chairs lined stiffly against the walls and a table in the center.

"Ten minutes," he said. He spoke quickly to the guard, who nodded and settled himself on the chair nearest to the door. He remained there for the whole interview, gazing at us steadily with an expression of bemused fascination.

"Ten minutes," Güney repeated, this time to the boy. He pressed my hand in his soft palm and wished me the very best of fortune.

"Do not worry," he said as he left, "about discretion. The guard speaks no word of English."

The door closed behind us. Raven and I looked at each other.

"Why don't we sit down?" I said.

"Why not?" he agreed cheerfully. We pulled chairs up to the table and sat down opposite each other.

"I don't suppose you've any American cigarettes?" he said.

"I don't smoke."

"Pity." He lit a new cigarette from the stub of the last. His hands trembled slightly, belying the cocky self-assurance of his manner. He licked the corner of his mouth and with the edge of a nail scratched off a scrap of cigarette paper stuck to his upper lip.

"So you're the lady who's going to get me out of this mess," he said.

"Is that what they've told you?"

"Someone better pull me out. I don't fancy spending the next ten years in a Turkish jail."

"What have they got you for?" I asked.

"It's a frame-up," he said. "They caught me with this much hash"—he held up thumb and finger barely apart to indicate the minuteness of the amount—"and now they say I'm a full-time pusher. The stuff was planted anyway," he added unconvincingly.

His accent was a strange amalgam of American and Australian, with traces of his native Lancashire. He'd been so long on the road, hearing such a mixture of languages, he'd forgotten what English English sounded like; instead, he'd acquired the speech patterns of his fellow travelers. He'd been drifting across Europe, North Africa, and the Middle East since he was seventeen. There were no jobs for him when he left school, and once he'd crossed the Channel he'd never bothered to go back. He'd met plenty of people who'd been to India, but he'd never got there. Wars and revolutions had closed the road. He'd liked Morocco best. He wanted to go back there.

"How long have you been in Turkey?" I asked.

"Too long."

"Have they told you why I'm here?"

"You're looking for someone," he said. "They think I might

have seen him. 'Tell the lady what you told us,' they said, 'about the trouble.' "

It was only an hour or so since Edmund Chance had told me his version of the truth about Robert's presence in Turkey. I think I had accepted it so readily because I wanted to. It fitted my own instinctive feelings about Robert. I would rather have had him a secret agent than the drunken dilettante his friends were so tolerant of. But now, at the mention of trouble, I would have given anything to be able to say, "Whoever you met, whatever he was involved in, it couldn't be my husband because the only trouble he would be in would be falling down in a bar."

I said: "What trouble was that?"

Raven hesitated. He said suddenly: "Exactly who are you?"

"Why do you ask?"

"Because you're out of place. You're not like the girls I've met on the road. You look too innocent to be mixed up in this sort of business. What's all this to you?"

I said: "The man who's missing, the man I'm hoping you've seen is my husband."

"Jesus Christ, you'd better hope not," Raven said, "because if it is, it's likely you're a widow."

The Turkish guard shifted in his chair. He looked ostentatiously at the clock hung on the opposite wall and made a clicking sound with his teeth.

I made myself sound very calm. "Just tell me about it," I said, "and let me decide. We haven't got much time."

Raven leaned back in his chair. He inhaled the smoke of his cigarette and attempted an air of nonchalance. "How much pull have you got with that smooth little runt you came in with?"

"I met him for the first time today," I said. "I've no pull with anyone."

He snorted. "Not much! Bringing me over here, private room, private interview, don't tell anyone, keep it quiet. I'm asking myself exactly what I've got into, whose racket I've stumbled on.

Drugs, currency, arms? Are you the front for them? Nice young girl, pretty as a picture, English just like me. What have I got to tell you that means so much to your friends, eh? What have you got to coax out of me that I don't know I know? You tell me what this is really all about. You tell me what kind of deal you can offer me, and then we'll see if I'll talk."

I pushed the table away and stood up. The guard leaped expectantly to his feet. I couldn't speak. I turned my head away. I wanted to take hold of Raven's thin shoulders and shake his story out of him.

"All right," he said. His tone was different, uncertain. I looked back at him, and this time he was the one who turned away, but not before I'd seen the dismay in his eyes. I knew then that he would do or say anything to prolong his temporary freedom. But since he didn't know what these mythical racketeers wanted of him, he could only repeat what he'd told the police. There would be no point in his telling me lies.

I sat down. Raven stubbed out his cigarette on the edge of the table and spread his right hand flat on the surface. There was a thin, livid scar, newly healed, slashed across the back of it.

"My souvenir," he said, "of that night."

It was two, three weeks ago, he couldn't remember exactly. Time didn't mean much to him. He said he couldn't remember exactly where it had happened either except that it was somewhere in eastern Anatolia on that great dusty plain that seems to stretch from nowhere to nowhere. He wouldn't say where he'd been or what he was doing there, but with charges of drug pushing floating around, it didn't take much imagination to see why the police had found him so suspicious. Drug smuggling was a long-established profession, and the roads from Asia to Europe converged on that area where Raven had been doing his innocently aimless wanderings.

He was traveling with another man called Carl, and they'd thought themselves lucky when they got a lift in a truck going all the way to Ankara. In late afternoon it broke down with an overheated engine, and they all went to sleep by the side of the road until it cooled. Raven and his friend woke to see the truck grinding away into the distance, taking all their stuff with it.

"Even the sleeping bags," Raven said bitterly. "He could have thrown those out."

It was getting too cold at night to sleep in the open. They began trudging along the empty road. No more traffic came through, and from experience they doubted whether any more long-haul trucks would till dawn. There were soldiers around, though. They'd seen dispirited-looking groups by the roadside way back, and now, as they walked, they saw the dust of an approaching convoy. Soldiers get curious about lone foreigners on the road as far east as that, Raven said. They didn't want to risk being stopped and searched, so they turned off before the trucks reached them. He didn't say what they were carrying on them that they couldn't risk being found, and I didn't ask him. They walked cross-country and eventually ended up on a rough road winding north through low hills. They'd decided to stop at the first village they came to; but the children threw stones at them, and they didn't like the look of the men hanging round the one café, so they walked on through. On the outskirts of the village they came face-to-face with one of those savage dogs the shepherds use, with his great spiked collar and vicious mouth. There was no sign of a shepherd, and the dog wouldn't let them pass. When they tried to drive it away with stones and shouts, it only backed away a few feet, and when they began edging past it, it went for Carl and got him in the leg.

"I kicked the dog off and dragged Carl away, and we got back into the village," Raven said. "We stumbled into the café with blood streaming down Carl's leg, and I pushed through into the kitchen, shouting for water. It was full of women scurrying around like startled hens. Carl was getting hysterical, convinced the dog had rabies, and the men were all crowding through the door, thinking the mad foreigners were attacking their women. We got it sorted out in the end. They washed the bite clean and put some kind of a bandage on it, and I persuaded Carl the dog was just a typical wild Turkish dog and he wasn't going to die in agony. He couldn't walk, though, so we had to stay. There was a room above the café with four beds in it. The owner said two were taken but we could have the others. We didn't know who had the other beds. When we sat down in the café to have something to eat, there wasn't anyone there who didn't look local. We were the great celebrities now after all the fuss; everyone wanted to look at us. The little boys hung round the street door, staring, following every move we made, fork to plate to mouth. The men pulled chairs up and watched us, too. They fingered the cloth of Carl's jacket, looked at our boots, discussed us as if we weren't there. Carl had hocked his watch way back, but I still had mine, and one of them, a great big fellow built like a Japanese wrestler, decided he'd like to buy it from me. He couldn't understand that I didn't want to sell it. Things got tense when he tried to take it from my wrist and I grabbed hold of his arm to stop him. I was wondering how we were going to get out of it without me losing my watch, and my front teeth as well, when a man who'd been sitting with another at a far table in the corner and hadn't joined in the circus got up and came across and began talking to the big man. I don't know what he was saying, the Turkish was too fast for me, but it must have been a pretty good joke. Everyone laughed; the big man roared and let my wrist go and clapped his great arms round the other one; then someone produced a bottle of raki, and they all began to drink.''

"What did you do?" I asked.

"Kept very quiet," Raven said. "We were starving, so we finished up the meal, and then, first chance we got, we slid out and up the stairs to the room above before anyone noticed we'd gone. By that time it was quite a party. The small boys had all come inside and were sitting on the floor, gaping at the big man, who was now pretty drunk with his arm still round the shoulders of the one who'd saved us. That one noticed us going. I saw him say something to his friend, and after a few minutes the friend came up the stairs and into the room after us. He didn't say anything, just picked up a canvas bag and began checking the things in it and putting them back. I asked him if he had one of the other beds. As soon as he answered, I knew he wasn't a Turk, an American maybe, and though his friend downstairs hadn't any accent that I could detect, I thought then it was pretty likely he was no Turk either."

"What did they look like?" I asked.

"That was what the police asked me," Raven said. "I told them they looked like peasants, same clothes, same dirt, same stubble on their faces, same smell. The one who stayed downstairs was the taller and the younger. The American was a bit shorter, stockier. He seemed to let the other take the lead, maybe because he spoke the language better."

"Did he tell you anything about themselves?" I asked.

"No. Only that we'd better be prepared since things might get rough. It seemed the big fellow was the headman of the village and what he said went. When he spoke, the others jumped, and when he wanted something, he got it. Hence the trouble over the watch. Well, what he wanted now was the American's friend. He'd taken a real fancy to him, he wanted him to go over to his house to spend the night there and unless the friend could talk his way out of it, things might end up a bit noisy. I asked what they were doing there, but he shook his head and said nothing. He got some stuff out of his bag, disinfectant or something, and put it on Carl's bite and retied the bandage. Then he got on his bed, put the canvas bag under his head as a pillow and lay there, waiting. We could hear the voices and singing and laughter coming up through the floor, but after a while I fell asleep. I'd had too busy a day to stay awake. I don't think I slept long; the creak of the door woke me. I opened my eyes and saw the man who'd saved us talking to the American. 'He's gone outside,' the tall man was saying. 'We've got about two minutes to get out. We'll go through the kitchen.' He was speaking in English, with an English accent, so there was no doubt about his nationality anymore. They picked up their bags and slipped out. I wasn't going to be left there when the big fellow found his prey had gone, so I started shaking Carl awake. At that moment there was a great roaring and shouting and thunder of feet and the stairs shook and the door burst open and the American and his friend were backing in with about twenty Turks after them. The big fellow was behind, very drunk and howling with frustrated rage, yelling at his men to stop them. I got knocked down in the rush, and my hand was slashed as I rolled under the bed for safety. The American went down, and I heard him shouting to his friend to get out. I heard the smashing of a window and cries. Then the stampede went into reverse, and we were left with a kind of terrible silence. I crawled out and found Carl looking down at the American. Someone had used a knife to stop him. He was quite dead. His friend, Carl said, had done an Errol Flynn out of the window. Smashed it with a chair and leaped through it. We could hear them after him, like dogs hunting him down."

I said: "Did he get away?"

"I don't know," Raven said. "We didn't wait to find out. When we looked out of the window, there was only a passage below leading out to the main street. If they caught him, I don't think he'd have had any chance. The mood that big fellow was in, he'd have beaten him to death."

There was a long silence in the room. Raven's Turkish guard was getting restless. Our allotted time was long since over. I said: "What did you do then?"

"We got out," Raven said, "before any of them came back. We put as much distance as we could between us and that village. Carl didn't seem to find his leg so much trouble when it was a question of his life being at stake. Next morning we got back to the road, and four days later we were in Istanbul."

"You didn't report what had happened? Send the police to the village?"

He looked slightly amused at my naïveté. "People like us keep away from the police. How much of that story would they believe? How much have they believed? We didn't even know where the village was or what it was called. If the police ever do find it, there won't be any sign of foreigners there, dead or alive, you can bet on that, and no one there will know what on earth they're talking about."

"How did this all come out then?" I asked.

"Because the police picked me up and found this stuff on me and I told them it must have been planted on me there. By the American, while I slept. So they wanted to know who the American was."

"Have they found out?"

"Not yet, but I told them Carl might know. In the dark and the hurry, he picked up the American's jacket. By mistake, he said. Later he found a passport sewn in the lining. He was going to sell it, but he liked the idea of having an American passport. He thought of using it himself. As far as I know, he's still got it."

"What was the name? Did you see it?"

He shook his head. "No. Carl kept that very much to himself. I know where he is, though. At least where he was a couple of days ago. If he's heard they've picked me up, he might have split."

"Will you give me the address?" I said.

"Sure. Why not? But it's a pretty rough place, and if you find him, he may not want to talk. Have you got anything to write with?"

I passed a pen across and a piece of paper from my handbag, and he wrote down the address. He didn't know Carl's surname, he said, but anyone would know Carl.

"Do you think it's your husband?" he asked curiously.

"Not the American," I said. "The other."

Raven shook his head slowly from side to side. "Well," he said, "I'd sure like to know what the hell they were up to. It was bad luck, you know, sheer bad luck that killed the American. If that big fellow hadn't found your husband so attractive— He must have had a smooth skin. Some of those hairy old fellows, they can't resist a smooth skin. I hope he got away. I hope you find him."

"Thanks for talking to me," I said.

"Oh, it's all right," Raven said. He looked depressed. "It's a bloody awful country. I wish I could get out of it."

I tried to see Nejat Güney again before I left the lawcourts, but though one old fellow obligingly went off down the corridors, ostensibly to search for him, I think it was more a gesture on his part. He was soon back, saying he couldn't be found. I decided to get his address from Madame Ağaoğlu later and write to thank him for his kindness. I'd say how forthcoming Raven had been, too, in case that might help him, and I'd also ask Halim Ağaoğlu if he could do anything to get Raven treated leniently—though I didn't know why I was thinking of helping someone who'd first tried to blackmail me and then told me my husband had probably died a violent and degrading death in the wilds of Anatolia without either of the two men he'd helped lifting a finger to save him.

For I was convinced in my own mind that the Englishman was Robert. The description, vague as it was, fitted him. The man appeared to have behaved in a way I could imagine Robert behaving, he was with an American, we knew Robert had left Paul Andriades's camp with an American and it had all happened in an area we might expect Robert to be. And Robert had been missing all this time.

If I could find this other man, this Carl, and make him talk to me, he might remember things that Raven had missed or forgotten. He might have noticed more, he might be able to describe the men better. After all, hadn't the American dressed the bite on his leg for him? They could have talked while he was doing that; the American could have said something that might help to identify his tall companion. And if Carl still had the passport, wouldn't that show the date and place of entry into Turkey as well as give a name to the American, a name Paul Andriades or others back in Athens might confirm as that of a friend of Robert's?

The important thing was to know. If I could get confirmation one way or the other, I could plan what to do. All the firm intentions I had set out with from Greece had become muddled and confused in the light of what had happened to Tom, of what I had learned from Edmund Chance, what I had just heard from Raven. My ideas now seemed naïve in their simplicity. It was no longer a question of heading east and hoping to pick up word of Robert. If I went east at all it would have to be secretly, deviously, with due regard to the danger I would be placing myself and Robert in. Edmund Chance wouldn't help me. He wanted me out of it, back in England. But I couldn't leave now, not without knowing, not without making any attempt to find Robert.

I wasn't rational about it, or I would have obeyed Chance's logical demand that I return to England, where, if I couldn't help Robert, there was less chance of my harming him. But although I saw the sense of that argument, I couldn't act on it. I was in the grip of emotions too compelling to deny, impulses that were driving me to seek Robert out so that I could protect him, fight beside him, die with him perhaps, but never be separated from him again.

The Europa Palas Oteli was not the kind of establishment to be found in the lists of any reputable travel agent. The grandeur of its name was in inverse proportion to the squalor of its interior. I had a hard time finding it. Struggling through the maze of street markets, avoiding touts, money changers, peddlers, the hunched porters stooped beneath their loads, skirting the slow-moving groups of slightly bewildered tourists, I emerged in the wrong street, going in the wrong direction. When I asked the way, no one had heard of the place. It was another ten minutes before a glance down a side street changed things. I was now in one of the poorest quarters of Istanbul, where the shabbiness had no patina of romantic Orientalism to glamorize its dirt and decay, no secret courtyards with hidden fountains or single shady tree, no tiny decorated mosques tucked between taller buildings, no antique relics of the past, only a dead cat at my feet and the aftermath of what seemed to have been a minor riot in the middle of the street.

There were two groups of men, still aggressive, still jeering at each other. Turkish youths confronting a bunch of bearded, tangle-haired Europeans, the Turks making darting ritual movements of attack that never culminated in actual blows, shaking fists, pantomiming the action of flinging stones, the Europeans crowded, as if for protection, round the open door of a narrow, flaking house, shouting obscenities back at them. A police car was parked between them, the bored driver, taking no interest in the affray, leaning against the hood, picking his teeth. There was a flurry in the doorway, and two uniformed policemen came briskly out. One got into the car; the other, revolver in hand, strode between the combatants, gesturing fiercely with his gun, pushing at any within reach, ordering them to disperse. Sullenly the Turks began to drift away. The second policeman called to the driver, and they both got into the car. The driver roared the engine a few times in a final warning, then drove away fast up the street. The Europeans slunk back inside the door. Above it I noticed inscribed in fading paint across the face of the building the words "Europa Palas."

I crossed the street and went inside. The lobby was small, dark, smelly and crowded. Behind the reception desk a thin man with the drawn face of a consumptive was arguing volubly with his tattered guests and receiving the same sort of replies as the Turks had outside. I pulled at the arm of the man nearest me.

"What's going on?" I said.

He looked down at me. He was a tall man of about thirty with a skin worn and wrinkled by too many changes of climate and a weary manner to match. When he spoke, it was with a thick German accent.

"Some man got beaten up by Turks, here in hotel, left for dead. Many people here in lobby when Turks come out as if nothing happened. They get attacked. They shouting, others coming in, fighting starts, police called. Turks say man drug dealer, stole money from them, wouldn't pay money owed. Police take injured man away, Turks run away. These people mad they weren't arrested—" He shrugged. "Stupid business. Now they want us all out of hotel. Very bad for foreigners here now. Not as it used to be. A friend of mine was shot a few weeks ago in Izmir. I came back to Istanbul. Now I leave."

I asked him if he'd been staying at the Europa Palas for long.

"Off and on. Whenever I come here to Istanbul. Cheapest place to be found. No water, too many fleas, but cheap."

"Do you know a man called Carl?" I asked.

"Sure. Carl's the poor bastard who was beaten up."

For a moment I felt as you do when you miss a step and tread on air. I realized I'd been relying on finding Carl. I'd depended on him as the next link in my search for Robert. It was hard to know what to make of what had happened. If the violence had really been about drugs, then it could be pure coincidence that Carl had been the victim. If it was something else, if it meant Robert's pursuers were on to Raven's story—

I asked the German if they'd taken Carl's belongings when they took him away. He didn't know, but he could tell me which room he'd been staying in: second floor opposite the staircase. He was quite incurious about my interest in Carl. He merely said: "If you're going up there, don't touch the walls of the staircase. They are not too clean."

No one appeared to notice as I made my way past the back of the crowd to the stairs. They smelled rather worse than the lobby. High slit windows on the landings gave some light and showed me the open door of the second-floor room opposite the staircase. The open door . . . well, why not, since the occupant was gone? I pushed it wider open and went in.

The room was, as the whole building appeared to be, more of a flophouse than a hotel: a bare floor, three beds, no window, lit by one overhead bulb. Standing by the bed farthest from the door, stripping the lining from a tattered jacket, was Mr. Okyer.

There was no hesitation on my part. I recognized him at once. What was disturbing was that not only did he seem to recognize me, but he knew my name. He looked up at me, not in the least alarmed or put out at being found in that situation, and put one hand up and said: "Mrs. Denning," in that low, guttural voice I remembered from that brief encounter in the taxi on the road to Fethiye.

I backed away. In my imagination, I had built up the menace of this man from the two meetings we had had, abandoning Bernice and me on the road below the temple, coming out of the cabin opposite ours on the boat to Istanbul, and also from the report by Bernice of his escorting the sultry Cleo to a car in Athens and from his signature in the visitors' book at Andriades's dig. The reality was even more threatening than my imaginings. He was big and solid and powerful, and if anything was needed to confirm that it had been Robert in that village in Anatolia, then Okyer's presence in that room would have been enough to satisfy me. I'd been foolish to suppose there was any particular secrecy about Raven's story. Gossip, rumor, bribery, it wouldn't have taken much to track down Raven's companion in that adventure, and so Okyer had got here before me. He'd arranged for Carl to be dealt with, and now any evidence Carl had had was lost to me. If Okyer was one of those unnamed men Chance had told me was searching for Robert, and I felt little doubt of it now, then my sudden appearance at the Europa Palas must have seemed like a gift from heaven. The little mouse strolling unconcernedly within reach of the cat's paw. I wasn't going to wait for the paw to descend. I took another step nearer the corridor.

He threw the jacket down on the unmade bed and came after me.

"Mrs. Denning," he called, louder now, commanding me to stop. I turned and ran.

I took the unsavory concrete stairs two at a time. I plunged through the complainers in the lobby and burst into the street and came to a sudden halt. Where the police car had been, there was now the oh-so-familiar black sedan, and sitting in it, waiting for me like two fat black spiders in the web, were Tom Shaw's murderers. Looking back, I saw Okyer closing in on me, and from that moment panic, not reason, directed my actions. I simply fled, down one side street, along another, in and out and down the hill into the street markets, and all the time singing away in my head was the terrible thought: Robert's dead, and now they can kill me. When I finally came to my senses, I was among the bookshops of the Ankara Caddesi with the faded glories of the terminus of the Orient Express before me. I thought I'd got away from them completely, but with the sudden instinct that hunted animals develop, I felt, out of all the strangers surrounding me, there was one whose whole attention was fixed on me.

I slowly turned and found behind me on the pavement the unlikely figure of John Nairn.

"You're a hard girl to catch up with," he said. "What were you doing? Practicing the hundred-yard dash?" He was smiling, as if pleased to have been able to surprise me, but my face must have expressed more than I knew, for his smile faded and he put his arm around my shoulders to support me and said only half-jokingly: "Hey, I'm not going to have to pick you up off the floor again, am I? Don't faint on me, will you?"

He'd a week's leave of absence due, and after my last phone call to the Bloomsbury flat, he'd decided to take it now and come to Istanbul to help me find Robert.

"I figured you could do with a little help," he said simply.

On arrival he had telephoned the Agaoglus' house and had been told by the butler that I was at the lawcourts.

"Did he tell you, just like that?" I said. "Without asking who you were?"

"Well, perhaps not just like that," Nairn said. "I did imply that I was from your embassy and had to get in touch with you rather urgently."

"Even so—"

"Not much security, you're thinking. If I found you so easily, others could."

"Yes."

"So it's as bad as that," he said.

"Yes."

"You'd better tell me all about it. But if it's any comfort to you, I drew a blank at the lawcourts, and so would anyone else. I couldn't find anyone who knew if you'd been there or not. It was pure chance I saw you tearing down the street while I was waiting to pick up a taxi to the hotel."

It was to his hotel he had taken me to recover, and now we were sipping tea in its civilized surroundings near Taksim Square and I was savoring the comfort of being with someone I could talk to freely. In a way, for all their kindness, I had not been able to talk to the Ağaoğlus; John represented someone who had no ax to grind, no government department to satisfy, but a straightforward desire to find out what had happened to his friend.

He listened intently as I told him about Tom's murder, of my meeting with Edmund Chance, my interview with Raven, my encounter with Okyer. He was fascinated to learn how often Okyer had come into the story and especially about his connection with Cleo, his own mysterious tenant.

"I suppose they, whoever they are, knew it was the most likely place Robert would come to in Athens and slipped Cleo in to trap him. That night you say everyone thought him hopelessly drunk was probably their attempt to kidnap him. She must have got him drugged before he caught on to her and managed to get away."

"Only just," I said. "If we hadn't come out of the taverna at that precise time—"

"Now don't start worrying about the things that didn't happen," Nairn said. "We've got enough to deal with with the things that did. This story by the hippie, do you think that was Robert in that village?"

"I'm sure of it," I said.

"And the other side knows it, too. Do you think they got the name of the place out of this man Carl before they dumped him?"

I shook my head. "Raven said neither of them ever knew it."

"Is there any point in our going to the police to try to see this man Carl? You were going to talk to him to see if he could confirm that the tall man in the café was Robert. Now you say Okyer turning up in the place is confirmation enough. I agree with you. I don't think we'd get anything useful out of Carl. Anyway, he seems to have been beaten up so thoroughly it could be a few days before anyone can talk to him, and we haven't got days to play with."

I liked all that talk of "we." It eased that cold, despairing loneliness I'd carried with me ever since the moment of Tom's death.

"Did you know anything about Robert's real profession?" I asked.

"If you can call it a profession. No, I took him at face value. There was enough to take there, without delving below the surface. He came and went so erratically, with no pattern to it, that people no longer expected anything staid and methodical about his behavior, not even a regular job. He was simply Robert, and you were glad to see him when you did. Of course, I knew about his father, and I did sometimes wonder if Robert was in touch with him. He was very defensive about his father."

John Nairn leaned back in his chair. He looked exactly as he had in Bloomsbury: calm, capable, full of common sense, a shoulder to lean on, which was exactly what I had done during the journey to the hotel. I'd liked the feeling of that shoulder beneath the thin jacket, the warmth of it, the comforting solidity of it. He had kept his arm round me all the way.

He said: "Do you think Edmund Chance knows of these latest developments?"

"You mean, have the police told the embassy about Raven's story? I don't know. He said he would be getting any of the same information Halim Ağaoğlu managed to get, but the police might think Raven's story too vague and suspect to make official."

"I was only thinking," Nairn said, "that if Chance does know, he'll very soon guess that's where you intend heading, and then you'll find yourself being escorted, in a no doubt gentlemanly but firm manner, to the London plane."

I looked across at him. He smiled gently. "What I mean," he said, "is why don't we get a jump or two ahead of the old fox, get to Van, which is probably the farthest east we can get without a travel permit anyway, and start searching for what traces of Robert we can find from there?"

All the time Raven had been telling me his story, there had been at the back of my mind the thought of Maurice Arden's village, the village where he had first been shown a griffin's head from a Urartian caldron. That had been somewhere in eastern Anatolia, too. Somewhere north of Van, going towards Ararat. Had Arden chosen that village to be the rendezvous with his son, so he could show Robert the site of his hidden city, so he could look at it again himself? And then I remembered something else.

"What is it?" Nairn asked, watching my face.

"I'm not sure if it's significant," I said. "But do you remember seeing a chessboard in Robert's study?"

"Yes."

"He told me he was playing a game by post with a friend from Istanbul. It had been going on for months. There was a pile of cards in his desk. The last card to arrive was by the board. It had a photograph of the fortress of Van on the back. Marvelous-looking place. But not the sort of card you'd find readily in Istanbul, I wouldn't have thought."

"You're saying the card was a message about his father? Could it be? Did it have anything written on it that you could see?"

"Only a move in chess," I said. "K to R or R to K, I don't really remember."

"K to R," Nairn said slowly. "King to rook, the other name for a rook being, as you know, a castle. And a photograph of a castle on the back. The king was going to Van. Do you remember anything else? Any number. There would most likely have been a number, K to R three or whatever."

"I don't remember," I said. "I'm sorry. I didn't pay all that much attention to it. But I think now it must have significance, or why would the burglar take that and leave so much else?"

"The postcard was all that was missing?" Nairn said.

"That and the golden bull," I said, and remembered as soon as I'd spoken that I had never told John Nairn about the bull and that now, when we were about to become partners in the search for Robert, I was going to have to reveal how little confidence I had had in him when I concealed that theft.

He told me he knew nothing about it, that Robert had never confided that part of his family history to him, but since I had betrayed the secret already to Paul and to Bernice, I saw no reason now to keep it from John Nairn. He listened to me in silent fascination and, when I had finished, pulled out a paperback guide to Turkey from an inside pocket and flicked over the pages until he came to a map of Anatolia.

"There's Van." He stabbed at the name with his forefinger. "At the southeast corner of Lake Van. And here"—he traced the thin red line of a road northeastward—"is Mount Ararat. It's practically on the Iranian border, can't be more than twenty miles or so, and the Russian border is nearly as close. See here, this narrow strip of land like a corridor between the Russian and Iranian borders which ends in a point where the three frontiers meet. My guess is that Maurice Arden's first attempt was a direct one, slipping across the Turkish-Russian border somewhere north of this area, near his excavations. I'm not surprised it came to grief; that's one of the most closely patrolled borders in the world, ditches, lights, watchtowers along a barren stretch of country with little cover. His second attempt, I would think, was rather different."

"What do you think happened between the first and second attempts?" I said. "Where do you think he was?"

"Moving, hiding, I don't know, but moving south. I see there's a railway from Van that crosses the border. Perhaps he came in on that."

"And at Van he was supposed to meet Robert; only something went wrong."

"I would guess so. But the only thing we can do is to try to follow their trails. That card with the photograph of Van—I would think the number would either be the date he planned to be in Van, or the number of days he would wait for Robert there, or the number of days after sending the card it would take him to get there."

"I'm sorry," I repeated, "I can't remember."

"I wouldn't worry about it," John said. "I don't think it makes any difference now."

His words depressed me because they emphasized the time I had lost before even beginning the search for Robert. Whatever had gone wrong at Van would have happened before I'd left Canada. And how many weeks had passed since Raven and Carl had seen the American die in the upper room of that café? Two, three?

"You know a lot of Robert's friends," I said. "Have you any idea who that American could have been?"

He shook his head. "Doesn't sound like anyone I know. Probably someone who joined Robert just for this job."

"An intelligence officer, you mean, like Robert."

He nodded.

"But Robert's doing this unofficially, going against direct orders, in fact. The American's bosses wouldn't have let him get mixed up in this affair, surely."

"Not officially perhaps. But perhaps they didn't know any more than Edmund Chance did. Perhaps he came as a friend."

"If that is so," I said, "I can imagine how Robert must feel about his death."

John Nairn leaned forward and covered my hand with his. "It doesn't do, Frances," he said softly, "to let emotion in on this. Look on it as a puzzle, a game of hide-and-seek. Now tell me again where this village might be."

I moved my hand away from his and picked up the guidebook. "Raven said they were on their way to Ankara when the truck left them. So I should think they were on this road from the border of Doğubayazit and Erzurum."

"And they turned off and wandered about and they didn't say in which direction?"

"Raven said they ended up on a track going north."

"They could have gone around in a circle."

"Yes."

He gave a short, impatient sigh. "It's a pity Robert wasn't more communicative. Why the hell didn't he tell me about it? I'd have gone with him."

"Now who's letting emotion come into it?" I said.

He looked up at me and then sat back squarely in his chair. "You're right. Let's go."

"Where are we going?"

"Collect your things and on our way."

I thought of the men in the black sedan and Okyer, their master or their colleague?

"I'm frightened," I said frankly. "I think those men will have gone back to the Ağaoğlus to wait for me. They're murderers, and now Okyer's with them. I'm afraid they intend to kidnap me or kill me, and you wouldn't be able to stop them. They killed Tom Shaw, remember."

John paused, thinking about it.

"You're hardly dressed for the wilds of Anatolia," he pointed out.

"I could buy something round here."

"Do you think you'd find jeans to fit? Turkish girls don't often have legs your length."

"These shops are quite international. I'm certainly not going back to the old town."

But he was making me feel foolish. They wouldn't try anything, would they, in broad daylight, at a house like the Ağaoğlus? Night on the road or day in the rough neighborhood of the Europa Palas Oteli was one thing; the environs of a wealthy villa in a prosperous suburb, another.

"All right," I said. "Get a taxi and tell him to go fast up the drive to the house. When we get near the house, I'll hide until we're through the gates. I can't afford to buy new clothes at the prices round here anyway. And besides," I added, "I want to say good-bye to Madame Ağaoğlu."

John said quickly: "Don't tell her what you're doing, will you? Let her think you're going back to England."

"Are we going to tell the police about Okyer and the others?" I said. "Shouldn't I telephone Edmund Chance about it?"

"And be put on the next plane back to London? Somehow that doesn't seem to be what you want."

"Then let's go," I said, and gave him what I hoped was a brave rather than a nervous smile. "Let's go."

CHAPTER 6

Sun glittering on water, the music of a distant band, gardens filled with flowers and children, nothing could have seemed more alien, more at odds with the tension of our mood than that drive along the Bosporus. The normality and beauty of the scene made the events of the morning seem totally unreal. As we approached the entrance to the Ağaoğlus' house, it became ridiculous even to think of crouching on the floor of the taxi in the melodramatic way I had described, but John Nairn gently pushed me down and kept me there, his hand firmly on my back, until by the turning of the car I knew we were through the gates.

"Not a sign of the notorious black car or of anyone else," he said cheerfully. "If they are here, they're very well concealed."

The whole visit was an anticlimax. Madame Ağaoğlu had not returned, and the house, emptied of her personality, was as impersonal as a hotel. I told the butler I was returning immediately to England and would leave Madame a note. While I was writing it, he sent a maid to pack my things, but she took so long, folding and arranging each garment with such meticulous care, that I became impatient and rather ungraciously sent her away so I could finish the job myself.

I had taken John's advice. In my note I explained that a friend from England had arrived and I was leaving with him at once for London. I said I would write again later and thanked her once more for her kindness and her help. Since I could not decide how much to say about my visit to the lawcourts and Raven's story, I said nothing. I thought she would be surprised and possibly a little hurt by my abruptness, and I even delayed the moment of my departure in the hope that she might suddenly return, but when I rejoined John in the waiting taxi, there had been no sign of her.

We drove quickly back to John's hotel, and this time I waited while he packed, made telephone calls to airlines and tourist offices and finally paid his bill. He had decided that the airport was very likely being watched, but not the station, so instead of taking a plane direct to Van, we were to take the night train to Ankara and fly from there.

I love trains, and I felt safe in the cocoon of metal rattling away through the darkness; but once in Ankara, looking bleak and cold in a gray morning light, I could not wait to get out of the city. I felt exposed there, with a dry, cold wind catching at the edge of one's nerves, foretelling the end of summer. I was suddenly conscious of the vast landmass stretching east to the frontier and of the enormous difficulties of the task we were undertaking. The dangers that, the day before, even in my terror, had possessed an almost operatic quality now seemed cold and bureaucratic, coming from men without heart, killing for policy without even the full-blooded excuse of rage or hatred to justify their actions.

I was disturbed, too, for another reason. I found I could not make my mind up about John Nairn and why he had come. I sometimes had the feeling that it was to help me rather than Robert. Something in the way he looked at me, his protectiveness, his clear concern, made me uneasy, as if I were going to take his help under false pretenses. But since nothing was spoken, since all this was beneath the surface, there was nothing I could do about it. I had to decide whether to accept his help or send him away, and ruthlessly I accepted it. I needed him and I was prepared to exploit whatever nascent feeling for me I glimpsed in his eyes, and that revelation of my own character was what disturbed me.

At the airport John left me to guard the luggage while he made more phone calls: to Van to confirm a hotel, to his own embassy to ask about restrictions in travel, to inquire about the latest political situation. Newspaper placards had spoken of riots in the east, and while driving out of town to the airport, we had passed a procession of silent people carrying banners I could not read. The taxi driver had turned away down back streets to avoid them or, rather, he explained, to avoid the soldiers who could be coming to break the procession up. Who were they? I asked. He shrugged. Religious fanatics, trade unions, communists, what did it matter? It always meant trouble. Later we had heard gunfire.

The plane to Van made two stops along the way, at Malatya and Díyarbakir. It was full of army officers heading for Van and beyond, and engineers bound for the oil fields at Díyarbakir. There seemed very few tourists. The only ones we identified were an aging foursome, two sprightly matrons who referred to themselves as the girls and their balding husbands as the boys. When John asked them why they were risking going to such an unstable part of the country, they said that a few local disturbances weren't going to put them off fulfilling their tour schedule, that they'd been in the Philippines during an attempted revolution and in Pakistan when rioters burned down their hotel. They seemed to carry these experiences like battle honors. Nevertheless, they, too, left the plane at Díyarbakir, heading for its black basalt walls. We traveled on, surrounded by the army.

A captain sitting behind me touched my shoulder to make sure I would not miss my first view of Lake Van. Its size was immense, its color extraordinary, a brilliant intense blue, its setting breathtaking, ringed by its guardian mountains.

"And there is Van," the captain said helpfully. "You know the saying: 'Van in this world, paradise in the next.' "

"I didn't know that saying," I replied, "but I can appreciate it."

"An old Armenian dictum," John whispered. "This was their chief city, but of course, there are no Armenians left there now."

And before the Armenians, the Medes and the Persians, and before them, the Urartians. This was their capital, that massive limestone rock was their citadel, the unknown, mysterious people who were such great engineers and who had vanished so completely, leaving almost nothing behind. No wonder Maurice Arden was fascinated by them. An air of mystery and tragedy seemed, even before we landed, to envelop that remote, majestic scene.

Once we were down on the ground, the political tensions of the latest crisis soon swept away any romantic speculations about the past. Police and soldiers at the airport outnumbered civilians, and even though we had come in on an internal flight, we were required to show our passports before being allowed to leave. They were given no more than a cursory examination; the fact that they were British and American seemed to suffice. Our nationalities, apparently, were not the suspect ones.

The captain was right behind us. He intercepted the passports as they were being handed back, glancing quickly at the names before returning them to us with a military click of the heels. For some reason it appeared he had decided to adopt us. Where were we staying? he asked. Had we transport arranged? Would we please allow him to escort us? It was difficult for visitors at times like these. He would not wish our arrival to be marred by any bureaucratic stupidities.

The captain was a tall, fleshily handsome man, with a neat mustache and excellent French. His English was more erratic. He had been visiting his wife and family in Ankara. They had formerly lived with him in Van, but he had sent them west six months ago. It had been obvious that trouble was brewing.

"You think worse is to come?" John asked him.

"This time it will blow over," he said. "Next time—" He shrugged. "The Kurds have been reasonably quiet through all this, but they are like a teakettle on the boil. They may blow up at any moment. There was an incident last week, I've been told, reports of shooting, but when the patrol went to look, nothing! They vanish into their mountains and wait."

He did not seem impressed by our hotel and wanted us to

move to another, but John insisted it would do very well, and by comparison with some I had stayed in with Bernice, it was in the luxury class.

"Then you must dine with me. I insist. The Officers' Club. Anyone will direct you." And with another flourish and click of his polished boots, he was gone.

"A popinjay," John called him.

"He looked quite competent to me," I said.

"He was trying to impress you. Why do you think we had all that attention? When we go there, stick close to me."

"We are going to dine with him then, are we?"

"Yes, of course. We're going to look and to be seen. We need to make ourselves conspicuous. We want people for miles around to hear about the two foreigners wandering about, asking questions."

"And if that doesn't produce any results?"

"We start moving northeast and begin again."

"John, do you honestly think this is the way to find Robert?"

"We have no other way," he said. "We must let him find us."

"But the others will find us, too. Okyer and his men, and Edmund Chance."

"I think we've got a day, perhaps two, before anyone catches up with us. Anything can happen in a day."

We dined with three other officers at the club, calm, sensible men who seemed to regard their more ebullient colleague with tolerant amusement. After preliminary gallantries to me, however, the captain appeared intent on demonstrating his more serious side, plying John with questions about American politics and what he considered an ambivalent foreign policy.

"Strong men are what we need," he declared. "Strong but flexible. Rigidity in a politician can be fatal."

"Not for him, unfortunately," one of the others added with a smile, "but for all those who become the victims of his decisions."

Their forecasts of events in the next few years were hardly

such to raise my spirits; but they lived on a frontier, and they had the frontiersmen's casual expectation of conflict. It was why they were there after all.

Tension was always present, they explained. There was a two-mile-deep militarized zone all along the Russian border. It had been possible for tourists to visit the cathedral at Ani, right on the border, under escort, but this had been stopped these past months. They went on to describe the watchtowers, the lights switched on nightly by the Russians all along the line, the constant patrols. It seemed literally impossible for Maurice Arden to have crossed anywhere in that region.

"Do any people get through?" I asked.

"Why should they try?" they replied. "Easier to slip on a boat across the Black Sea or go through the mountains."

I exchanged a glance with John.

"You spoke of a shooting incident in the mountains," I said to the captain. "Was it on yours or the Russian side?"

"I regret I cannot say. We have never yet picked up a defector from Russia, but there is always a first time. If they have the help of the Kurds, they would have a chance, no doubt of that."

But they considered it doubtful. The more they talked, the more depressed I became. Looked at in the cold light of reality as presented to us by experienced men who were both friendly and unbiased, Maurice Arden's attempts at escape had been doomed from the start. Edmund Chance had come to the same conclusion when he forbade Robert to go that second time. He had not been an enemy to Robert; he had been protecting him. I wished he had succeeded, for I was becoming more and more convinced that Robert's long silence could have only one explanation, that our hopes of contacting him were pitiable in their guilelessness, that the only news I should ever receive of him would be the news I dreaded to hear.

We declined the offer of a lift back to the door of our hotel. After the hours on the plane I wanted to walk, and I wanted the silence and anonymity of the night. At that time the long boulevard lined with acacias was almost empty, the soldiers were back in barracks, the few tourists were in their hotels and in the side streets we saw only a handful of men playing cards in a coffeehouse and a straggle of Kurds on their way to the truck park.

We had spoken little on the way back. Crossing the road, John had taken my arm, though there was no traffic to be wary of, and he had not let it go again. At the hotel he came to my room bringing a half bottle of whiskey and two glasses. We drank in silence.

At last I said: "Do you think there's any hope?"

He looked at me strangely. He said: "I'm sorry, I'm sorry." And began to kiss me, at first tentatively, then with increasing urgency, with a growing passion.

I welcomed his kisses. I longed for the comfort of his human warmth, his body close to mine. I wanted the safety of his arms round me, to feel for a few moments no longer so lost, so terribly alone. But I liked him too much to do that to him, to make use of him like that. I wasn't foolish enough to make that an argument. I could imagine the response he would give to that. I simply said no as gently and insistently as I could, with my mouth and with my body and, when he let me, with my voice.

He left without another word and went back to his room. In the morning when we met, he behaved as if nothing had happened. He was neither cooler nor friendlier than before; his smile was as natural, the tone of voice the same. I took my cue from him, and neither of us mentioned the incident again.

The bright autumn sunshine had revived my spirits. It was another day, and with it came renewed hope. Anything was possible, particularly where Robert was concerned.

"Today we'll go look at the old city," John said.

He had said he wanted us to be noticed, and he was as good as his word. Our progression was slow and deliberate, and all the way John stopped to talk. He talked to the hotelier; he talked to street cleaners; he talked to the men in the dark café where we stopped to take tea; he talked to assistants in the shops, and the women at the market stalls, and the bus drivers who traveled round the lake. As I was beginning to get tired, we were hailed by an officer in a jeep. It turned out to be the blond lieutenant who had been one of our dinner companions the night before. When he heard we were on our way to the old city, he offered to take us there. He brushed aside our polite protests.

"You don't want to walk all the way, and the bus is no good. Jump in. I have time. I shall enjoy it."

So it was with appropriate military escort that we arrived at the citadel of Van.

I had never been to a place which seemed to me more haunted or more desolate. The great cliff rose red-gold in the honeyed light above the broken ruins of its town. It stood, massive and dominating in its isolation, amid the silent marshes where once the lake had flowed, populated now only with ghosts and darting water birds. Once it had teemed with people, had heard the trumpeters of kings, had seen ships clustering its harbor. Xerxes in triumph had carved his name and works upon the rock three times, in three languages, high above the inscriptions of the usurped Urartian kings. The Armenians had made it prosperous, the paradise they were to lose forever, full of rich gardens tumbling with abundant fruit. Tamerlane had sacked it; Turks and Persians had fought over it. It had survived as a city, with Muslims and Christians living side by side, until the First World War, when the Russians, by taking it and then abandoning it, signed the death warrant for its Armenian inhabitants, unmentionable traitors to the Turkish mind, and a Turkish general razed it to the ground.

Now all had gone: mosques and chapels, gardens and mansions, streets and markets. All that was left was the rock, crowned with its citadel, honeycombed with caves and tombs, crisscrossed with rising steps cut painfully from the stone. Climbing those ancient stairways, standing in those empty chambers, placing a hand on slabs of rock smoothed by time and the hands of dead warriors were for me an essay in communication with the past that failed. It disclosed nothing to me of the spirit of the people who had lived there. The mystery remained.

"There is a Urartian palace or a temple, I'm not sure which, not far away at Toprakkale," the lieutenant said. "Not much to see, a mound surrounded by ramparts. They've been excavating on and off for years, found quite a lot of stuff, I believe."

"Can we go there?" John asked.

"I'm afraid it's not possible," the lieutenant said. "Toprakkale is a military depot, out of bounds for visitors."

We were upon the citadel itself, gazing down over the southern rim at the old town. I saw movement among the ruins.

"Who could that be?" I asked.

"Shepherd boys," the lieutenant said.

"What would shepherd boys be doing in the city?"

John smiled at me. "Looking for lost sheep?"

"Looking for goats, more likely," the lieutenant said. "Shall we go down?"

Walking away across the soft turf toward the lieutenant's jeep, I turned back to look once more at the cliff. Sunlight shone full upon it, revealing in pitiless purity the vain marks vanished men had left, like the scratchings of children on slate.

Not all the men had vanished. One was standing at the entrance to a tomb, a tall man leaning negligently against the rock, binoculars to his eyes. They were directed at us. I gave a cry. I pulled at John's arm, forcing him to stop and turn.

"Robert!" I whispered. "It's Robert!"

"Where?"

I looked again. The rock face was empty, the figure gone.

"He was there," I said. "He must have gone into the cave. Come on!" I was already beginning to retrace our steps.

John held me back. He spoke in fast, urgent tones. "No. If he hid when he realized you'd seen him, it must have been for a good reason. By the time we climbed up there again he would be gone. Don't worry. If it was him, if he recognized you, we'll hear from him soon."

"It was him," I said. "He's alive, John, he's alive."

We stared at each other, his hand still gripping my arm.

He said: "You're sure you're not mistaken? It could have been a shepherd or a tourist. Or a shadow, a trick of the light."

"It was him," I said. "It was Robert."

The lieutenant looked back at us. "Something the matter?"

"No, no, we're coming." John put his arm round my shoulder, exerting a gentle pressure, and reluctantly I went with him.

I spent the journey back consumed with impatience and doubt in equal measure. Had it really been Robert? Or had my wishes deceived my eyes? What was he doing here? Was the rendezvous with his father still to come?

I began to wonder if John intended to return to the citadel alone. He seemed as restless and uneasy as I was.

At the hotel I asked him: "What do you think we should do?"

"Wait," he said. "My dear, there is nothing else we can do."

I couldn't remain in the hotel room. I couldn't stay in any one place. John took me out to eat, and afterwards we walked towards the lake.

"Do you think he's still out there at the rock?" I said.

He shrugged. "I don't know. But I know him well enough to realize he'll get in touch with us when he's ready, when it's safe and not before."

"How much did you tell the captain last night?" I asked.

He looked surprised. "Nothing directly about Robert. You know that. You heard everything that was said."

"I thought you might have been more specific, have said something to the captain while I was talking to the others."

"No. What makes you think that?"

"I was wondering about the lieutenant," I said. "Being there with the jeep, being so obliging. I thought I might have betrayed myself when I saw Robert."

John paused. "I told the captain we were waiting for a friend to join us here, that we were afraid we might have missed him, that he might have arrived before us and gone on."

"The same story you gave the hotel receptionist, in fact."

"Yes, the story we'd agreed on."

"I sense the lieutenant knew more. That he was under instructions to keep an eye on us."

"That wouldn't be unlikely," John said. "There are not too many foreigners here. It's late in the season, and besides, the troubles have put off the tourists. I suppose the military are suspicious of all travelers. Let's go back. I don't feel we should wander off too far on our own."

"You think it's dangerous?"

"Foolhardy, perhaps. After all, we don't know the situation."

I looked at him. "Then you do believe it was Robert I saw."

"Oh, I believe you," he said. "I saw your face."

When we returned to the hotel, there was a postcard waiting for us. It must have been brought by hand, for there was no stamp on it, but no one could recollect its being delivered. It was addressed to me. On one side was a photograph of an elaborately decorated church. On the other, in the space left for messages, was written the single figure 5.

"Is it from Robert?" John asked.

"It must be."

"You can't tell? From the writing?"

"You probably know his handwriting better than I do," I said. "But it must be from him."

"I keep forgetting how short a time you two actually spent together," John said, "how little you really know him."

We went to the nearest coffeehouse and sat with the card between us on the table. Outside, a file of soldiers marched wearily up the dusty street towards the barracks. Flies circled in lazy spirals beneath the stained ceiling. It had grown very hot.

"Who else would send a message like this to us," I said, "and for what reason?"

"To trap us?" John said.

"It is from Robert," I insisted. "We are to meet him at five, at this place."

"Aktamar."

"You know it?"

"No. I'm reading what is printed on the back of the card. 'The Church of the Holy Cross, Aktamar.' I'll ask about it."

The proprietor was playing cards with a group of cronies at the back of the room. John went across. He was greeted with grave courtesy and offered a chair, but once he began talking, his inquiry was received with indifference or a reaction even more puzzling than that: shrugs, frowns, heads turned away, a resumption of the game, which had ceased through politeness when he arrived. Only the proprietor continued to give him any attention, replying with brief reluctance to John's questions.

He came back to our table, pulling a face as he sat down. "Not the best bunch for me to pick to ask about the church. It is apparently one of the tourist sights of the lake; but it is Armenian, and since they are convinced that some terrorist trouble in the region a couple of months ago was instigated by Armenians coming over from Russia, they are not too happy to discuss any previous Armenian presence here. Anyway, it is on a small island in the lake. There was a palace and a monastery, but I gather the church is all there is to see now. It is covered by sculptures of 'holy men,' as they put it, saints and prophets, I presume, and animals and birds and flowers. You can see it quite well from the steamers that go up and down the lake, but if you want to visit the island, you have to go to a town called Gevaş and get a boat from a pier about five miles from there. He says it is so small an island that it is hardly worth visiting. He says the regular boats that go every two hours will have stopped by the time we get there. We will have to find someone to take us ourselves."

He put his hand on mine. "I've decided that you shouldn't come. I'll go alone. I want you to wait in the hotel."

"I'm not waiting anywhere," I said. "I'm coming."

"Robert wouldn't want you to risk yourself. Remember, he doesn't know about Tom Shaw's murder, or the two thugs who've been following you, or the mysterious Mr. Okyer. We don't know who might be following us now, who might be waiting for us."

"Robert sent that card to me," I said. "He wants to see me, and I want, God knows, to see him. I haven't come all this way to stay behind at the vital moment. I'm going to that island church with all its beasts and birds and prophets, and nothing's going to stop me, not Okyer, or you, or whole hordes of invading Armenians."

He smiled. "All right. I know when I'm beaten. Let's go back to the hotel. I think you should get some rest. There's an hour or so before we need to start. I'll see about hiring a car to get us to Gevaş."

I went up to my room, but I couldn't rest. Excitement, apprehension, fear, impatience were tearing me apart. I forced myself to calmness with practicalities: packing my bag, counting my dwindling money, checking that I still had my passport. I wondered what clothes to wear, how cool it might become on the lake at the turn of the afternoon. The endless lake that was like a sea, with only the encircling mountains to mark its farther shores; the lake of incredible color and beauty, the sulfur springs of which killed the fish and poisoned the plant life on its banks; the lake that was seven times larger than the Lake of Geneva, the captain had told us, in autumn and winter a prey to sudden terrible storms, with a barren coastline and few settlements. Was it across that water that Robert intended to take us; was that to be the escape route?

I opened the window to try to get some fresher air into the hot staleness of the room and saw John Nairn crossing the street towards the hotel. His pleasant face seen unaware had a serious, preoccupied expression, a tension that I suspected echoed my own. If his emotion last night had been as genuine as it seemed, he must have his own ambivalent feelings towards Robert or perhaps towards me. I was hardly the first woman to come between two friends, but that was not a situation I was going to allow to develop. If I could help it, that is.

He came to my room with that solemn, concerned face and told me that something had happened that must change all my plans. When he went downstairs, the receptionist had told him that an international telegram was waiting at the telegraph office. Thinking it must be from his office, he had gone to collect it.

"Only it wasn't for me; it was for you," he said. He handed me the thin, much-folded piece of paper. It had been sent from Athens and addressed to me simply at Van. It read: "Urgent. Mother desperate. Return Vancouver first flight." There was no signature.

I was stunned by its unexpectedness, by the sheer impossibility of its arrival.

I said helplessly: "Where did it come from? Who sent it? 'Mother desperate'—what can that mean?"

"I should think it means desperately ill," John said. "It must have got mangled in transit. I'm very sorry, Frances. Is there anything I can do?"

I stared blankly at him. "I don't understand. My mother has no idea I'm in Turkey. She had no idea I would be in Greece. As far as she's concerned, I'm in London. She would have cabled London."

"What about your cousin Bernice? Perhaps they cabled her when they couldn't get hold of you. She could have sent it. It's come from Athens."

"Yes," I said. "Of course. They got in touch with her when they couldn't reach me. She knew I intended coming to Van. She sent this—" I looked down at the cable. "She must be back in Athens. I'll ring her. She'll know what this is all about. Better still, I'll ring Vancouver direct."

"That's not possible, I'm afraid," John said. "You can't make international calls from here. I suspect the nearest place is Ankara."

I was still considering the cable. "It's addressed to Van, nothing else. How did they find me?"

"That's simple enough," he said. "The operator asked the police to check on recent foreign arrivals. It's not such a big place. It didn't take them long to call the hotel." He looked at me with those kind, considerate eyes. "They tell me there's a flight out of Van in half an hour, the last this week. So don't worry. It's not too late."

"Yes, it is," I said. I was thinking of my mother as I had last seen her. The courageous smile of farewell, and then the telltale slump of the shoulders when she thought I had gone. I thought of her tears and her loneliness, and I knew what that "desperate" could mean. But she'd let me go. She wouldn't call me back. I knew her.

"She didn't send any cable to Bernice," I said. "She didn't ask anyone to send for me."

"Well, obviously not your mother," John said, "if she is so ill—"

I gazed at the paper that was like a ticking bomb in my hands, about to blow everything to pieces. Why couldn't they have said more, whoever they were who had sent the first message? Why couldn't they have made it clear, so that there could be no doubt as to the right action to take? Could she really have become desperately ill in the short time since I'd left her, barely two weeks? A heart attack? If so, then it might already have been too late by the time the telegram arrived. On the other hand, if she was still alive, there was an even chance she still would be in forty-eight hours or however long it was going to take me to get there.

Whatever had happened I had to go to her, but not now, not till after five o'clock.

"I could run you to the airport," John was saying. "I've got a car outside. Not much of a car, but it should do."

I said: "John, I'm not going yet. I've got to keep that appointment with Robert. I'll go when I've seen him."

"You can't do that," he explained patiently. "You've got no choice. This is the last plane. There isn't another till next week."

"Then I'll go by train."

"The nearest railway is at Tatvan, a hundred fifty kilometers away."

"You could drive me there. Or perhaps the captain could spare us a jeep."

"I don't want to sound like an alarmist, but suppose something goes wrong on the island," John said. "Suppose something happens to prevent you from leaving?"

"I'll have to deal with that when it happens. Oh, I wish Bernice had sent a clearer message. You say I can't telephone Athens from here. What about telex? Could the army post help out?"

"It's not that sophisticated a place. There won't be any telex here."

I got up and walked to the window. Outside, a crowded bus lurched up the street, top-heavy with bulging suitcases and baskets of provisions. Two young men walked past, hand in hand. There was, at last, a faint breeze from the lake.

I said: "Then I shall have to take the risk that I'm doing the wrong thing, but I'm not leaving till I've seen Robert."

John came up behind me. He put a hand on my shoulder.

"All right," he said. "If that's your decision."

I turned to face him. I found myself stumbling over my words. "Thank you, John, for being so understanding. I don't know what I should have done without you these past few days."

He said quietly: "It's not important now, but I happen to love you. I can't help being concerned. And now, if we're going to get to that island by five, perhaps we'd better start. I don't know how reliable the car is."

As we went along the corridor, he took my hand briefly in his. Perhaps he had read on my face what it was costing me to say no to that plane out of Van. I knew what I was doing, and I believed I was right; but it took more effort that moment to follow the judgment of my own instincts than anything else I had done.

The heat had gone from the sun by the time we drove into Gevaş, and when we reached the pier, the long shadows of late afternoon were spreading across the land. The distant mountains were as still as a painted backcloth. Little waves whispered into the shore. The lake stretched calmly before us. A mile out lay the small hump of the island.

Most of the boatmen had gone. There was one left, who for a price agreed to take us to Aktamar.

As John took my hand to help me into the boat, he looked at me, briefly, with a strange expression that seemed a mixture of sadness and regret. But he turned away almost at once and began to question the boatman about other visitors to the island.

There had been none that day, the man said. There had been none for weeks. They said people weren't coming because there was going to be a war. All he knew was that it was hardly worth keeping the boat on. The ferries had stopped for the winter. He thought he would, too.

I watched, fascinated, as we came nearer the island. I could see the church, small and in color a rich chocolate brown, standing on a rocky terrace amid the ruins of some other buildings. It had a cone-shaped dome like other Armenian churches I had seen, and beneath this was a frieze in high relief of stylized animals, hares, dogs, lions, horses, foxes, gazelles; below them were carved rich clusters of fruits and plants, vines and pomegranates, with human figures among them, and then below that, on the walls of the church itself, those prophets and saints John had spoken of, biblical scenes easy to recognize: Noah and his Ark, David and Goliath, Abraham and Isaac.

"Is there only the one landing place?" John asked.

"We always land the same place," the man said. "It is very steep, the island. Boats only come to this side."

"Good." He stood up as we approached the jetty and jumped quickly ashore. The hand he offered me was impersonal. He said: "I think we should go up to the church as quickly as we can."

I began to climb the path. When I looked back, the boat was already heading back to the mainland. I had a sudden sense of panic.

"Why has he gone? Why didn't he wait for us?"

"It'll be all right," John said. "Don't worry." And this time he took my arm.

I had half expected a guide, some black-robed, none-too-clean old man waiting to show us all the glories of Aktamar, but the surroundings of the church, the island itself, seemed deserted. I looked at my watch. Five minutes to five.

"We're early," I said. "Do you think Robert can have arrived? Do you think he's here?"

"Let's find out, shall we?" John said, and pushed open the door.

It was cold inside, with that insidious, damp cold of ancient buildings never used. There was a smell of dust and stale air and what might have been the lingering fragrance of nine centuries of incense. It was some moments before I realized that the walls were covered with frescoes, the life of Christ, it seemed, faded here and there, and flaking.

The church was built in the shape of a cross, with the dome rising some sixty feet above us. We walked round it slowly, like tourists, returning to the entrance by which we had come in, as if instinctively wanting to make sure of our escape. And then I saw him. He came out of the shadows and stood quietly some way off, looking at us. He must have been there all the time, but so still, so camouflaged by light and shadow that we had passed by without seeing him. The ability to merge into the background had not left him.

"Robert!" I said. "Thank God."

I took a step towards him, but John's grip tightened on my arm, holding me back. And Robert made no effort to come nearer. He stood there, watching us, his face tired, his eyes wary. When he spoke, his voice was controlled, without emotion.

"Hallo, my love," he said. "So you didn't come alone. I thought perhaps you might not. Are you going to tell me who your companion is?"

It took seconds for the implications to hit me. I glanced at the man beside me, then back at Robert.

"John Nairn—?" I began in a questioning tone.

"No," Robert said. "John Nairn is dead. He was stabbed by some excitable Turks in a village fifty miles from here. They nearly got me, too, but luckily I managed to escape."

"Then who—?" I swung round to face the man I knew as Nairn and saw why Robert hadn't moved. Nairn was holding a gun, and it was trained on him. So it was a trap, and I was the one who had let him set it up, the one who had led him to Robert.

"He's got Nairn's passport," I said to Robert. "I've seen it."

"Yes, I imagined he would have. One of those scruffy individuals stole it, I presume, and they got it off him."

"A man called Carl," I said. "They beat him up." And as soon as they'd got it, they slipped it to their agent, who had already been passing himself off as Nairn, and he was able to appear to me, fully documented, as Robert's best friend come to the rescue.

He spoke to me at last, not looking at me, his concentration fixed on Robert. His voice was harsh.

"Why didn't you go?" he said. "Why didn't you believe the telegram?"

"I did believe it," I said.

"What telegram was this?" Robert asked.

"He brought it to me at the hotel. It was about my mother. I was to fly back to Canada at once."

"Well, well," Robert said. "Having scruples about killing a girl? I hope you've not been trying to console her? I worried a little that you might have reported me as dead. But of course, you couldn't, could you, until you'd found me?"

"All that time," I said. "From that first night in London— You're a good actor. You quite convinced me, you know, with your sympathy, with your kindness. They broke into the flat, Robert, the night before I was due back. They took the golden bull and the card with the message about Van on it. I'd come back early, and when I interrupted them, they knocked me out. That was what happened, wasn't it?" I said to the man who was holding me against his side as tightly as a lover. "You were the burglar."

Then he did look at me. He said: "Yes. I'm sorry." And there was on his face that same expression that had puzzled me before, that mixture of sadness and regret: regret that I hadn't taken what had been my last chance to get away? Sadness for what might have been?

Later I was to wonder what might have happened if I had stayed behind at the hotel, as he had asked, and let him come to the island alone. Would he have returned, saying that he had been too late, that Robert had been killed by his pursuers? Would he have stayed around a little longer than he had been ordered to, to comfort me, and might I not in the end have been ready to accept his comfort, on any terms? For it seemed to me, for that one moment in the church, seeing his face, remembering his words, that it might not have been totally a lie when he said he loved me.

I said: "What is your name? Who are you?"

"It doesn't matter," he said. "Why don't you go on calling me Nairn? It's the name on my passport."

I was thinking how we could get the gun away from him, how I could distract him so that Robert could bridge the distance between us and reach him. I knew we had to get away before the others came. I believed I knew who the others would be, and the thought of facing those two men who had hunted Tom Shaw and me all the way from Greece was enough to frighten me into any impossible action.

Robert said, as if he'd been reading my thoughts: "How long are we going to have to wait here, in this drafty building? When are your fellow thugs charging in for the kill?"

"There'll be no killing, not yet," Nairn said. "Not until you tell us where your father is."

"I wish I knew," Robert said. "I was hoping you'd tell me."

"Do you expect me to believe that? He may not be on this island, he may not be in Van; but you've got him hidden somewhere, and we want to know where."

"If I knew," said Robert, moving a fraction closer, "you'd hardly expect me to tell you."

"You will," Nairn said, "if you love your wife."

Robert sighed. "You've reverted to type pretty quickly, haven't you? The gallantry already evaporated. Are you going to do the dirty work on her yourself, or let those two apes of yours loose on her? And here, in this holy place? Not very commendable."

"Stop joking."

"I'm not joking," Robert said. "And are you aware that my wife is about to attack you, to try to get that gun from you? I'm warning you because you might not expect it of her, and I don't want her hurt. I know how quick your reactions would probably be, and they'd be instinctive, wouldn't they, like mine? You wouldn't think about what you were doing."

"What do you want me to do, Robert?" I said.

"Nothing," he said. "You're doing fine. We just have to wait."

We all heard the sound at the same instant. Someone was approaching the door. I froze into a stillness that owed everything to fear and nothing to the calm waiting on events that Robert was displaying. The man I still thought of as Nairn and I were standing slightly to one side of the entrance. He didn't turn his head. He kept his eyes on Robert. There lay his immediate danger. There was no danger to him from the man at the door. After all, he knew who it was.

The door opened, and Okyer stepped heavily into the church.

It was like the culmination of a nightmare. The man who seemed to have been haunting me for weeks, whom I'd escaped from so narrowly in that hotel in Istanbul, had finally caught up with me. There wasn't going to be any escape from him here.

He looked larger and uglier and tougher than ever. His suit was stained and dusty, and he needed a shave. He ignored me and glanced at Robert, and Robert nodded and then things happened too fast for me to follow. Just as Nairn was relaxing his hold on me and beginning to turn to greet his colleague, Okyer suddenly seized him by the shoulders and flung him headlong against the wall with all the casual violence of a dog shaking a rat. His head cracked against the stone with a sickening impact, and he slid into a huddle at my feet.

I stared from Nairn to Okyer in bewilderment. He said dryly: "I don't think your wife was quite expecting that, Robert. I think she has been seeing me as the enemy."

"Nice timing," Robert said, joining us. "Were the others any trouble?"

"They weren't expecting me either," Okyer said. "So they were no trouble. I tipped them into the lake. They won't be found for a while."

I looked at Nairn. "Is he dead?"

Okyer shook his head. "No. But he's out of the game now. He won't be any more trouble to us."

Robert's hand clasped mine. He bent and kissed my mouth. "Thank God, you're all right," he said. "You are all right?"

"Yes," I said. "I'm fine. This was a trap you set up, wasn't it? He thought he was catching you, while you were catching him."

"We had to get rid of those particular pursuers, and we had to get you away from him, so we thought we'd coax them over here. It's a nice isolated spot. The ferries stopped weeks ago, and the tourists with them. I knew once you'd seen me, you'd come to whatever rendezvous I set, and I knew he'd be with you and his friends not far behind. So we came here a little early and waited for them. I was to keep your would-be lover occupied here while Nazim dealt with his friends."

"Would-be lover? Why do you call him that?"

Robert smiled. "He was, wasn't he? Why should he try to send you to safety when he most certainly had orders to take you as well as me? Besides, he betrayed himself in the way he spoke to you. I'm a jealous man, you know. I can recognize someone else's love when I see it."

Nairn's face was gray. Blood was seeping from the wound on his head. Okyer touched him gently with his foot, then glanced at me.

"There is no need for you to feel tenderhearted, Mrs. Denning," he said. "He intended to kill you, you realize, along with Robert."

"Yes," I said. "I know. I'm not quite used to this yet."

"You're not quite used to me either, are you?" Okyer said. "But you won't run away from me this time, as you did in the hotel in Istanbul. We both got there too late. They had already taken the passport."

"You're from the police?" I said.

"Attached to them. A department rather like Robert's. He and I have worked together on and off for some years now. Let me introduce myself since your husband is too bemused at having you back safe and sound to think of such mundane matters. I am Nazim Okyer." He bowed formally and shook my hand. His palm felt as hard and leathery as his face.

"For God's sake," Robert said, "we haven't got time for all that. Let's get out before his friends on the shore decide to come and see what's happening."

"You mean there are more of them?" I said.

"As soon as he knew you'd found me, he would have sent for reinforcements. There are more in the area. Nazim and I have come across them already. But we didn't give him time to get too well organized, and with any luck we'll be away before anyone else turns up."

"He sent the boat back," I said. "That would have been to pick up these other men?"

"Don't worry," Okyer said. "No one had arrived at the jetty on the mainland five minutes ago. I checked on that. But you are right. The sooner we get on our way, the better. You go ahead, Robert. I'll see to our friend here, then join you."

It wasn't until much later I realized what "seeing to" Nairn must have meant. Okyer wouldn't risk leaving him behind to link up with his friends. The only safe place for him was the sea, and although I never asked him, I think now there is no doubt that that is where Okyer put him.

At the time I didn't even think about Nairn's fate. I was more concerned with our own.

"Where are we going?" I asked Robert.

"Quite a long way," he replied. "Quite a long way."

There was an inlet on the other side of the island, just big enough to conceal a small boat. Okyer climbed in first and held it steady in the water while Robert and I got aboard. The engine started with what seemed a shattering explosion, then settled down into a quieter purr as we nosed out of hiding into the lake.

The light was changing with the dying of the day. It came directly at us, turning the gently swelling sea into an expanse of shimmering gold. The mountaintops were touched with pink and violet; the dusty trees of the mainland flowered into brilliant greens. By the time we landed, some miles west of Gevaş, the color was draining from the sky and the sharp outline of Aktamar was fading into a rising mist. I stood shivering in the new cold as they moored the boat to a broken jetty, and Robert took off his jacket and put it round my shoulders. His lips brushed my hair, and I caught his hand and held it tightly.

"Have I put you in danger?" I said. "Coming out here after you?"

He didn't answer directly. "You were in danger wherever you were," he said, "as long as they were still searching for me. We were more vulnerable apart than together."

"Edmund Chance came to see me in Istanbul," I said. "He wanted me to go back to London."

"What was he doing in Istanbul?" Robert asked.

"Looking for you. He came over from Ankara to see me. You know Tom Shaw was killed?"

"Nazim told me. I suppose you now know most of what there is to know about me? I'm sorry I didn't tell you. I wanted to keep you out of it. I'd hoped it would be over by the time you got back from Canada."

"What went wrong?"

"I'll tell you later. We had better get going. Nazim's waiting."

The jetty had belonged to what was now an almost deserted village. Walking up the track towards it, we came upon a dilapidated pickup truck that looked as if it had been going since before the last war. It had lost its bumper and half a mudguard; the windshield was cracked and the bodywork crumbling with rust. On its battered black paintwork someone had inscribed the pious motto "God Preserve Us," and I felt much the same sentiments when I realized that this was the vehicle in which we were to travel Robert's "quite a long way."

"Nobody takes any notice of an old heap like this," Robert said. "They're ten a penny in the country. Don't worry, it's got a good engine."

He reached into the back and produced a shapeless long black skirt and a shawl.

"A simple but effective disguise," he said. "Put it on and we'll be three peasants off to market together."

"At least we'll all smell together," I said. "How long have you been wearing this jacket?"

"I don't think I've had it off for a month. After a while, you know, you'll stop noticing our earthy peasant aroma. Have some goat cheese, and you'll notice it even less."

The driver's cab was a long way off the ground. Okyer lifted me up to it with no apparent effort and climbed in beside me. Robert was to drive. Before we set off, we ate the bread and the strong cheese and drank from a bottle of rough red wine; then Robert nursed the pickup, clanking and groaning, up the rest of the track and through the village to the main road and turned west along the lake towards Tatvan.

CHAPTER 7

It was a long drive we began through the encroaching darkness. As the landscape receded into the dusk, the cab of the truck became our world, an enclosed, cramped, juddering, chilly world, as Okyer wound down the window to let out the stench of engine oil and Robert hauled us up the mountain roads by what seemed sheer determination.

He had said the truck had a good engine, and I suppose it had since it never actually broke down; but we had to stop at the top of the Tatvan Pass to let it cool, and it was there we really started to talk. I asked when he first learned that I was in Turkey, looking for him.

"When Nazim saw you in Istanbul," Robert said. "That was the first we knew. I thought all this time you must be in London. I expected you to worry about me, perhaps go to the police." He smiled. "That is, if all my friends hadn't managed to persuade you I was lying in a drunken stupor somewhere in the Greek islands, forgetful of my married state."

"They tried," I remarked. "Some of them tried." And then felt shabby because it was Tom Shaw who had tried the hardest and been killed when he went against his convictions in order to help me.

"Yes, well—" He touched my face gently. "I hadn't forgotten. It was impossible for me to get a message to you. Too dangerous for both of us. I did think you might have talked to Edmund Chance, who would have soothed you with some story and kept you safe in London."

"Once he found me in Turkey, he didn't exactly soothe me," I said, "but he did try to send me back."

"It is a good thing you did not go," Okyer said. "I think you will be safer now with us. They weren't very pleasant men, the ones who were following you."

"I thought they were with you," I said.

"I know. The man, the one you knew as John Nairn, was in the car with them at the hotel, you know. He must have hidden when you appeared, but when you ran off, he got out of the car and followed you, and I followed him. I was surprised when I saw in what a friendly way you finally greeted him. I was curious, so I came after you to the hotel and discovered he had checked in in Nairn's name. So now I knew you were in trouble and Robert in even greater danger. I decided to stick close to you. I was with you on the train to Ankara, and I took the next plane to Van after yours."

"I had no idea," I said. "I never suspected you were there."

"Ah," Okyer said. "I can be unobtrusive when I wish."

"Were those army officers working for you?" I asked. "They seemed so very anxious to help."

He shook his head. "No. We are a very unofficial pair, Robert and I. Officially we do not exist; we are nowhere near Anatolia. As a matter of fact, I am on leave. You see, Robert's superiors specifically requested that no help be given him. They didn't like this business at all. They thought it stank. Perhaps it does; but it was Robert's father who had been left stranded by his own countrymen, and Robert is an old friend. So—" He grunted. "I took my leave. As for the army officers who were so attentive to you, well, they don't get many pretty women in Van these days."

"Perhaps they'll look after my things then," I said, "at the hotel."

"Did you leave much behind?" Robert asked.

"No," I said, smiling at him. "And it doesn't matter. I was joking. But, Robert, Edmund Chance hasn't abandoned you. He told me that he was searching for you in his own way. He wanted me to leave so I wouldn't hinder him, apart from my presence being a danger to you."

"He's had a change of heart then," Robert said. "From the first he thought my father's name was being used as bait to trap our own people. After the first debacle he was sure of it. He didn't believe my father was anywhere near Turkey. He thought he had probably died of natural causes sometime before. Anyway, he wasn't going to risk anyone's life. It was a reasonable assumption, but I couldn't see why the Russians should try it a second time and expect us to fall for it, so when I got the second message, I was inclined to believe it."

"Was that the postcard of Van?" I asked.

"That was a confirmation of a date," Robert said. "Nazim here got the message to me on that boat where you and I met. We had to split up when things went wrong at that first rendezvous. We arranged to meet at a shepherd's hut not far from some ruins on the road to Fethiye. I gather from Nazim you know those ruins."

"My apologies," Nazim said to me gravely, "for taking your taxi. I sent him back as soon as I could, but it was rather a matter of life and death."

"Don't apologize," I said. "It didn't do us any harm. You'd come to warn Robert, was that it? It was you who fired the shot?"

"They had got hold of one of our group. They had learned where we would be meeting. They laid the trap very well. Two of them came quietly on horseback across country. They were dressed as soldiers. Even I had doubts for a while. I thought they had not arrived. I thought they wouldn't with the soldiers there. I realized my mistake at the same time as they saw me. I fired a shot to warn Robert and ran for it. Luckily we both got away that time. They didn't come after me; they went for Robert. They nearly got him on the boat before you came to his rescue. It pleases me that you two meet again and marry. I think it is fate for you, Robert. She is good luck for you, this beautiful, determined woman. She is like a creature out of a legend, coming to search for you, do battle for you. Now we are all together, as comrades, all will be well. You will see."

"That's the longest speech I've heard from you for days," Robert said. "Get the bottle out. We'll drink to that."

As we came down from the mountains and took the rough road north, along the shores of the sleeping lake, Robert told me what had happened in Greece. He had gone there from Turkey to arrange things with his friend John Nairn; but John was still away in America, and while he waited for him, he got involved with Cleo.

"Of course, John hadn't rented the flat to her. They moved her in when they found out he was away. I always stayed with him in Athens. Their intelligence is pretty good on things like that. In fact, it's been a bit too good for comfort all along. Oddly enough, it was when she drugged me and tried to kidnap me that I knew for certain that the whole business was genuine and that my father was still free."

"What happened to Cleo? She was still in Athens after we left. Bernice saw her."

Robert said briefly: "Nazim dealt with her."

I didn't ask how he had dealt with her. From the closed expression on his face, I don't think I would have liked the answer.

"I wish you had told me about all this," I said to Robert. "I wish you'd felt able to trust me."

"My God, it wasn't a question of trust," he said. "It was a question of safety. As long as you knew nothing about it, I was praying you'd be safe. You certainly complicated things for me. You were going to Canada. I was involved in all this. I couldn't waste a minute if I wasn't going to lose you. It was my good luck you felt the same. However, you knew something was up, didn't you? I didn't entirely pull the wool over your eyes."

"There was that phone call in the night," I said. "That really was from John Nairn, was it?"

"Yes. He was ringing from Greece. We arranged to meet there at Paul Andriades's dig. He was coming with me to make a third with Nazim here. Two of the three people I knew I could trust. I wasn't trusting many people by then."

"I'm sorry to spoil my image as the trusting wife," I said, "but I heard some of that call. You'd left the receiver off in the bedroom, and your voices woke me. The bit I happened to overhear was when you were telling him what a good liar you were."

Robert laughed. "And you still married me? I was referring to my colleagues in England. I wasn't intending to let Victor Ransome or Edmund Chance for that matter know my every move. I was going to create a slight smoke screen for my activities. I think it worked, for a while anyway, perhaps too well. Now it seems that Edmund is prepared to help me after all."

"Are you going to get in touch with him?"

"Not possible," he said. "I wouldn't risk sending a message anywhere at this stage of the game. If it was intercepted, we'd probably find a reception committee awaiting us, like the last time. We might not be so lucky this time."

"You haven't contacted your father yet?"

"Oh, we've had contact," Robert said. "But he's still on the wrong side of that line. It was to meet a contact that John and I went to the village where John was killed. One of my father's friends from the old days. It was a little tricky. He was frightened off by the interest the headman and his friends suddenly started taking in us. When it turned nasty, I had to wait in hiding outside the village until the fuss died down and slip in quietly just before dawn to see him. He told me John was dead. He'd got his things for me, but the jacket with his passport was missing. I told him to persuade the headman not to report the death to the local police for a while. I don't think he had much trouble about that. He was going to see John had a decent burial of a kind, until I could arrange to do whatever his family wanted."

"I'm sorry," I said. "Darling, I'm so sorry."

"Yes," he said. "That's been one of the bad things that's happened. And I wasn't too pleased to find a KGB agent taking over his identity and making an attempt to take over my wife as well."

"He was convincing," I said. "And he kept up the deception all the time. For instance, he pretended he knew nothing about the card from your chess-playing friend, the one with the photograph of Van on it, and I quite believed him when he said he also knew nothing about the golden bull. And yet he was the one who stole it."

"Oh, no," Robert said. "Not he. Hold the wheel a moment, will you?"

And while I struggled to keep the heavy vehicle on a straight line, he felt deep into his trouser pocket and pulled out a colored handkerchief which was wrapped round some object. He handed it to me and took back control of the truck.

"Open it," he said.

I unfolded the handkerchief and looked down at the small, vibrant figure of the golden bull.

"You took it."

"Yes," Robert said. "In the first message my father got to us after the original attempt failed, he said he'd deal only with me and that I was to bring positive means of identification. Passports, letters, photographs can all be forged. I decided to take the one object he couldn't doubt, the one very few people ever knew about."

"But they were searching for it," I said. "So they did know about it."

"I don't think so. I think they were simply searching the flat to find out whatever they could, some clue, some message from my father to me. Then, when you interrupted them, they must have thought it was worth seeing what they could learn from you by winning your trust. The most plausible one stayed and became your rescuer and husband's old friend. You notice he didn't join you in Turkey until they knew for sure John Nairn was dead. That was the same reason he kept away from Greece. But you knew so little of my life and my friends that it was possible to deceive you. It was a gamble that brought him quite a long way."

"It proved they don't know where your father is."

"Yes. It's nice to have that confirmation."

"But you know."

"Yes. I know," Robert said. "We're on our way to meet him. He's making the attempt tomorrow night. We've a rendezvous with him on Mount Ararat. A fitting meeting place, when you think of it, for an archaeologist with his interests." He stroked the curved back of the bull with one affectionate finger. "Perhaps you didn't know, but Ararat is the biblical name for Urartu."

We spent that night in sleeping bags in the back of the truck, huddled together for warmth on the hard floor beside the spare cans of gasoline. At first light, Robert touched me on the shoulder to wake me. He lifted me down tenderly from the truck and led me away by the hand to the soft shore of the lake, and there in the silent, pearly dawn we made love by its quiet waters. We bathed naked in those waters, so buoyant that no effort was required to keep afloat, so soft they left the skin silky and smooth like a child's. When we returned to the pickup, we found that Nazim had already walked the two miles to the nearest village and back, bringing with him fresh bread and honey, yogurt and small sweet apples. He produced an ancient Primus stove in a tin box and made tea, which we drank in companionable silence, watching the light changing on the eastern mountains across the empty blue depths of the vast inland sea.

It was the best morning of my life.

The road that day was north all the way, through Erciş at the northern end of the lake, through Patnos to Ağri, where we joined the main route to the Iranian border and turned east for Doğubayazit. It was hard driving across the high plateau. The men took it in turns, pushing the old engine to its limits, conscious of the distance still to cover.

"Is this the same truck you drove from Greece?" I asked Robert.

He laughed. "Good God, no. That was a very sophisticated vehicle John got for us. We left it at Doğubayazit. It was a bit too conspicuous for our purposes. We'll be using it later, if it hasn't been picked clean by now."

I was very concerned that thinking the bull had been stolen and therefore presuming its existence was known, I had told so many people about it, even the pseudo John Nairn. Robert assured me that it no longer mattered. "If they get the bull, it means they've got me, and if they've got me, the game is over anyway."

Nazim's job in their plan was to make sure no one did get Robert. He remained behind when Robert and John Nairn left Greece, going instead to Athens to learn what he could from the unfortunate Cleo. What he found out sent him back to Turkey fast to prevent Robert from walking into another trap, for it seemed the rendezvous with his father at Van had also been blown.

"How?" I asked. "How did they know?"

"I don't know," Robert said. "One reason I took that card with me was that anyone comparing its message with the game set out on the board would have realized it had nothing to do with chess. Nazim thinks it was one of my father's contacts on the other side who told them the location he was making for. I think he trusted someone and chose the wrong person. Anyway, we managed to stop him from coming. Since then we've been waiting. Moving around, keeping in contact and waiting. At one time I thought the blowup in the village where John was killed was a put-up job, but now I'm convinced it was simply bad luck."

"That's what Raven thought," I said. "He told me it was sheer bad luck, but it seemed to me he contributed to it."

"Could be," Robert said. "Too late to worry about it now. How did you know about the truck I left Greece in?"

"You were seen," I said. "A young American girl was hoping

for an assignation with you. She caught you in the act of moving out."

"Those young girls who like digging up old skeletons," Robert said, "are all inclined to be a little too earnest for my taste."

"After digging up dead men," Nazim observed, "they must find live ones almost too exciting. Let us change over, Robert. It is my turn to drive."

"Why are they so anxious to get your father?" I asked Robert a little later. "Why are they putting so much effort into it? They are not hesitating to kill to get to him, are they?"

"That puzzles me, too," Robert said. "Edmund has always assured me that he was in no danger in Russia, that he was sending over low-grade general stuff. I wouldn't have thought he would know enough to warrant this all-out campaign. It may simply be a demonstration of power. Once in their system, no one can opt out, especially those suddenly revealed as double agents. And there is now another development. He's not coming over alone. Who it is he's bringing with him, I don't know. Maybe someone who knows how to get him across and whose price is that he be given asylum when he gets here. But what sort of bird we're going to find in our net is another matter. He might be no more than a soldier who knows a few passwords or the way through the minefields."

"Nairn, the false Nairn, thought he might come through Iran. He behaved as if your father would definitely be making for Van."

"That was to draw me out of the mountains," Robert said. "It was an easier area for him to set a trap. No, I've no idea how he's going to do it. It's a completely off-the-cuff job. If we'd organized it, it wouldn't have been easier, but it wouldn't have taken quite so long. And you wouldn't have been in the danger you were. I find it hard to forgive Edmund for washing his hands of it. Matter of policy, no doubt; decision imposed on him from above maybe. It's still a dirty trick to play on a man who, no matter how much of a traitor he once was, has spent twenty years playing a double game for him."

"Is Frances coming on the mountain with us?" Nazim asked across me.

"She's going to be safer with us than waiting around in Doğubayazit," Robert said.

"Possibly," Nazim said. "Possibly not." He nudged me with his elbow. "But if the shooting starts on the mountain, get down and stay down until it stops."

"The mountain is in Turkey, isn't it?" I said. "If he arrives there, surely he'll be safe."

"He won't be safe until he's in London," Robert said. "And then only if I look after him."

"Edmund Chance said he was ill."

"Yes, he is," Robert said. "But I'm not persuaded that he is dying. I don't intend to let my father die."

From Tutak to Ağri we followed the valley of the Murat, soft and green and full of birds. It was on the banks of the river that we rested awhile, finishing off the bread and the cheese left over from the previous night and filling the old truck's panting radiator with fresh water.

There had been traffic on the road but none we could identify as Nairn's reinforcements in pursuit.

"I think we've got well ahead of them, Nazim," Robert said cheerfully.

Nazim grunted. "Once they've checked we've left Van, they won't waste much time coming north, trying to pick up our scent."

"At the speed the truck's going," I said, "they may even have passed us."

Nazim gave a deep throaty chuckle. "Perfect. Let them pass us; then they will be going round in circles, chasing their own tails, while we quietly go our way."

There was now a tension, a sense of anticipation in the cab

of the pickup that was infectious. The adrenalin was beginning to flow. I found I was looking at every peasant, every village, every van or car with a heightened alertness.

On the road from Ağri to Doğubayazit we were stopped by a military patrol demanding to know our business and see our permits. Nazim got down from the truck and stood by the front wheel, talking volubly to the soldiers and producing well-thumbed documents in great profusion. Whatever his story was, it convinced them. They waved us on.

"Is the village near here?" I suddenly asked Robert.

He knew which village I meant. "Southeast of here," he said, adding without the slightest trace of bitterness in his voice, "In the wilderness."

It was still light when we reached our destination, light enough to study in some detail the immense mass of Ararat rising from the plain in solitary splendor. It dominated its surroundings. For miles it had been impossible for me to look at anything else, broad-shouldered, capped with a brilliant crown of ice, a volcanic cone as symmetrical as a child's drawing. The closer we came, the grimmer and less welcoming it appeared. I could see the snowfields that spread like spilled icing down its sides, the black rock strewn with loose boulders, the rough pastures of the Kurdish shepherds.

"This was the heart of the Kurdish territory in the old days," Nazim told me. "Great robbers and bandits. Old Bayazit was a fortress, very important when the Russians held Iğdir, on the other side of Ararat. But the old town no longer exists. They sent all the people away after the Kurdish rising and built a new town, Doğubayazit. Of course, it is still a border post. Few people here but soldiers. The Turkish alpine troops train on the mountain. Ararat itself is a military zone."

"Then how are we going to get on it?" I asked.

"Ah!" He patted his pocket. "We have permission. It is

possible, you see, to obtain permission in Ankara to climb Ararat. It is discouraged, particularly in the past couple of months, but if you have the right contacts, as I have, it can still be arranged. It is for myself and group, so you see, you are already included."

"You don't really expect to drag me up that mountain, do you?" I asked. "I can't climb."

"A gentle walk is all that will be required," Robert said. "We don't intend to go past the snow line. It's quite easy."

I remembered then that he had climbed Ararat, that he knew the mountain, and that reassured me as much as anything could.

I was glad we were not going to spend long in Doğubayazit. I did not take to the place. It had all the charm of an army headquarters anywhere in the world, with a special added flavor of its own, made up of the smell of goats, the reek of dung fires, dust and heat and flies. I was left, reluctantly, in charge of the truck while the two men went off together. I wrapped the shawl round my head and pretended to be invisible. From a butcher's shop along the street, a sheep's bloody head regarded me mournfully. A yellow dog snuffled at something in the gutter, shying away when a boy threw stones at it. Loud, wailing music droned incessantly from a teahouse, relayed, so Robert had told me, from Russian Baku.

About twenty minutes after Robert and Nazim had left a man in a ragged suit began taking an interest in the truck. I had not seen him arrive. I became aware of him only because of his unmoving stare. He walked round the truck, stared at me again through the windshield and at last went off. Five minutes later he was back with a friend. His friend hoisted him up to the level of the cab, and he began to mouth at me through the closed window. The more I ignored him, the angrier he seemed to get. Suddenly he disappeared, and when I saw him again, he and his friend were mouthing and gesticulating at Nazim, who got rid of them by the simple method of advancing a step towards them, waving a peremptory hand of dismissal.

"What did they want?" I asked him when he opened the door.

"A lift to the border. They mixed us up with some other truck which does the trip. Would you like to get down now? We're leaving."

Behind the truck, Robert was sitting at the wheel of a Land-Rover. Beside him was a small, thin man in the uniform of a policeman. Tossed in the back were bundles of equipment which I presumed were what mountain climbers required, together with a shotgun.

"For the wolves," Robert said straight-faced in Turkish. The policeman nodded. His mask of official impassivity was shaken a little when I hoisted up my skirt to climb into the truck, revealing my jeans underneath. I wondered if they had planned for him to accompany us or if he had been imposed on them.

Nazim, meanwhile, was handing down cans of gasoline from the truck to another policeman. He placed them carefully into the Land-Rover, shook hands with Nazim, climbed up into the cab of the truck and drove it lurchingly away.

I was sorry to see it go. In the past hours it had come to represent a safe world to me. As long as we were together in its cab, simply traveling, no harm could come to us. Now I was being thrust back into the cold world of action, about to embark into the unknown.

Nazim got in beside me. He pulled two tins from his capacious pockets and showed them to me.

"I saw them in a shop. Stuffed peppers. They are very good."

I looked at the stained labels with a certain apprehension. His face cracked in a sudden grin. "No, really, you will see."

Robert turned round in his seat. "We're ready to go."

"Yes," Nazim said.

"Everything fixed?"

Nazim gave a slight, evocative shrug. "As much as it can be."

"OK." Robert looked at me with a smile. "You can take that skirt off," he said. "When we get there."

We began by following the road to the frontier but after a

few miles turned off onto a track that seemed to lead across the plain towards the foothills of Ararat.

"It's about twelve miles," Nazim told me. "We are in good time."

I indicated the policeman, sitting ramrod-straight by Robert. "Is he coming with us all the way?"

"He is doing me a good turn," Nazim said. "I have a good contact in Doğubayazit. I bring him letters from important people in Ankara. He is happy to oblige me. It is due to his good offices that the Land-Rover was still intact when we reclaimed it. This young fellow is to guard it for us when we leave it at the foot of the mountain."

"I thought Robert was to get no official help," I said.

Nazim put a finger to his lips in a heavy parody of secretiveness. "None of it is official. No one will remember having offered any help when it is over. It is a question of a few favors to be repaid, a few friends who act upon their friendship, a little bribery here and there to oil the wheels. Nothing official."

My black shawl and skirt were being spattered with fine black dust.

"Volcanic soil," Robert said. "Every piece of rock on the mountain is black. On a bright day the views from the summit are stupendous, but it is not a mountain I feel a great affection for."

It would be dark before long. I looked at the immense dome rising ahead of us. How were we going to climb in the dark?

The Land-Rover took us beyond the plain and some way up into the foothills. There was still a glimmer of light when Robert pulled off the steep track onto a relatively level piece of ground and tucked the Land-Rover into the shelter of a broken wall. It was a relief to be free of the bone-shaking jolting we had endured for the past hour. On those slopes I decided I preferred to walk.

The men took the bundles from the back, and from one of

them Robert produced a man's soft wool sweater, a brand-new anorak and a cap and handed them to me.

"Where did you get these?" I asked him.

"American army issue, courtesy of NATO," he said. "Strictly on loan, of course," he added solemnly. "We shall return them later."

I took off the black skirt and shawl and put on the new clothes. They hung loosely and warmly about me.

"I ought really to have brought you some trousers to go over those jeans," Robert said. "You're going to find the jeans chilly tonight."

I knew he was right, but it was as yet hard to believe. There was still a close, sultry heat even at this height. I couldn't guess how far we had come, but we were way above the level of the plain. There and at Doğubayazit it had been like an oven.

Robert and Nazim also changed into sweaters and anoraks. They rolled up their thin jackets and put them into the back of the Land-Rover, Nazim transferring his two tins of peppers into a light rucksack. They shouldered a rucksack each, leaving me free. I was grateful for that. I was having serious doubts as to how far I would be able to keep up with them. As if reading my mind, Robert said: "You could stay here with the truck if you'd like to."

"For how long?" I asked.

"A night and a day?"

"No, thank you! I'll stay with you."

He laughed and kissed me. "You don't know how glad I am that you're here."

"Really?"

"Who else have I got to make me laugh?"

Nazim was drawing out from a long sack two lethal-looking rifles. Whether these too were on loan from the NATO forces, I didn't inquire. The shotgun apparently was being left for the policeman. With his own sack of provisions and his gun he was settling himself down comfortably for his long watch.

"Are there really wolves on the mountain?" I asked Nazim.

"So they say. And the occasional bear. The wolves take the goats and the horses, not the men. As for the bears, I have never spoken to anyone who has actually met one. It has always been a cousin."

"You know this region well?"

"Tolerably well. I was stationed here at one time."

"Is it always as hot at this time of year?"

"It varies. The summer was late starting this year. It seems to be late ending. It has worked to our advantage. The Kurds have not yet left for their winter quarters. Another week and who knows? There would have been few left on the mountain."

"Is that important?" I asked.

"It is important to us tonight," he said. "Don't worry about the climb, Frances. I shall be behind you. It is not as difficult as you may think."

"All these constant reassurances about the ease of the climb," I said, "make me realize just how difficult it's really going to be."

He gave his throaty chuckle and clapped me on the shoulder in a friendly gesture. Robert said, slinging the rifle across his back: "Ready?"

I nodded; Nazim grunted; we said good-bye to the policeman and set off. I don't know how many hours that climb took us, but it seemed to go on forever. At first, Robert walked with a powerful flashlight swinging from his hand; but the moon rose early, bathing the barren landscape in an eerie light, and I had no trouble discerning my husband's figure in front of me. He looked gray, as the cropped grass of the rough pasture we were climbing looked gray, and the boulders strewn treacherously across our path, and the long fingers of snow that clutched at the rock above us. The whole world shrank to the length of the path in front of me, the distance between myself and Robert. I could hear Nazim behind me, but I didn't look back. I kept on following Robert, one foot in front of the other, always upwards, always hard and stony and dangerous underfoot, going on and on until my knees and ankles ached from the strain and the sweat ran down my back. We seemed to be climbing in a great curve across the southern flank of the mountain towards what destination I didn't know and hadn't the breath to ask.

Suddenly Robert halted. From behind me Nazim asked: "What is it?"

"Up on the snow line," Robert said. "Lights. Someone signaling."

I strained my eyes in the direction he was pointing. I could see nothing, and neither, it seemed, could Nazim.

"Whoever they were," Robert said, "they've stopped."

"Ours?" Nazim asked succinctly.

"I doubt it," Robert said.

They didn't say any more, but they hardly needed to. We continued to climb at the same steady pace, only now there was an added tension, an urgency we all felt, and the long rifle on Robert's back was no longer there for any hypothetical purpose, such as stray wolves or bears, but for a more deadly and to me more frightening reason.

It was not long after this that a third man joined us. One moment Robert ahead of me was alone; the next a shorter, squatter figure was beside him. They didn't pause. They talked in low voices as they walked. Then, with a quick glance back at us, Robert turned right, away from the direction we had been following. The man with him seemed to be the guide. He led us some four hundred yards from the place where he had joined us, and all at once in the moonlight, there were the shapes and smells of animals, the sharp barking of a dog, the low glimmer and acid aroma of a dung fire, the dark outlines of skin tents. Two men came forward to greet us. Through the open flaps of the tents I could see women squatting and curious children peering at us. We had arrived, I realized, at a Kurdish encampment.

To most modern Turks, and no doubt especially to a man like Nazim Okyer whose job was involved in security and order, the Kurds were an anachronism. Still clinging to their tribal organizations and their independent life as nomadic herdsmen, the proud men and their wild, handsome women, with their pigtails and their layers of petticoats and flowered dresses, rejected any attempt to make them live a more settled life and showed a stubborn refusal to pay attention to authority. Their reputation remained as bandits and troublemakers, and in a frontier area such as Ararat they were doubly suspect. But it seemed in some cases suspicion could be replaced by respect and trust. Nazim Okyer had been clasped by the Kurdish chief in a dignified embrace. Robert was talking to the other men as if he knew them so well the social niceties could be abbreviated and the real business of our visit got down to without delay. We sat down beside the fire and were brought glasses of hot tea. I couldn't understand a word being said around me. The speech was too fast and the accent too difficult for me to grasp. If I had not been so tired, it might have been easier. Now that we had stopped I knew I could not walk another step that night. My head ached from the effort I had made and from the change in altitude.

Suddenly the discussion was over. A decision had been made. The men shook hands again. We stood up. My calf muscles were trembling. I was assaulted by a great wave of weariness. But how could I say I could not go on? There was no place for a passenger on this expedition. I began painfully to follow Robert and Nazim away from the fire. They halted by a rough wicker fence erected around one side of the encampment. They slung rifles and rucksacks off their backs onto the ground. Nazim extracted a bundle of cloth from his rucksack and began to put up a tent.

Robert shone his flashlight into my face. "You're very quiet. Are you all right?"

"Are we staying here?" I asked.

"Yes," he said, and smiled. "I'm sorry. I thought you'd understood. We spend the rest of the night here. We move on in a few hours."

He put his arms round me and hugged me close for a moment. "You look worn out. Get some sleep. I'll wake you when it's time."

We were offered food, but I was too tired to eat. I waved away the yogurt and the cheese and Nazim's stuffed peppers. He sat cross-legged beside the tent, eating them out of the tin with much enjoyment. I kissed Robert and crawled inside a sleeping bag and was asleep before my head touched the stony ground.

It was still dark when Robert woke me. "We're leaving now."

I sat up. "Who's we?"

"Nazim and I and two of the others."

I pulled myself out of the sleeping bag and blinked at him. "And me."

"No, darling."

I stood up. I said fiercely: "And me."

He nodded. "All right," he said softly. "God knows I'd worry about you wherever you were. Come on!"

Nazim seemed not at all surprised to see me rejoining the party.

"Not quite such a long walk this time," he murmured. "Not quite so steep."

If that was supposed to encourage me, the reality of that trudge through the predawn darkness soon wiped any eagerness off my face. It was worse than before. The track they followed was steeper, rougher, harder; the pace they took was faster. The two Kurds led the way, Robert was next, then I, then Nazim bringing up the rear. If it hadn't been for that strong, sympathetic presence behind me, that gruff, solid piece of teak of a man whom I had found so frightening before, I wouldn't have made it. It was he who kept me going. I don't think Robert ever knew quite what an effort it took.

When the sun burst over the mountain, flooding it with life-giving light, we had been climbing for three hours. Far below, on the distant plain, I could see a road winding its way towards the frontier with Iran. The settlement where we had slept last night was a huddle of black dots. The mountain above us had lost its symmetry. It was nothing more than a cruel jumble of ice and snow and rock. We were almost at the snow line.

Robert turned to look at me. His face was strained.

"We're here," he said.

I looked about me in genuine bewilderment. Nothing I could see was any different from any other part of this mountain. The place we had stopped was as harsh, infertile and unfriendly as the rest of Ararat. It was also incredibly still. There was no movement of air, no sign of life, no eagle, no buzzard, no bears, no wolves, no other men. It was like a dead planet.

"This is a place many climbers make camp before going on to the snowfields," Nazim told me. "It is a recognized stopping place."

"Is this it?" I asked. "The rendezvous?"

He nodded.

"Robert didn't want me to come," I said. I watched Robert as he went forward a little, talking to the two Kurds, using his binoculars to scan the slopes to the northeast, towards Russia.

Nazim squatted down on a large, flat boulder. He kept his rifle cradled in his arms.

"He needs to keep his mind clear," he said. "That's all."

"I shouldn't have come," I said. "I'm going to distract him at the wrong movement."

"Not you," Nazim said gravely. "Not you."

Robert came back and sat beside me on the cold ground. He looked at his watch. "All we can do now is wait."

"How long?" I said.

He shrugged. "Half an hour, perhaps more, perhaps all day."

Nazim grunted and, after putting down his rifle, began to roll himself a cigarette. The two Kurds had gone on, disappearing out of view. After a while Robert said: "My father and his companion were crossing somehow in the night. From Russia itself across the river Aras, or from Iran somewhere near the Turkish State Farm Center, which is the way I would have tried to bring them. I don't know. But somehow, down there in the night, they will have changed to respectable climbers, all set to tackle Ararat.

They will have made their way across the lower slopes, up to the saddle between Great Ararat, where we are, and Little Ararat, to the east of us, and now they will be climbing up towards us, wondering if they will find us here, wondering if they have been seen and followed, wondering if they have been betrayed yet again and are climbing up into a trap. Not the best sort of exercise for a man with a bad heart."

"But he knows it?" I said. "Your father knows the mountain?"

"Yes," Robert said wearily. "He chose the rendezvous."

There was a sudden movement beyond us, and the Kurds were back. They were smiling and pointing. Robert leaped to his feet. He turned his binoculars the way they were pointing. He said: "That's it. There they are." He handed me the glasses. I put them to my eyes.

At first I could see nothing. The landscape seemed no different. Then I realized I was searching too far down. I raised the binoculars and caught them. Two figures, nearly close enough to have distinguishable faces, one in front of the other, climbing slowly as if each step were an intolerable effort. The first was a tall man, nearly as tall as Robert, but stooped as if to move his body forward took every last scrap of his energy. Behind him a shorter, squarer figure, with a scarf and a cap. They, too, had rucksacks on their backs. They carried no guns.

Robert was in a torment of impatience. He could not remain still. He took the glasses back from me and gazed long and hard at the two struggling men. Suddenly he called to the two Kurds and set off at a blistering, slithering run down towards his father.

Nazim hadn't moved. "Let him go," he said calmly to me. "He's waited long enough."

I was becoming as restless as Robert. "Nazim, can I borrow your glasses?"

He handed them over to me, and I raised them to my eyes in time to witness that triumphant reunion. Robert didn't wait to produce his solemn evidential objects. His documents of identity and the golden bull remained in his pocket. I saw him fling his arms round the first of those two figures and hug him to his chest. I saw him shaking hands with the second man. I saw him waving to the Kurds to come forward and beginning the final stretch of the climb up to us, his arm protectively, encouragingly round his father's shoulders.

I realized when I met Maurice Arden from whom Robert had inherited his charm. His face was tired and worn, his complexion gray, tinged at the mouth with the telltale blue of the heart sufferer. His eyes were full of a pain suppressed and ignored. His smile was like Robert's smile. He took my hand and said: "Worth coming over for, Robert," and they laughed as if they had never been parted.

His companion was first introduced to us by a letter only. "Colonel A," Maurice Arden called him. "Formerly of the KGB. My passport back to freedom."

Whether or not it was dangerous to remain on the mountain too long, we had no choice. Maurice could not go farther without a rest. But it was impossible to stop him from talking. Robert had given him the golden bull by now, and he held it in his hand, his thumb occasionally moving over the curve of its back, as if touching a talisman.

"It was my friend Colonel A who, out of the blue, warned me not to make that first attempt to get home. He told me information had reached him from an impeccable source in the West, one of their long-term agents, giving every detail of the plan. I couldn't warn you, Robert, but my friend here, whom I shall from now on call Alexei, was eventually able to let me know you had got safely away. He volunteered to maintain the contact with you and to help me plan another attempt, so long as he could come, too. His wife was dead; his only son had been killed in a rocket accident. For a long time he had been finding his life soulless, worthless and degrading—I think those were the words he chose—and whether or not that is his real motive for defecting, those were the reasons I chose to believe. What is more, he was the one man who could exonerate me in the West, the one man who could give me back my honor and my life."

Alexei had made no comment throughout this lengthy speech. Now he raised his head and said: "Why don't you save all this until you get down this mountain? You will exhaust yourself even more."

"Who says I will get down the mountain?" Maurice said. "I may not make it even halfway down. But I don't care. I don't give a damn. I'm out of that bloody country. But, Robert, wait till I tell you what I found over there. I've brought one of my monographs with me. It's in the rucksack. We'll get it published in English. It will be some justification for a lost career."

The first jubilation had left Robert. I could tell it from his face, and so, it seemed, could his father.

"You are thinking of the problems," he said. "You are thinking they won't let me back into England, the traitor, the defector, the notorious Arden. Well, it may be a bit of a struggle to convince them. I thought the only man who could help me was dead. I thought there was no way out, until I met Alexei. Now I know what double-dyed treachery from a 'smiling, damned villain' really is. I know who wasted my life, and that knowledge has made me angry enough to make a second and third attempt until here we are. The first time I was coming because I knew I was dying, but now I'm here because I'm angry. You're married now, Robert. I'll have grandsons someday. I don't want them to carry a name they're afraid to use because the world, mistakenly, believes it belongs to a traitor."

He emphasized that word "mistakenly" so that every syllable had its weight. I caught Nazim's glance, and he raised an eyebrow. Robert said: "You're not a traitor? You never were?"

His father put his rucksack against a boulder for greater support and leaned back against it.

"When I was a young man," he said, "there were a great many what we used to call parlor pinks, passive supporters of the communists, idealists, most of whom changed their politics with the approach of war, but there were others whose early beliefs were

nursed and encouraged and praised, who were flattered and sometimes tricked into becoming part of a wider organization, who
were persuaded to devote their lives to it, who saw the concept
of patriotism as naïve and betrayal of their country as unimportant. There were men in our intelligence service at the time
who were anxious to discover who the recruiters of these young
men were. I was approached by an intelligence officer, called,
shall we say, Brown, to see if I could help them track down any
of this fifth column." He broke off and smiled wryly. "That's a
dated phrase, 'fifth column.' Is it still in use? And by the way,
Alexei, have we any of that brandy left?" He took the flask his
friend offered him and swallowed some of the liquor. "We got
here on brandy, didn't we, Alexei? Damn cold at night down in
those Persian marshes."

"So you came that way?" Robert said. "I wondered if you
would."

"Alexei had a magnificent idea of us donning the uniforms
of high-ranking officers, marching up to the Turkish frontier and
requesting an interview regarding some breach of border regula-
tions. Then we thought that the Turks would hardly be likely to
let two Russian army officers take off into Turkey when the interview was over, and if we revealed ourselves, it was likely to
blow up into an international incident and we might even have
been sent back. So we did the sensible thing. Alexei's papers and
authority got us into Iran, and last night we found a quiet way
over the border, not too far from the track leading to Ararat.
Alexei had the bright idea of bringing gold. Gold greases more
palms than paper money ever could." He turned the golden bull
over in his hand. "You see, gold never tarnishes, unlike ideals."

"What about Brown, the intelligence officer?" Robert prompted
him. "Did you agree to work for him?"

"Indeed. Most successfully. I worked solely for him. No one
else knew what I was doing. It had to be convincing, you see, for
me to be trusted or even approached by the other side. But I was
duly approached, and such a bright star did I prove to be that

before long I was promoted to being a recruitment officer myself. I had one or two successes; most had the sense to back out before they became too involved. But of course, Brown had the names of the ones who were willing to be corrupted, and my suspicions and in one or two cases my certainty as to who the organizers of the schemes were."

"You are saying you were playing a double game from the beginning," Robert said. "It was Brown who asked you to defect to Russia?"

"Indeed, it was not. I never intended to go to Russia, to exile myself from my country, my family, my work. I was blackmailed into it. You see, Brown died, and with him all evidence that I was working for British intelligence, not Russian. There was one other man who knew, a man ambitious for Brown's job, a man he had trusted. He inherited his job, his confidential private papers which included a statement setting forth my position quite unambiguously. This man, who, in the ridiculously secure way they had, was known to me only as Black, destroyed that paper. We had an interview in a house he had off Grosvenor Street—he was quite a wealthy man—in which he put my new position in equally unambiguous terms. The evidence was there in plenty that I had tried to recruit students to work for a foreign power. There was now no evidence, and no single person alive, to prove otherwise. He wanted to send me, in a blaze of publicity, over to Russia to settle myself in as a mole. He gave me no choice, prison, possibly even a contrived suicide, or exile. Your mother, Robert, who was the only other person who by that time knew the truth, didn't want me to go. She wanted me to face it out, try to cause a scandal, name names and so on. I didn't get the chance. In the end Black lost patience with my hesitations and had me 'hijacked,' I suppose we call it now. I was on a plane for Moscow before I knew what hit me. They told me your mother committed suicide, but I have always believed he killed her. Well, I got on with the remnants of my life. I accepted the acclamation and the blame. I did what work I could. I sent as little as I could to Black. I had no wish to bolster his reputation. For I had learned a little more about that gentleman. His revelations about me successfully put an end to investigations of other possible agents in high places. They'd found the villain, so they could all relax. I was the scapegoat, and Black got his promotion. He is a very important person in your intelligence service now, Robert, and in Alexei's, too. He has been one of their most important agents, you see, for over thirty years. I only learned that and his real name when I met Alexei. And so I'm coming home to expose him."

"So that's why they had to stop you," Robert said. "That's why it's been so important to them. To blow the cover of a man embedded as deeply as he is—" He broke off.

"You know him," his father said. "You know his real name."

Robert looked across at Alexei. "Yes," he said. "From what you have told me there can be no doubt. His name is—"

"Edmund Chance," Alexei said.

"Yes," Robert said. "Edmund Chance."

There was a long silence on the mountainside. Robert sat looking at his father, and the expression on his face frightened me. Hamlet being called to avenge his father. Maurice Arden had even quoted from the play. Edmund was the "smiling, damned villain" who had, if not murdered him, wrecked his life.

It was Nazim who introduced a cool reasonableness into that taut atmosphere.

He said calmly: "I think, if you feel rested enough, Mr. Arden, we should start down. We don't want to stay too long in any one place. There are, I believe, still people looking for you. Remember the signal lights, Robert?"

Under his instructions, we formed ourselves into a line and began the long climb down towards the plain.

It was a strange journey. The lower we got, the more intensely that unseasonal heat rose to meet us, and the more worried Robert became about his father. There was a kind of febrile brilliance about him. We stopped frequently to let him rest. His breathing was difficult; his color was bad. He made jokes about his illness.

"When Alexei discovered they knew not only about our first rendezvous but that second planned meeting in Van, he knew he had no option but to come over, too. Isn't that true, Alexei? Isn't that what pushed you into this final desperate throw? When we discussed ways and means, I said the only way they would never expect me to come would be over a mountain. They would think it too much of a strain for a man in my condition. 'Let's meet Robert on Ararat,' I said. 'At least there one can see who's coming. And if I'm stranded there, I'll be in good company with the Ark.' "

"How is your condition?" Robert asked him.

In response, his father showed him a bottle of tablets. "If I fall to the ground, shove one of these down my throat. No, I'm all right, Robert. Don't worry. I'll make it. I haven't come this far to collapse on you now."

He grasped Robert's arm for support and stood up.

"It's ironic, you know," he said. "If Edmund Chance had let me quietly return when I wanted to, he would have been perfectly safe with me. I didn't consider him my friend, but I didn't know the truth about him at that stage. He realized I was ill, and even spies should be allowed to retire. No, it was his action then that is going to finish him now. By the way, do you know where he is?"

"He is in Turkey," I said. "Looking for Robert."

"Ah . . ." He nodded at Nazim. "I understand the need for hurry. A desperate man is a dangerous man. And the Russians will know about Alexei by now. Gentlemen, let us get off this damn mountain."

I didn't find it hard to accept their revelations about Edmund Chance. I remembered the ruthlessness I had sensed in him, the egocentric streak in his character. But his behavior to me didn't seem to fit in with his other actions. I fell back to wait for Robert and ask him why, if everything they said about him was true, Edmund had tried so hard to make me go back to London.

"Because at that stage the man taking Nairn's place couldn't come to Turkey. As far as they knew, the real Nairn was still with me. And Edmund wanted you being looked after in London by the pseudo Nairn. He had to know exactly what your plans were and exercise as much control over them as he could. The last thing he wanted was to have you wandering freely all over Turkey. He must have been shattered when you went to the Ağaoğlus after Tom's murder. He hadn't realized you had any friends in Turkey, let alone friends with police contacts like Halim Ağaoğlu."

"Robert," I said, "how ill do you think your father is?"

"Ill enough," he said. "But anger is going to carry him through. He's going to stay alive for as long as it takes to get Edmund Chance convicted." He paused. "How are you?"

"I'm all right," I said. "Apart from my feet."

He laughed and put his arms round me. Ahead of us, the taller Kurd and Nazim were leading Maurice Arden and Alexei round a gently shelving curve that disappeared behind a rocky ridge. The second Kurd was behind us, bringing up the rear. We had fallen behind as we talked. The van of the party was out of our sight for about two minutes. When we joined them, we found they had halted again.

Nazim turned to us. "Your signal lights of last night," he said to Robert. "There seems to be an alpine patrol they forgot to tell us about in Doğubayazit. Look." He pointed ahead, up and to the right where a group of eight men were descending in a diagonal line towards us. At that angle they would cut directly across the path we were following.

Alexei was frowning. "Do the Turks know we are coming?"

"No," Robert said. "It's a chance, that's all. A coincidence."

"They appear to be turning towards us," Maurice Arden said. "Mere curiosity do you suppose? Or something more official?"

"Don't worry," Nazim said. "I have all the necessary papers."

"Good," Maurice said. "I have no desire to be detained in Doğubayazit."

"They are not all soldiers," Robert said. "There are two civilians with them."

"Then there are other climbers on Ararat," Maurice said. "Do you suppose they were sent to help them? Perhaps there has been an accident."

Alexei had taken Robert's glasses and turned them on the

patrol. Now he handed them to Maurice and said with a kind of amused resignation: "I don't think so, Maurice. Those are not genuine Turkish soldiers. As for the civilians, one of those climbers has been working in my own department for the past five years. The other I think you will probably recognize yourself."

Maurice put the binoculars to his eyes. He handed them back to Robert. "Edmund Chance," he said, "unless I'm very much mis taken. Take a look."

Robert didn't waste any time. He examined the group and nodded. "You're right."

Maurice laughed. "He can't wait to confront me."

"Daren't wait, you mean," Robert said. "You're too dangerous to be allowed off this mountain. Get behind the ridge. It will give us some cover."

We backed away behind the shoulder-high pile of rocks. The men unslung their rifles. Alexei produced a heavy revolver. Only Maurice Arden and I were unarmed.

As soon as they saw us taking cover, the patrol increased its pace. When they were almost within range, Robert fired a single shot that spat up the dust before them. They halted. The taller of the two civilians came forward.

It gave me an odd sensation to see Edmund Chance in those surroundings. He had seemed a man more fitted for London clubs and the offices of senior civil servants than a bare mountain. He was wearing goggles against the glare off the snowfields or perhaps as a disguise to deceive us as long as possible. Now he pushed them up on his forehead out of the way.

"My dear Robert," he called, "it's no use. You must realize I could never let your father pass. We've been waiting for you. Because I know him, I gambled that he would choose to come this way, the most surprising and the most dangerous for him. Congratulations, Maurice, on getting this far. You see, I can still read your mind. I was always the better chess player. How is your heart standing up to this unaccustomed exercise? I hope we don't have to carry you on a stretcher back to Russia."

Maurice said urgently: "Let me talk to him." But Robert pressed gently on his shoulder to keep him down.

"The moment you show your face," he said, "they'll kill you."

He called out to Edmund: "We're all armed, and we're the ones in a friendly country. I don't think the Turks are going to take kindly to your men masquerading as Turkish soldiers. That's going to take some explaining."

"We shan't be here by the time any Turkish soldiers arrive," Edmund said. "I know there are no maneuvers planned on Ararat until next week. You knew that, too. That's why you went ahead. As for your Kurdish friends, you're still a long way from their camp. Face it, you're on your own and outnumbered. It would be rather foolish to start a shooting match. You'd only be killed, all of you. You don't want your wife killed, do you, Robert?"

One of the Kurds said in Turkish: "They intend to kill us all and blame a Kurdish feud. Don't listen to him. Let us deal with them while we can." He raised his rifle.

"We are hardly outnumbered," Robert called. "And if it's a question of waiting it out, we can certainly outlast you. You are the ones in the vulnerable position."

"I don't think so," Edmund said. "Look behind you."

Coming up behind us, hidden until that moment by the bend in the path, were six more men dressed in the ill-fitting uniforms of Turkish privates. Their guns were trained on us in a dispassionately businesslike way.

"Well, Edmund," Robert said, "my father must certainly have frightened the hell out of you to make you lay on this elaborate charade."

"Throw your guns over here," Edmund said. "Then come on out with your hands on your heads."

"Edmund," Maurice called. "I'm unarmed. I'm coming out first." He brushed aside Robert's restraining hand with a strength remarkable in a man so exhausted. He paused for an instant beside Alexei. Their eyes met, and without a word the Russian handed him his revolver. Before Robert could stop him, Maurice had left the barrier of rock and taken one, two steps forward. On the third step he raised the revolver and shot Edmund Chance through the head.

It had happened so fast no one could have prevented it. The shot echoed round and round the mountain. It seemed to go on forever, to be evoking an answering thunder. I waited for the shots that would kill us. I was aware of Robert flinging himself on his father, bringing him crashing to the ground out of the line of fire, protecting his body with his own. There were armed men in front of us and behind us. We had no chance of survival. But the suddenness, the unexpectedness of Maurice's action had thrown the soldiers off-balance. Their leader was dead, no one had ordered them to fire and so they hesitated for vital seconds. In those seconds, Nazim took aim and shot the other civilian, the man from the KGB.

The tall Kurd beside me swung round and began firing at the six men coming up behind. As they answered his fire, I heard him grunt and felt his body sagging against me. I fell under his weight, that noise still in my ears, and as I did so, the ground beneath me seemed to give way. The hard rock I fell on quivered and shook; the ground rippled like a cloth shaken by a giant hand; there was a tremendous deafening roaring in my ears, like an express train hurtling past within inches of me; there was a rushing wind; dust filled my eyes and mouth; I thought my head would explode with the noise. And then it was over. The ground steadied; the noise died away. I could hear other sounds, a groan, someone choking on a cough. I pulled myself free of the Kurd's body and staggered to my feet.

I was standing at the tip of an arrow. The shaft was the stretch of relatively untouched mountain that fell directly away from our position. The arrowhead was the triangular ridge of rock that had been our shelter. Now it was twice its original size, built up by the pile of boulders jammed against it. The enormous avalanche that the earthquake had triggered off had split and divided against that ridge as a tumultuous racing wave breaks and divides against a rocky outcrop in the sea. The overwhelming noise beating me down into the ground had been the thunder of tons of rock, torn loose by the tremor, hurtling down the steep mountainside. They had cut a swath either side of us fifty feet wide. The avalanche had swept the slopes clean. There was no sign anywhere of the soldiers in their faked uniforms or of the bodies of Edmund Chance and his Russian colleague. It was still and calm and deathly. They had been wiped out as if they had never existed.

I looked round fearfully, but our small party was safe. Robert had dragged his father into the protection of the ridge just in time. Shaken, covered in dust from head to foot, we were incredibly all there, and all alive. Even the Kurd, though the side of his head was streaming blood, was only superficially hurt, knocked out by a bullet which creased his scalp. His friend helped me stem the blood and retied his turban to keep the makeshift bandage in place.

As for Robert's father, he was most interested in estimating where the epicenter of the earthquake must have been. Southeast, he thought, towards Tabriz. He stood gazing at the chaos below us, the upheaval above, the great boulders flung a thousand feet as if they were no more than feathers to be tossed in a light breath of air. Any one of those great rocks could have crushed and killed us.

He turned to Robert and said calmly: "Well, my boy, the golden bull seems to work quite well as a talisman. I've a feeling it's used to earthquakes. You had better keep it from now on."

Far below, on the stricken mountain, small figures could be seen working their way upwards. The remaining men from the Kurdish encampment were setting out to search for us.

Before we left the kingdom of Urartu, before we set off for Ankara and Istanbul and London, to be swallowed up in the controversy, the publicity, the legal arguments, the political bargaining and international recriminations that had to be borne before Maurice Arden was able to hand back to his son a name clear of the stain of traitor, we made a short diversion south of Doğubayazit, east of Patnos, north of Van, to a broken village whose single street of houses lay collapsed into mounds of mud from the force of the earthquake.

From there we drove some three miles until we came to a long, steeply rising hill, pitted with ravines and gullies and tumbled rocks. We got out of the Land-Rover and walked a little way up this hill.

"It has changed," Maurice said. "The contours are different. Look there, at that raw scar of earth. The earthquake has changed it yet again. It is somewhere over there that I found the golden bull, but I cannot recognize the place. It is all changed. I'm not even sure now that this is the same hill."

His face was touched by an ineffable sadness.

"Too late," he said. "Too old and too late."

Robert stooped and drew something from a narrow fissure between two solid slabs of rock. He held it up lightly in his fingers, turning it so that the light revealed its fragile coils of twisted wire, the dulled jewel at its center, the delicate swinging droplets of beaten gold.

"An earring for a queen," he said, and smiled at his father. He held it to my ear, so that I felt its gentle touch against my cheek. Maurice gazed at it wonderingly as if Robert had performed some feat of magic. Robert took the earring to him and placed it into his hand.

"Where there is one earring," he said, "there must be two. Where there is one tomb, there will be another. We'll come back one day and find your city. It is all here, beneath our feet."

Then he took his father's arm and, with his other hand clasped tight in mine, led him back down the hill to the waiting car.